QUANTRILL

QUANTRILL

by William Goede

QUADRANT EDITIONS

Acknowledgement

I wish to thank Pauline Siegfried Fowler at the Jackson County Historical Society for her invaluable research, Gary Geddes and Terry Byrnes for their encouragement and advice, David Greer for editorial assistance and Marilyn Goede, without whom all this material had forever lain in a drawer somewhere. I am pleased to aknowledge the grant of the Ontario Arts Council which helped me to complete this book.

Typeset by Robert & Ursula Dawson, Hatley, Quebec

Printed in Canada

PUBLISHED IN CANADA BY QUADRANT EDITIONS

Editorial Office: RR No. 1, Dunvegan, Ontario, K0C 1J0.
Distribution: English Dept., Concordia University,
1455 de Maisonneuve Blvd. West,
Montreal, Quebec, H3G 1M8.

ISBN 0-86495-013-6

Published with assistance from the Canada Council
and the Ontario Arts Council.

For my Father and Mother

ONE

The day before Christmas they set out for Blue Springs, the six of them. Two rode horseback, and four were in the long farm-wagon with the tall sides. Below wormeaten mouldy grey blankets and bald buffalo skins on the plank floor of the wagon lay a narrow black wooden box that had been nailed shut.

They left the daylight of Kansas and burrowed into the darkness of Missouri. John Dean handled the team and was told to keep one eye out for the Star of Bethlehem, but he informed them they were headed the wrong way for any Star of Bethlehem and besides he was following the slow steady shadow of the man in the road ahead of him.

"Charley Hart," he said, "he's supposed to be a wise man, you know."

The moon fell down over Westport and smiled at a sign pointing southeast to Blue Springs. In the back of the wagon Plunk Ball drew the crisp buffalo skin tight about his own hide and watched the man beside him heave the jug again over his head. You could tell by the sound there wasn't much left in it because of that goddamn Morrison, who sat up there beside Dean with a shotgun across his lap. At least now they had the jug, and they would make sure there wasn't a whole lot left for Al Southwick, who rode behind the wagon in the dust, because Southwick was a Baptist and you couldn't trust Baptists with a jug that had something less than three fingers in it.

"Christ, Lipsey!" he growled, "you'll drown in that stuff unless you come up for air now and then."

Chalk Lipsey cradled the jug. "I shouldn't even be here," he growled. "I don't know why in hell I come this time."

"You want me to tell you?" Ball took the jug and swirled it around, listening to it. "Money."

"You like to put a dollar on everything, don't you?"

"Five dollars," he said, sucking at the jug. "A quarter a head."

"You got it all worked out. People like you give niggerin' a bad name."

"Yeah," he said, lowering it. "People like me got no principles. Ain't that what you mean?"

"That's what I mean." It was a good moon, they could see each other's features. "Now give me that jug."

Ball passed it back and watched him shoulder it and lay the beak onto his lip. "That's because people like you, Chalk, own all the goddamn principles. There just ain't enough of them to go around to everybody."

Chalk thumbed the cork into the neck. "The way I look at it, it hasn't got nothin' to do with principles, niggers is human just like the rest of us."

The words were loud and clear. The man out in front of the wagon turned and looked back.

Dean spun about on the seat. "Quiet, you two!" he said. "Even Charley can hear you. Now pass that jug back up here where it belongs."

"What about Southwick?"

"To hell with Southwick."

"Anyway," said Dean, quieter, "you heard what Charley said about the other side of the Iron Bridge."

"What would he know?" said Lipsey, sinking.

"Charley figures if they're going to stop us," said Dean, leaning close to Morrison, who listened, "they'll come at us somewheres between Iron Bridge and Fire Creek."

The country lay about them like a moonlit corpse, and they appeared to be its undertakers, their long wagon rattling over the

8

gravel roads. The land was empty, hushed, as if waiting for something to begin. Once a stagecoach came ringing out of the gloom and vanished again into the darkness. They met a tall muffled horseman, a long Kentucky rifle crossways in his saddle. He rode like a dead man and stared straight ahead as if only he knew what he was looking for. It was a night for churches, steeple-starward, blazing with candles, resonant, skirted all about with wagons and buggies, democrats, mule carts. In among the yews along the road before the cemeteries the Blacks, who waited beside the horses and vehicles, set up their painful counterpoint against the foursquare glad tunes that sprang from the churches, and they watched the wagon move slowly on down the road.

"Charley Hart seems to know everything there is to know about niggerin'," said Dean. "But . . ."

"But what?" said Morrison.

"Nothin'."

"Why'd you say 'but'?"

"Well," he said, leaning, "I got the most peculiar feeling the other day when he come into my shop that somewheres a while back I met him, only he didn't look the same."

"This is one hell of a place to be getting suspicious!"

"Pipe down up there!" said a voice from the box. "And pass that jug back to the troops."

They crossed over a small creek tumbling north through Major's Mill and Fristoe's Fish Trap and the Osage Nation before emptying into the Missouri, that freighted it along to the Mississippi and out among the Seven Seas. Being the source of it all, it still bore a modest title, Little Blue, like everything else in this part of the world, a misnomer, because in the spring, swollen with winter rain, it became a monster tearing its way past all landmarks with little or no regard for man. Little Blue lay just east of Big Blue, its older brother, which also snaked its way down to the Missouri, and to the east, further still, up against the hills, the Sniabar, which watered the lands of White Oak Woods and Texas Prairie. It was a series of high plateaus rich in cotton and Black slaves.

Just short of Blue Springs Charley Hart stood ahead of them in the road pointing off to a winding path that went down into a grove of cottonwoods. They followed him across the flat land and down through the trees until they came to a level clearing alongside a creek. Dean pulled the team up, and everyone sprang to the ground. Charley Hart sat on his horse watching them rubbing out the pain from the long ride.

"You boys know the plan," he said. "Chalk, Ed, Plunk, you boys follow me into the house. I'll go in first, you cover me. They'll be asleep. I want them all held in their rooms while I go out to the barn to secure us all fresh mounts. John, you and Al will wait until we're in the house before you hightail it in the wagon down around the field to those slave quarters. Get those slaves into that wagon as fast as you can. If you have to use guns to do it, well do it! We can't foul up just because some nigger says he doesn't want to go to Canada. Now, once we got that wagon full and I got those fresh mounts out front, you boys in the house should be back outside and ready to go. We got to be back on the other side of that border by dawn if we expect to make Lawrence by noon." John Dean was lighting lanterns. "Now, I'm on my way, but I'll be back as soon as everything settles down for the night. You boys be ready when I return. This has got to have good timing or it won't come off." He turned his horse and rode up into the moonfilled meadows.

"Let's get at it," said John Dean.

Ball pulled the long black box onto the tailgate and pried the lid off it with a hammer. He ripped it from the box and held it up to the lantern. "Now, this here gift," he said, beginning to laugh, "is addressed to 'The Emigrant Aid Society', that's us, and it comes from the Reverend Henry Ward Beecher . . . back in Boston. Why, look here, he's even written on the outside of the box what's inside it."

"What's it say?" said Southwick, suppressing his laughter.

"It says, 'Bibles'. Yessir, that's what is says. It says, 'Bibles'."

"They must be 'Beechers Bibles'!" said Chalk Lipsey.

Ball reached down into the straw and pulled out a carbine.

"Praise the Lord!" said Ed Morrison, holding his gift close to the lantern and studying it.

10

TWO

He came straight across the yard and secured his mount to the head of a brass serpent, stepped onto the porch and lifted his black hat, stared at the door for a moment and was about to lift the knocker when a song broke from within. Silent Night, Holy Night, All is Calm, All is Bright. He knew the words, had sung them all his life, and his mouth obeyed his instincts, but somewhere in the middle of the second chorus, he stopped and went to the window.

He had seen James Morgan Walker once before, in a bank in Independence. He stood with his old gnarled hands fixed to the shoulders of his wife, who punched at the harpsichord. Across from them, building harmony, three men who were spit-and-vinegar of the old man, and yet another, a step away, fat, slick, sweating, his fingers full of gold rings. Next to him was a fine woman, in a long wine-coloured velvet gown, her ivory neck edged with pearls, her long cinnamon hair brilliant with combs and small flowers. Away from all the rest, a smaller woman, plain, most likely older than she looked, worried that somehow she had lost her place in the music.

It was a handsome room, carved out of mahogany and oak, resplendent with oiled and shimmering surfaces, the walls lined with great portraits of the Walkers of past times, sober, disapproving, rimmed with gold. He remembered the great houses in Canal Dover, Ohio, where he was born. Houses he would often

11

visit by windowsill late in the night, when everyone was singing and laughing. It made him sad to see it because in his own small dark house nobody sang or laughed, ever.

Thoughts that had simmered all the way over from Lawrence now boiled over into words. "I knew you'd be in there behind that harpsichord singin' like that," he said, his breath clouding the glass. "I even dreamed about it. Why, I'd be damn disappointed if you were any different because . . . I need you, like this." He figured he knew these people, knew how and where they would move even before they themselves knew it. Why, they had been put on earth for the sole purpose of making him outguess them. "Look at it this way," he said. "I don't owe you a thing, not a thing. And what I'm doing, see, I'm doing you a favour. Look at it that way, I'm doing you a favour."

He watched them until the song ended and slipped back across the porch to the door, wheeling his Kossuth hat in his hands, lifted the brass knocker and let it fall. It rang out across the moon-blanched fields as he smoothed back his wheat-coloured hair and straightened his tie.

The door opened and a man stood in it. "Boy," said Charley Hart, "you go in there and tell Mr. Morgan Walker I want to talk to him." But the man merely stood there as one who seeing, still did not believe in ghosts. "You think you're clever enough to remember all that till you get back inside there?" Still, he refused to move. "Now git!"

"What's the name, sir?" he said at last.

"I don't have one. What's yours?"

The lips moved slowly. "Abraham Lincoln," he said.

This was going to be difficult. "Well, you go tell Mr. Morgan Walker the name's Jeff Davis."

"Mr. Walker, he busy tonight. It's Christmas, you know. Why, can't you hear them back there? Mr. Walker, he—"

"You git back in there, boy!" he hissed, leaning close, "and tell Mr. Morgan Walker if he wants his niggers to spend Christmas at home, he better come along out here and talk to me."

The servant stepped back, and turned and rushed back through the house. The song died in middle flight, someone

12

cursed, and, after the door was thrown open, out came the men, scrambling to see who could get to the door first. They were dressed fit to kill, formal jackets, red waistcoats, watchchains, gold watches, long black cotton trousers, tapered at the leg, shiny black boots.

"What is the meaning of this!" snarled the old man, hurling himself out in front of all his sons. He planted himself in the doorway. "Just who are you and what do you want?" His face had turned the colour of his waistcoat and his left eye twitched. "Don't you know it's Christmas Eve?"

"One question at a time," said Charley Hart, trying to slow down his own blood. The women came and stood behind the men, and the servants behind the women, up on their toes, amazed. "I don't have a whole lot of time and you'll have to listen real close. I know you're mad at me but you'll just have to hear me out. I think I know a way to save both our skins."

"What's your name?" said Mr. Walker.

"My name is Hart. Charley Hart. I came over from Lawrence with a crew of Redlegs and they're out there right now waiting for me to give them the signal and they'll be coming to get your niggers and taking them back to Mr. Jim Lane. They're Quakers." He felt the words rushing at him. "Now, you and I, Mr. Walker, you and your family, your niggers, we all have a lot in common and I'd like to tell you about it. Yet I maintain that we share nothing in common with the boys down in that ditch, you and I." He looked at the others. "Now we can work our way out of this if you just listen to me."

Morgan Walker turned to look at his son. "Andrew," he sighed, "what's he talking about? Is this Redleg talking English?"

"Look, mister," said the young man, "it's Christmas. We don't want any trouble tonight. Why don't you climb onto your horse and go away?"

"I'd love to do that, but those boys down in the ditch aren't going home till they get what they came fifty miles to get. It's that

13

simple. All I got to do is go out there in the yard and raise my hand and they'll be here.''

"I say shoot the bastard!" said the fat man.

"Sure, sure, that'd do it. Shoot. They'd be in here so fast you wouldn't get a chance to reload. Now, why don't you just listen to my idea?''

"Listen to what the man say," said the black man who had met him at the door. "Niggers don't study spendin' Christmas under no buffalo skin in no cold wagon goin' out to no Lawrence, Kansas.''

"Andrew?" said Mr. Walker.

Andrew Walker stepped in front of his father and narrowed his eyes. "Why don't you tell us what you got on your mind and then we'll decide whether you're crazy or not?''

Going on midnight he was back again; this time the others had come along with him. John Dean drove the team, Al Southwick alongside him on the seat holding a primed Sharps across his lap, Plunk Ball and Chalk Lipsey on the tailgate, armed, their eyes driven through the hard moonlight, and Ed Morrison out in front of the wagon, riding with a carbine held in front of him like an axe. The moon was snared in the high branches of the cottonwoods and a long low peal of bells echoed throughout the empty prairie. The wagon was drawn up just inside the gate. Plunk Ball and Chalk Lipsey took up positions in the middle of the yard while Ed Morrison tied his horse to a post and came into the yard to stand in between Ball and Lipsey facing the house. Charley Hart rode up to the dark house and tied his mount to the porch, stepped up onto the stones and walked to the door, cocking his carbine as he moved. He turned to make sure everyone was in his place and found the moon above the house making all the shadows run away from him out toward the road. The white light made it possible for him to read what was written on their faces.

He stepped back until he felt the door, put his rifle to his shoulder and pointed it at John Dean.

Someone spoke and the door fell inward, the rifle exploded, its lead flying straight up through the roof, the gunman sent sprawling back into the dark room, his head striking the floor. The night was full of thunder and the cries of angry men, but someone had him by the shoulders, had him spun over onto his belly, his arm cranked up along his backbone.

He couldn't move without pain shooting his full length. A candle flared, another and another, filling the house with crazy faces.

"All right, Zach!" said a woman's voice. "Let the snake up."

His arm was loosened, and someone stepped away. He sat up to find himself in a room full of women who watched him as if he had been pulled out from under a bed and might make another run for it. A crowd of black women circled up the stairwell and along the balcony, and on the top stair stood old lady Walker with a Kentucky flintlock pointed at his head.

"I wouldn't want you to think you were the first Jayhawker I ever shot, Mr. Hart," she said.

He sat on the floor listening to the gunfire out along the road. In time it grew quiet and the men came back into the yard talking among themselves. The door was thrown open, and Mr. Walker came into the house, followed by the others, his sons and neighbours, all of whom wanted to see what the man on the floor looked like.

"We got one of them," said Mr. Walker. "There's two more of them down in the bottom but it's too dark to go down there tonight and look for them. One's been wounded anyway. I doubt if either of them could get very far tonight."

"And the wagon?"

The old man squatted beside Charley Hart. "Boy, that wagon is halfways back to Lawrence by now." His eyes were full of tears. "That isn't quite what you had in mind, is it?"

15

THREE

Christmas morning they saw the smoke and set out on foot along the road until they reached the woods that thickened along the draw toward the bottomland. Andrew Walker led them down through a thicket that darkened and fell toward a bluff overlooking a deep crevice. Pointing his gun toward a small clearing near the creek, Mr. Walker indicated the source of the smoke and asked who was willing to lead them the rest of the way. Charley Hart stepped forward, but old Clint Williams, Morgan's neighbour, hauled him back again and looked mean-eyed at his comrades.

"Not this one," he said.

"There's only one way I can clear myself," said Hart, "and I'll need a gun to do it."

"Don't take no chances," said Clark Smith, a tall, thin man who leaned against a tree, out of breath.

Andrew Walker stepped into the centre, swivelling his head and burning his eyes into them. "It's only right he should do it," he said, and, turning to Hart, extended his double-barrelled Kentucky rifle out to him. "You got only the two shots," he said, exchanging a long look with Hart, "and you better not waste either of them. You know how to shoot this thing?"

"I think so," smiled Hart.

Walker swatted him on the shoulder and placed both hands on his hips. The men watched the Jayhawker look the rifle over carefully, smile at Andrew, and slip off down the hill toward the white smoke.

They waited. There were two shots and they waited to see if there would be three. They saw him waving at them from the trees and went down and found Plunk Ball and Chalk Lipsey face down in the creek.

The sheriff came down in the afternoon from Independence with a posse. Mr. Walker went out into the yard as they dismounted and told them the problem had been solved, he wasn't intending to press charges against the young Jayhawker from Lawrence. "I should've come up and visited you, Mr. Burris. It would've saved you boys a long ride."

"Where is he, Morgan?" said the sheriff. "We want to have a good look at him. Bring him on out here."

Charley Hart stepped out onto the porch, and Andrew Walker followed and stood alongside him.

"Well," said Mr. Burris. "So you're this Hart." He turned to the others. "You boys know this fellow?" The sheriff was a portly man, well-dressed, successful. "You seen him before anywheres?"

"He's one of Lane's all right," said a bearded man. "He's been over here before."

The sheriff studied his face. "That right?"

The young man surveyed the men in the yard. "Yes, I used to ride with him," he said in a low voice, "but last night I burnt all my bridges."

"If it wasn't for him," said Andrew Walker, with a note of anger in his voice, "we wouldn't have our niggers today. It was all on account of him."

Mr. Walker went to the sheriff. "I set my store by the boy, Mr. Burris," he said. "He's like one of my own now. You ride back into Independence and let me handle this. I'll see to him."

The sheriff thought about it for a while. "There are things outstandin' here, Morgan. But if you see it that way, well, I won't stand in the way." He climbed onto his horse and looked at Charley Hart. "You stay close, you hear? Any trouble and we'll have to come lookin' for you for an explanation."

17

Mr. Walker watched the sheriff and his men turn the corner and head for the King farm. He went to Charley Hart and smiled. "I'm going to take care of you," he said. "I have a little filly for you to ride and I want to pay you a reward. I think maybe you ought to go down and stay with Andrew for a while just in case Jim Lane comes looking for you."

"In that case," smiled Andrew Walker, "you'd better keep him here for your own protection."

The long bevelled mirror reflected a row of blue German chinaware, and the servants filed into the room and stood along the wall, staring at the floor. It was quiet in the room when Mr. Walker launched a long home-made prayer about The Young Man Sent from Lawrence on Christmas. The subject of the prayer was not a man given to such practices and chose, meanwhile, to study the faces of his new family. Walker, with his dry leather face, long thick nose and ears, his generous silver locks . . . Polly, his wife, small and mean, aristocratic, with slow studied steps. . .eldest son, John, a bachelor, serious and shy, with hard blue eyes . . . Andrew, easily the strongest of the three sons, bronzed, heavy chin, determined walk, a young Morgan Walker in the face . . . and last, Zach, too large for his clothes, awkward, silent, a finger gone from his right hand.

"Let us know Thy Will," sang Mr. Walker.

Nancy was the youngest. She sat next to her husband, a man named Slaughter, flashing her eyes at him when she thought no one was watching her, twisting her rings nervously, smiling at him; she had cinnamon hair and an ostrich feather in her hat that kept getting into her face. The other woman was Beth, Andrew's new wife, a woman who seemed by each word and gesture to be reminded that she had married above her station, by each board on the floor that somewhere beneath her was a room they would one day put her into for good.

The servants fled at Mr. Walker's Amen, and the family began to eat with dignity and silence, exchanging pleasantries and avoiding the subject most central in their minds. You could see Mrs. Walker was the one who would break the solemnities;

she had been observing the young man from Lawrence for some time, her face already set for the moment when she would ask him the question that was on everyone's plate.

"Why did you do it, Mr. Hart?" she finally said.

"Polly!" said Mr. Walker, who had seen the question coming. "Let Mr. Hart finish his meal."

"It isn't as if you merely crossed the border between two neighbouring states," she said, impervious to her husband's glare. "It's more like going to the moon. Your're a Northern man, I gather it from your accent. This is the South. We're Southron people."

"Mr. Hart has his own reasons," said Andrew, defensively, watching his mother as if he expected her at any moment to mount a broomstick. "We're not Kansans, we don't demand such loyalties."

"The North and the South have nothing in common," she continued, bravely, "and indeed shall shortly come to the point where we can no longer continue as one nation. The point at issue is the Nigger. At the moment he is ours, but the Northerners want him so that they can put him to work in the factories instead of the fields. It is purely an economic argument, but it means war and you have just changed sides. I think we deserve some kind of an explanation, Mr. Hart."

"My name is not Hart," said Charley Hart. "It's just a handle I use over in Lawrence. My real name is Quantrill. Charley Quantrill. Well, it's really not Charley either. It's William."

"William what?" said the fat man, grinning.

"Quantrill."

"Are you sure?"

"What's your daddy do over in Lawrence?" asked Nancy, pushing the family off the subject.

"Oh, we're not from Lawrence," he said. "My father was a schoolmaster in Canal Dover, Ohio. You know where it is?" They gave no indication, but he moved on anyway like a man escaping from a fire. "When I was nineteen, my father sent me to a school in Kansas to teach for the Emigrant Aid Society, you know, the abolitionists."

"The barnburners!" snarled the fat man.

"I guess I wasn't cut out to be teacher," ignoring the heavy looks around the table, "and so as soon as I heard my brother Frank was on his way to pan for gold in California, I went up to Lawrence to join him. He had this nigger he picked up in town, and the three of us set off early one morning in '58, middle of June. We got to the Cottonwood River and set up camp for the night." Often when he got to this point, he felt the need to improvise, depending on his audience, and now, facing these farmers from Missouri, it was time to invent a wild but probable event. "I don't know exactly what happened, but I looked up and found them kicking the fire into shape and tossing more firewood on it, and my brother Frank jumping to his feet and running for his horse, but they shot him in the back and grabbed the nigger and put him on Frank's horse. Two of them tied me down and the other three came and told me we had stolen a slave and they were taking him home to his rightful owner. I heard my brother moaning, and, as they staked me face down onto the sand, I asked them to put him out of his misery . . . but they only laughed. I got a good look at them, I memorized their faces. One of them grabbed me and forced my mouth open and another one poured sand in it, and then they all rode away. I watched my brother on the ground, he couldn't move, he just lay there moaning, bleeding. I tried to talk to him, but I don't think he heard me. He . . . died about an hour later, the moon came up and I saw wolves come out, one by one, smelling blood." Beth excused herself and left the room. "I'm sorry if I—"

"What happened next?" said Polly Walker, a silver fork poised in her hand.

"Early the next morning a rattler curled up beside me," he said, quietly, letting the force of the words carry the conversation, "and I just gave up, stopped squirming and yelling, just curled up and waited for his tooth. And then, I heard a shot. I opened my eyes and saw an Indian on a horse. I figured I was next. I couldn't speak an inch of Indian and he an ell of English and I just gave up. But then he climbed off his horse and cut me loose, and we buried my brother right where he died. The Indian took me home with him. He couldn't say Quantrill and I couldn't say his name, and so we called each other 'Spybuck'. He taught me how to speak Shawnee and eat Shawnee and dress and think Shawnee, and then he taught me Shawnee warfare.'' This much was true: he always felt better when he got to this hard soil in his narrative. It somehow made the rest of the story fair game. ''He wanted me to become a Shawnee, but I told him I had to find my brother's killers and so I went back to Lawrence. I had put on weight and grew a moustache, and so I figured nobody would recognize me. I carried wood and cleaned out fireplaces for Mr. Stone, at his hotel, and at night I helped wash the dishware, but from night to morning, I looked for my brother's killers. I found one right away in his shop, Mr. John Dean, he was a wheelwright. He didn't recognize me, and so I started to hang about the shop waiting for the other four to come, hoping they were still friends. One day another man came, I knew him, and then another and another, until they were all there. They whispered a lot and I finally found out why. They all were niggering for Mr. Jim Lane. It wasn't against the law, but it wasn't something you bragged about either. Anyways, I finally went to Dean and told him I wanted to go to work for Lane, and he was delighted with the idea. I worked for him for over a year now, did his dirty work.'' His voice darkened. ''Then one day he told me I was done. I asked him for a reason and he wouldn't tell me what it was. I knew I had to move fast and so I told Mr. Lane I wanted to take one last niggering, and he let me do it. So I took the five who killed my brother Frank and put them right into the wagon. In that way I got my revenge . . . don't you see? Against everyone, even against Jim Lane.''

''No,'' said Mrs. Walker, ''I don't see. Revenge only bequeaths revenge. Now Mr. Lane has a good reason to come over to Missouri and burn everyone out trying to find you.''

The men rose from the table and retired to the sitting room, where a fire had been laid and a crystal decanter of rosewater and box of Havanas left on a round table. The doors drawn, Mr. Walker poured the tiny glasses full and beamed. ''Here's to Quantrill, William Quantrill,'' he said.

21

"You can call me Charley."

One by one came oranges and dates, Boston creams, coffee, tea, and they took to watching the strange young man from Lawrence. The chair in which he sat, with its bronze rosebuds and clever gold leaves, its dark-veined maple arches, eagleclaws clutching glass marbles that rolled him across the carpet. He felt the rosewater mount in his head as he turned in the chair tracing the intricate patterns in the room, the rosewood loveseat, harpsichord, its secret inner lid describing a scene in which shepherds and shepherdesses cavorted among the animals, the corner secretary desk stuffed with envelopes and newspapers from St. Louis and New Orleans, New York, London, the cut-glass bowls in the windows, reconstituting the falling December afternoon light, and the banjo clock with its pendulum moving back and forth across a scene of a naval battle, measuring and weighing the hours.

He tried to find himself in these patterns.

"Charley," said Mr. Walker, breaking into his thoughts, "I want you to have this." He placed a small envelope in front of him on the table. "It is a token of our esteem for what you have done for us. We know that you can't return to Lawrence, even if you so desired, and so . . . we want you to stay here, with us." He opened the envelope and saw that it was stuffed with money. "There's plenty of work to be done, both here and down at Andrew's. Your days of wandering are over, young man, this is probably where you were going anyway."

They laughed, and Andrew took him by the hand and looked him straight in the eye.

"You're coming with me," he said, slapping him on the back.

Later, Andrew and Beth Walker loaded him into their democrat and drove him south to their farm. The moon was high, and it turned cold. He studied the countryside and realized it no longer looked so formidable to him, and he thought about what Mr. Walker had said, that at last he was finished rolling, that he had come to rest. Once in the house, he was shown to a

22

small cold room, where Andrew once again embraced him and walked out, leaving him alone with the candle. He lowered himself onto the edge of the bed and looked around the room. It was a pleasant room, wallpapered, chintz curtains, a chenille bedspread, patterned as a heart, a braided rug on the floor.

Then he heard horses in the night.

He blew out the candle and slipped quickly to the window. The moon rode high and showered white light across the landscape. Like a long snake out of hiding they came, at least a dozen of them, and when they reached Andrew Walker's gate, they drew up into a circle and stared down the lane.

"Andrew!" he shouted. He jumped to his feet and ran into the hallway, heard someone coming up the steps, slowly. "They're out there in the road," he said, his blood pumping. "I saw them."

"Who?"

"How should I know."

But when they returned to the window, they found the road empty.

"Perhaps I only imagined it," said Charley Quantrill.

FOUR

He was moved about the country like a plaster saint. The Tatums installed him in their sitting room after church, and Mr. Tatum made a speech and presented him with a gold watch and chain, and the Hallars gave him a new saddle for his new horse. The Kings invited their neighbours over, and one of them brought along a fiddle and made the three King girls dance a reel for him (he took a shine for the youngest, the one called 'Kate'), and the Vaughans gave him a spyglass to keep at least one eye out for Jim Lane. Even though they knew it by heart, the Hudspeths wanted to hear the story, and afterward showed him a newspaper in which he read about the bombardment of a Yankee ship in Charleston harbour. Mr. Hudspeth said it meant war. One Sunday afternoon he went down behind the barn with John Koger, who showed him a letter, creased and smudged, which invited the able-bodied young men of Missouri to run away from home and join the new Confederate Army being trained in Arkansas.

And so it went, this gathering in Sunday rooms that late winter, Quantrill telling the same story over and over, altering passages he knew so well that he could improvise without destroying the melody, and, when he was finished, their presenting him with gifts and peace offerings. The story affected them deeply, and they took to looking west from the windows as if they expected Jim Lane at any moment.

The story became so well known that even when he did

24

improvise upon it, they seemed to accept it as gospel truth.

But they wanted even more than improvisation.

They wanted a moral at the end of it, something easy but convincing. They needed an explanation that measured his curious defection, and revenge was not enough. He muttered something about being deep down 'a Southron man', but this struck them as especially shallow, and so he clung to a paradox, that Abolitionists were men less interested in freeing the Black men than in enslaving the whites.

This only deepened their skepticism, and so he began to slip away from them, if not actually to hide. He knew he had not even the beginnings of conversion to the Cause, nor could he be converted to a system of belief that turned Blacks into slaves simply because he had never *disbelieved* in it. Maybe this was it, this calculated refusal to believe or disbelieve in anything, this which had driven the people of Lawrence to turn their backs on him, because he took no positions, spoke no beliefs, uttered no prayers or vows, preferring instead to think of it all as a kind of hocus-pocus uttered in a moment of fear by one clinging to the slippery stones of a well deep and dark at the bottom.

He knew he wasn't about to fall into the water because he wasn't even curious enough to go look over the edge.

His father had been the first of them. He used to sit him down in a hard chair and weave back and forth before him trailing his long black robes. Often at night, still the figure of his father would return, and he would sit up in bed in a cold sweat. He no longer remembered precisely what he said, something about The Negro Race, something about Emancipation, and of course, everyone but him, the schoolmaster's son, was reading a new book called *Uncle Tom's Cabin*. His father! It had been a long process, but he had at last succeeded in losing the logic and even the subject matter somewhere in the vast murky swamp beyond the thickets at the back of his mind.

And his mother.

She would wait for the lecture to conclude, time the moment when she would waylay him, drag him by the collar into her sewing closet and warn him about Satan, who would swim to the surface inside you when you were ripe, say thirteen or fourteen, and you wouldn't know he was in there until suddenly you broke out in running sores or cramps or miseries of any kind or, worse, in those dark and insatiable desires and cravings for women.

He was surprised to discover his own dark and insatiable desire was to leave town.

Once he had attained something like belief.

His father had taken him to the gristmill one hot summer day and told him to stand in one place. There were twelve sacks of wheat between him and the mystery of the mill, which he found to be a constellation of gears and wheels, valves and axles and spindles and belts, and somewhere behind it all, a dark vowel. It was as if he had at last been given a chance to understand: everything seemed to be in movement, small wheels driven by larger ones, larger ones by still larger, belts walloping, spinning, all of which meant that somewhere, deep in the mill, there had to be an original wheel moving so slow and forever. He did not feel his feet at all, had no idea how he got there, only that he was standing in front of the vast abyss and heard, down below the last moving belt, the dark moan, where he bent to look.

He was saved at the very last moment by his father, who cursed and dragged him screaming into the night.

No, he had nothing to do with the refinements of belief. He figured himself a practical man. He had come out to Kansas to teach them to sit up straight and do what they were told. He had no time for believers. He was too busy defending himself against them, against his own father and mother, against the parents of his students, against the men who came to his schoolhouse with guns because they heard he believed in one thing or another.

No, it wasn't the time or place to justify or to believe in anything; it was time to learn how to carry arms and know how to shoot without missing.

Plunk Ball had come to his room at the Eldridge House in Lawrence late that November night and told him Jim Lane wanted to talk to him, that he was down in the office with the

26

mayor and others, such as old Jennison and Montgomery, for instance, and that the mayor had been having angry words with the old man. He left Ball standing there and went down the steps and along the corridor until he came to Lane's office. He rapped on the door and waited. In time the mayor came to the door and looked at him.

"Show him in," said Jim Lane, and he saw him sitting at his desk, pulling out his purse. He reached into it and hauled out a bill, laid it on the desk in front of him. "I hear tell you was real good at washing dishes for Nate Stone, Hart," he said. "Maybe that's more your line of work."

"He likes the scum!" laughed Charles Jennison, stretched out across a sofa at the back of the office.

He looked down at the money. "What's this for?"

"Walking money."

"Why?"

"Why?" said Jim Lane, roaring with laughter. "I don't have to give you no why. That there ten dollars is why."

He was being tossed into the street. After all he had done for him, Lane was tossing him into the street. The bastard! He was tossing him out.

"I'll take the ten dollars," he said, thinking there was no turning back. "But you'll have to let me earn it first. That'd be only fair and square."

"Take it and git!"

"No," he said, feeling his mind turning slowly like a machine. "No, that wouldn't be right. It wouldn't be right of me to just take that money." No, there was no turning back, he had to ride on ahead, Lane or no Lane. "Look, I already got a raid already worked out. John Dean's made me a new wagon and I got me a crew for it." Lane looked up at him as if he smelled something slightly foul. "We plan to leave out of here the day before Christmas."

"Bad timing, Hart. We don't go niggerin' on Christmas."

Maybe it was hatred, but it straightened him out all the same. "Well, there's twenty-five of them. Christmas Evening. Everybody home, the roads open. Wouldn't it look good for you

27

to roll a wagonload of slaves up to the front of the Eldridge on Christmas Day?''

Jim Lane sat back, pulling a long face; he turned in his chair and looked at the others. They seemed passive, and so he turned back again, his jaw set. ''Where'd you figure on twenty-five of them, Hart?''

''Morgan Walker's plantation.''

''Walker's!'' He roared with laughter again, and the others joined him. ''Why, you'll never be able to bring it off. It can't be done.'' Jennison got up and leaned over, spat something into Lane's ear and sat down again. ''How you proposing to do it?''

''Is it a deal?''

''Wait a minute!'' said Mayor Collamore, coming to Lane's chair and gracing it with a hand loaded with gold rings. ''I don't want this heathen anywheres in sight,'' he said, his eyes burning, ''if there's goin' to be a wagonload of niggers delivered to the front of this hotel.''

''Make a Christmas gift to the people of Lawrence,'' said Hart.

''I don't want *you* there!'' he said, jamming his rings at him. ''You or any of those Jake Herd animals!''

The mayor went back to the sofa and fell into it with a grumble. Jim Lane leaned forward on his elbows and examined Charley Hart. ''You heard what the mayor said.''

''Yessir.'' He tucked the bill into his pocket and smiled. ''The mayor won't find me anywhere in sight, Mr. Lane. I can promise you that much. No, you won't find me nowhere near that wagonload.'' He paused, altered the timing of his words. ''I'll take the money now but one day I'll be looking for you to give me one good reason why you're throwin' me into the street.''

Lane was insulted. ''I don't have to give you *no* reasons, Hart,'' he said, his face passive as a stone wall.

He went and stood in the hallway and waited until he heard the room ring with laughter.

FIVE

On Easter Sunday Mark Gill rode over to ask if he was interested in helping him transport his father's fifteen slaves down to Texas, where they would be sold to a new owner. It wasn't safe, he said, for any man to keep slaves in Missouri, and it might even prove more dangerous trying to reach Texas because of the Yankee patrols.

"I'd like to," said Charley Quantrill, "but I promised Mr. Burris I would stay close to Blue Springs." He had become a model citizen; he had turned over a new leaf. "You wouldn't want me to break the law."

"To hell with the law!" said Mr. Walker. "This country down here belongs to us."

"You've been a great help, Charley," said Andrew. "You've worked hard, you deserve a rest." He looked at Mark Gill. "Maybe you can show Charley where that new Confederate Army is down in Arkansas. You read about it, didn't you?"

Everyone had read about it, about the shelling of Fort Sumter, about the surrender of the Yankee garrison, the rattling of sabres in Richmond and Washington, the new nation arising out of Southern States, and about the call for volunteers to the new army.

"It's not my war, Andrew," said Charley,.

"There's going to be trouble here too," said Mr. Walker. "You don't think the Yankees are going to let Missouri out of the Union, do you?''

They would gather in the fields or down along the creeks and talk about the war. They would consider going down to Arkansas to join the fight because Arkansas had already made up its mind — along with Alabama, Virginia and North Carolina — to refuse to obey President Lincoln's call-up of the state militia to go fight the insurrectionists in the Carolinas. And they would exchange rumours about the incoming Yankees who would make sure that Missouri stayed 'free'.

"I don't need a war to settle my account with Jim Lane," he said.

On the way to Texas they heard about the shootings in St. Louis. Someone told them a Yankee patrol had turned on a crowd of citizens and killed twenty-eight of them, reported the government had fled, said that a man by the name of Sterling Price had come south to Wilson's Creek to build a citizen's army to go back to St. Louis and clean the Yankees out once and for all, and then install a government that would bring Missouri into the Confederacy.

"Let's go find Price!" said Mark Gill.

"What about these slaves?"

"On our way home?"

"Maybe."

On the way home a half-breed came out of the high grass and told them his name was Joel Mays. "It's time to make a stand." he said. "Come, join us. I'll show you how to destroy the Yankee."

Against his better judgement, Quantrill went along to the grassy sedge of the small southern Missouri stream called Wilson's Creek, but he learned nothing. General Sterling Price won the battle, chased away the Yankee patrols; he would win others, but he most surely would lose the war. It was time he oiled his own gun.

Early October he was back in Blue Springs. A hot wind swept in from Kansas bringing sand and wheeling weeds that collected along fences and high in the trees. He rode head-down, hat low over his eyes and his red bandanna across his cheekbones. He couldn't see but realized he was going in circles. It was time to find some cover. He dismounted and drew his horse along towards a row of cottonwoods, but he had not quite reached them when he saw the riders.

Groping, tentative, leaderless, dumbfounded, shouting words now of encouragement, now of despair, cursing, they came with the wind straight across the Divide and toward the Sniabar Hills in the east. He stood shielding his eyes, watching until they were gone. He tied his horse so the flank was toward the blowing sand and hid behind a tree with his head in his lap.

The dark riders came again and went again, and within the hour returned, undeterred, shouting slogans and cursing into the wind.

Who were these people? Where had they come from and where were they bound? Who was leading them and where?

When the wind settled and the sand fell, he began once more to see the shape of the land and sat waiting to see the riders in the light of day. But they seemed, with the storm, to have vanished, come with the wind and vanished into it.

He climbed up onto his horse and surveyed the landscape, realizing he was close to Andrew Walker's place.

As he remembered it, so it remained: the small white house and tall proud red barn backed into the long brown rise, jewelled about with orchards and gardens, cattle grazing along the bluff, trees silver and shimmer. "I thought I'd never see you again!" sang Andrew. "They said you'd fought down at Wilson's Creek and made yourselves heroes, you and Mark Gill."

"Goats, Andrew," he said. "Soon as we could find a way to come home we took it."

"You deserted?"

"Never signed on."

Andrew Walker saw a shadow fall across his face. He turned away and led his mount up into the barn.

"That sure doesn't look like Black Bess," said Andrew, following.

31

"Shoshone horse." He drew the saddle off and hung it onto a peg. "They shot Black Bess out from under me at Wilson's Creek." He sounded tired, defeated. "A fellow needs a warhorse under him if he expects a beast to understand him."

"Well," said Andrew, taking down a brush and walking to the other side of the animal, "I guess you won't need one of them any longer."

"Not if I can help it," said Quantrill, peering across the spine at his friend. "I'm a man of peace. You know that." Suddenly smiling, clouds rolling away. "Like you. Right?"

Later that night, after chores, the two of them strolled across the dry prairie. Andrew was quiet. He was waiting for an explanation. Both of them understood that it was the time to get it all down in words and be done with it.

"We come across a man by the name of Joel Mays and he took us on out into the sand and made us ride hard and learn to live on what we found in the marshes," he said, and Andrew drew out a hayseed and stuck it into his mouth. "And when he was satisfied with us, he took us to meet General Price. He had the right ideas, ol' Mays, but Price, he had no time for Indian ways. He broke us down and gave each of us a blunderbuss and we took instructions in how to stand up in the line of fire and load them. Hell, when the Yankees come, there was blood everywhere, all these people standing up in ranks looking ugly across the water at each other, waiting to see who went first to their knees." The crickets had begun their revolving choruses, the owls in the low places, the air was full of woodsmoke. It was autumn in Blue Springs, a good time, a good place, this, he thought. "The only thing that tipped the battle in our favour was when we heard that General Lyon had been shot, and that cheered us up. They must've heard about it at about the same time because they turned heel on us and ran up the hill towards the woods, Price onto his horse, leaping the creek, and the rest of us cheering and running after him." Quantrill laughed out loud, an echo bouncing back at him from the trees. "When we realized we'd won, the Arkansas boys went home to fight the Yankees along the Mississippi, and we were on our own. We chased the

Yankees for a while and when we weren't busy shooting them, it was all routines and lectures, standing around. If the Yanks had just dug in somewheres, why we would have run for cover. No, Andrew, it isn't up to General Price whether the Yankees take over Missouri.''

"Who do you think can?" said Andrew.

"Nobody. It's time to hide."

The next morning Andrew took Quantrill out to the back pasture and showed him his new steed. "I named him 'Charley'," he said, thrusting an apple into his great jaw. "He reminds me a little of you."

Quantrill stood before the horse as if transfixed.

"He looks like he could just fly, don't he, Charley?"

"Kentucky horse?"

"Bluegrass."

They rode across the fields, Quantrill holding to Andrew's horse as one who expected at any moment to fly off the face of the earth, riding circles about Andrew on the back of the Shoshone. It looked as if Andrew had planned it: they rode straight into the yard of the Hallar place and saw four men sitting on the porch.

"I guess you boys all know Charley Quantrill," said Andrew, jumping to the ground.

One by one they came to shake his hand.

Bill Hallar, skin the colour of river sand, a man with a shifting face, deep-set eyes, a nervous wren-like motion. Johnny and Jimmy Little, twins, bodies fixed like trunks to the soil, powerful, oaken, yet twinkle-eyed, quick smiles of men who always have a story to tell. Johnny Hampton, fine-veined, porcelain, like a jar on the shelf, poorly repaired, with the long blue seam that began somewhere in the scalp and ran along the face to the mouth. They looked like men who had been keeping a secret for a long time.

They took Charley Quantrill into the house and set chairs about the Liberty stove, leaned back into them and put their stockinged feet up onto the fender. "It's time you knew about Zach," said Andrew. "Judge Stanley wrote out an order on him. Put him up on the block. They were going to ship him out to St. Louis. Put him in the federal army."

"When they come for him," said Hampton, as if he had rehearsed the part, "we was ready."

"We didn't kill anybody," said Andrew. "We only scared them. We made them think twice about coming down to the Divide to get our boys."

The fire snarled at them. Jimmy Little teased him with his eyes. "We figured," he said, "we had a genuine troublemaker in you, Charley."

"I'm not looking for trouble," he said, at last. "I guessed this was a good place to stay out of trouble."

Bill Hallar went into the kitchen and returned with a jug of coffee, which he sent around the stove in stone cups. It had all the look, thought Quantrill, of a communion service.

"Once you crossed that border," said Johnny Little, "you changed your mind."

"I guess," he said, as if he understood.

"You been quiet."

"I'm a quiet man, unless I'm riled."

"We're all quiet men," said Andrew Walker. "But we have been sorely tested." The clock struck ten and the wind sang in the harp of the old house. "We're also Christian men but we run out of other cheeks. We also run out of words. The Bible doesn't say much about what you should do when they come in the night and shoot your folks in the head and spike your children and rape your wife right in front of you."

"They're just freeing the Blacks," said Quantrill, imparting a deliberate ambivalence to his words.

"We don't need the Bible," said Jimmy Little. "What we're looking for is guns and a place to hide."

"We live in a garden," said Andrew. "There's always good places to hide in a garden."

"What about you, Charley?" said John Hampton. "You a gardener?"

34

Quantrill spent the following week on the Divides thinking about the next move. The land had a natural shape: three high table lands cleared for cotton, creeks isolating the divides, three of them, Big Blue, Little Blue, Sniabar, all leaning north by north-west like barricades facing Lawrence, all with deep pools and heavy willow woods around the mouths of the many tributaries, such as Little Cedar, Fire Prairie and East Fork of Little Blue. These creeks had driven themselves down through limestone and sandstone beds to reach a good footing, leaving behind rugged cliffs, notches, ravines full of flowers and rattlesnakes. Papaw and willow and buffalo grass grew in heady profusion along the creeks and hid the wheeling springs from the tablelands. It had the look of a garden, some of it wild and dark, some laid to order in the light. It was twenty-five miles wide and twenty-five miles deep: six hundred square miles of hideouts.

"I figured it would be like this," he thought to himself. "Maybe this *is* where I've been heading all my life. Now all I have to work out is what to do to stay here and then do it."

Bill Hallar learned about the Yankee riverboat lodged in the sandbar below Wayne City Landing and said to hold arms bound for Lawrence. They asked Quantrill if he wanted to ride along with them. "Maybe this once," he said. They took a wagon up to Salem Church and over to Blue Mills on the Missouri and hid out in the bushes waiting for the sun to sink. The moon came out and showed them the boat, high and dry, and the small tent alongside it where the two guards sat and played cards. Andrew Walker walked in on them holding a wheel-lock while the rest of them went aboard the boat and found ten boxes of 'Beecher's Bibles', thirty boxes of cartridges and a thousand firing caps.

Quantrill rode on the tailgate and thought, "That wasn't hard to do. They don't ask too much out of you. Maybe this time it'll be easy."

SIX

October deep, the moon rose in the thorn of the dawn, the fog slipped over the prairie and farms drifted apart. You went out to the dooryard and found five or six of them comin' out of the fog holding guns, or you heard a noise out behind the barn and saw smoke and then heard them shooting your animals. Your children ran in from the field, and you went out and saw them shoot your husband in the traces, the horses bolting and being shot as they ran.

Sometimes Andrew Walker took his men down below Iron Bridge and made them stand like trolls, but somehow the Jayhawkers got loose, and they had to wait until the barns began to burn before they knew where to look for them. The Yankees at Independence heard about the little band of bushwhackers and came down to look for them, breaking down doors, taking names, hauling people off because they didn't like the answers. Ed Koger was one boy who had seen enough. He came looking for Andrew Walker's clan, but all he found was a small group of tired, angry boys who blamed one another for their troubles.

"Christ, Jimmy! You couldn't hit the broad side of a barn with that carbine!"

"It was your horse that tipped them off, John!"

"The goddamn carbine just went click! click! and nothin' happened!"

"Charley let that guy slip away from him!"

Mrs. Strawder, on the other hand, might have fallen into their laps straight from Heaven. It started when Jimmy Little rode into the yard at Andrew's house, bearing the bad news. "A goddamn baker's dozen of them this time, Andrew," he shouted, propelling himself to the ground. "Maybe more, I don't know. I didn't stop to count them. Nobody seen them come, they was just there. Like they was born right out of the mist. They shot old man Kromeroy in the back and left him for dead and went and burned down his house. Who knows where they went after that? Somewheres along the line they went to Maclean's and fired the barn and killed his cows. Then they come to Bill Hallar's place—"

"Oh my God!"

"He was out in the field, he seen them coming and run into the house but it was too late, they was everywhere and he got out the back and come running over to my place."

"Where are they now?"

"Last I heard they was headin' for Tatums'."

Andrew flashed his eyes at Quantrill.

"You're the boss, Andrew," he said, dropping his eyes.

"Maybe they figure they've done enough damage for one day."

"Maybe."

"Don't think they won't be down here at your house next," said Jimmy Little, kicking the dust.

It took them too long to get organized, to bring Hampton and Koger to Lobb Church, where Johnny Little and Bill Hallar stood waiting for them. They could see the smoke; it was like a black fang. They rode close together straight into it, following the debris: a bloodsoaked shirt, a torn hat, spoons cast into the road, a dead cat . . . it all led to Mrs. Strawder.

Squatting in the ditch with a dead child in her arms. Three small wide-eyed girls leaned against her, a cart tipped into the grass, a clock that had stopped, and a doll with a hole in its head. They pulled up before her, and she rose before them, slowly, off-centre, stood a moment, pushing her children away from her. She came, then, out of the ditch and straight to Charley Quantrill.

37

"You're that Redleg, ain't you?" she said. "I seen you ride past once or twice." The blood was dry on her face. "I even give you a drink of water from the well. You don't remember. I always fed the Redlegs. I figured they was just boys. I had six. Just these little tikes left, them and the baby."

She stood before him. "Get away from me, woman!" said Quantrill, snarling at her.

"It was Easter. You was with a couple of mean ones but you was kind to me. I says, 'You boys look like you could stand a pig's eye or two. My husband jest pickled some last week'."

Quantrill rode behind Andrew Walker. "Get her away from me!" he said again.

But Mrs. Strawder followed him and held up her dead baby as if it were an offering. He had to look at it. It looked like the dead doll in the ditch. Its eyes sewn open, a small hole in the head, just behind the ear.

"Sonofabitch!" he snarled again, wheeled away from her, his horse rearing . . . and then he raced off down the road, while the rest of them watched him.

Mrs. Strawder began to cry. "I know he's the one!" she said. "I went to the pump 'cause he wanted cold water and I give it to him."

It was all over even before they knew what had happened. Yet, afterward, when they sat down and tried to remember it, it seemed to go on forever, each second hammered thin, just like gold, until it took on a shape and design. The Jayhawker horses grazing in the yard, sun filtered through the dead willow tree, the men drawn to the edge of the porch watching the man ride toward them, curious, Quantrill high in the saddle, rifle jammed into his shoulder, levelled, leaping into the yard, firing once, twice, two of them punched back against the clapboards, splattering, the others running, dodging him, the Jayhawker horses frightened and racing for the woods.

"Jesus Christ!" screamed Jimmy Little, driving himself into the slipstream created by Quantrill's plunge, the others following, firing at the Jayhawkers, not in panic, rushing after their mounts, falling, dropping their guns. They saw Quantrill at

38

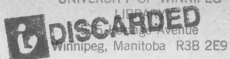
the corner of the barn, sighting his gun, firing at random, and they fell in behind him and emptied their carbines into the trees.

There were four dead men, two on the porch and two in the grass. "I have a confession to make," said Charley Quantrill, on his knee before one of the dead Jayhawkers. "I never killed a man in my life."

"But what about Ball and Lipsey?" said Andrew Walker. "You went down into the creek and we heard those two shots and found them in the water."

"They were both dead when I got there. I kicked them over onto their faces and fired two shots into the air." He turned to look at Andrew Walker, his eyes flung open wide. "It . . . come easy to me once I knew I had to do it."

They heard a noise in the road, turned and saw the funeral procession: Mrs. Strawder pulling the wagon, surrounded by the children, and wrapped in bloody blankets, the dead baby.

SEVEN

November brought them rain, and Jim Kelly.

He was a small man with chopped red hair and a yellow beard, about sixteen years old by the looks of him. He seemed to take real pride in his eating and always made himself a toothpick at the woodbox and sluiced out his mouth in the creek. He was a clean, eager boy; he had had enough of living in the caves above the Sniabar, and what with his mother gone off to Arkansas and the farm abandoned, he figured he had nothing to lose by joining Andrew Walker.

"The only thing is up there at least you could hide," he said. "Down here there ain't no place to go."

"Jim is right." said Ed Koger. "We need a place to hide." Koger was a big man, and he needed a big place to hide in. "We can't go home anymore that's for sure."

The folks tell me they put ten of them over at the drop behind Mork's barn," said Johnny Little, staring at the lamp on the floor of the haymow in Walker's barn. "My mom's got a way of riggin' the washing on the line so's me an Jimmy know when it's safe to come home." They sprawled in the hay, hypnotized by the gay little lamp. "We need a proper place to go every time. Where nobody knows."

The lamp hissed for a while.

"I know just the place!" said Bill Hallar, sitting up. "It's got to be right in the middle of things, right? And yet even when you look at it you can't see it?"

"I don't know," said Andrew Walker, "I don't think Beth would go out to Arkansas and I know my folks won't. I don't like being away from them either."

Early in the morning Hallar took them up into Hudspeth country and showed them the hill. Well, it was not so much a hill as it was two long bluffs on either side of Waldo's Pond, the two bluffs connected by an archway that ran in a bow above a creek. The first settlers called it Hudspeth Hill after the man who bought it, but the Osage looked beyond it at the sky and thought of it as an altar where they could lay their dead leaders. To the gods, however, looking down, it must have resembled a capital 'H', and so Jimmy Little called it 'Hell'. At one point a long draw came up both sides of the creek and made it possible to ride from one bluff to the other without leaving the few trees that graced the heights. Along the south slope and in among the shade trees they built their first camp, a dozen shelters rudely fashioned out of willows and papaw, and fenced in a corral. The meadows along the creek were generous, a little muddy at times, and a small pond at the one end made it possible to water both man and beast. It was indeed a veritable fortress, impregnable if not invisible, grand and even perhaps at times comfortable.

"I called him 'Spybuck'. It was a word he could say and me I couldn't pronounce *his* name any more than he could say mine, and so he called *me* 'Spybuck'." Things had been different since he shot the two Jayhawkers at the Strawder Farm: they looked at him differently, listening to him when he talked about guns, and especially Jimmy Little, who shadowed him night and day and then began to talk and act like him. The pair of them even went over to Six Mile for a week and Quantrill told him what Spybuck had said. "And the second man I learned anything out of was this Joel Mays, a halfbreed down in the reservations." Jimmy Little knew Skybuck's ways, and so when they all went up into Six Mile to learn the ways of Joel Mays, Jimmy became double-smart, and he and Quantrill would play out the ambush because it appeared as if only the two of them had the ability to outwit the others. Quantrill taught the men how to use their mounts as

41

weapons, how to get them to lie down and stay down, even in water, how to get them to stand silent; but mostly he taught them how to move and when to move and, moving, how to hit something else moving. He got them to pare down to get the right sort of saddle and how to convert it into an arsenal. He gave them each a new Colt revolver and showed them how to make it twice as effective as a Sharps rifle.

Andrew Walker, in the meantime, was on the road up and down the border, talking to the settlers about his little band of bushwhackers who were ready to defend the county from the Lawrence Redlegs if and when the settlers themselves saw fit to work out a system to let him know when the Redlegs were coming. It was all quite intricate, he knew, and intricacies are always prone to mistake, and so he made sure that at least one man was at the top of Hell with Charley's spyglass at all times.

Often, when Andrew came back to camp, he had the feeling of being the odd man out. He realized he had to earn his way back into the circle, and he did it by talking to them, explaining things, telling them about the war between the North and the South. The men were intrigued, they loved to hear him talk about the world above and beyond Hell. Curiously, at these times, Charley Quantrill would sit off to one side and merely commune with the bonfire. Even during quiet times, when the jug was passed around the fire, when they traded small observations, they could feel his withdrawal. It was more than withdrawal, it was more akin to contempt, boredom, melancholia. They noted how he always hid his eyes inside his head, how they receded, like the eyes of a wild animal, and he would lie there dormant. "Not much for talk, this man," they would laugh. "Charley stays away from fireside words because he don't know how to handle them." Someone would say, "It's because he ain't got a woman. He don't miss no one. If he ain't up on a horse, he ain't nowhere."

This they could have dealt with, this sullen smile, this stupor, the hat lowered across the cheekbones, the studied contempt. But what they hated about him was the way he would suddenly explode in anger, for no reason at all, simply blow up at them and then stomp off into the woods or go climb onto a horse and be gone all night. He was like a crocodile: you could stand right up next to him and do anything you wanted with him as long as those eyes were half-lidded, but then, suddenly, if they flicked open and the jaw wrenched upward, you'd better head for a tree.

Johnny Little waited one day after an angry display and a sudden disappearance, and then he told them what Charley Quantrill had said to him that very morning in the swamp. "We was riding along together," he said, "me and him, and me, I was just makin' small talk with him, you know. I think I was mentionin' something I heard Lincoln had said . . . anyways, all of a sudden, he says, 'Johnny, don't bother me with all that drivel. It's all hocus-pocus, you know. All that stuff about niggers and whitemen, about right and wrong, good and evil. It don't mean a thing, none of it. Don't fill your head up with that stuff.' That's what he said; 'course me, you know me, I'm a Christian man, I says, 'But, Charley, it's all written down in the Good Book, all you got to do is read it.' And he looks 'crosst at me and says, 'It's all a pack of lies. Nothing but lies. You been fed a pack of lies and me, I been fed nothing but a pack of lies. All that about Jesus Christ and Satan and all that, it was put together for a bunch of cave dwellers who were scared of the dark and didn't have a thing to do in the daytime.' I could see he was gettin' all riled up, but me, I was gettin' mad too, so's I said, 'We are all Christian men here, we're fightin' Christ's battles.' I said the Yankee was the Anti-Christ and all that. He just about blew up at that point. Why he come at me with them eyes of his, you know how he can fix you and melt you down with those eyes of his, and he says, 'The first thing you got to learn down here in the woods is you're up against somebody bigger and better than you are. All the rest of it is bullshit. Them and you. There ain't nothin' above you goin' to come down and save your skin for you and no bunch of follitydolly words is goin' to bring the sky down on the ones you got to beat by yourself. You got to learn to be where you ain't . . . and how to be more than you are, or less . . . how to get deep down inside your own head and see what you can do about

43

it and then deep down inside the head of the man starin' across his gun the other side of the swamp, because remember they ain't sent out a bunch of hayseeds to fetch you out of the Divide, these boys are all on a mission, and they got the best of them out of Boston and New York City and Baltimore and Cleveland, and now you got to beat them at *their own game*! Now listen! The minute you start after them because you're scared or because you're just plain mad or because you're drunk or because it says somewhere in that fancy book you boys kneel to, then sure as hell you're going to lose out. All that fancy good-and-evil stuff is made up to keep somebody in their place, and you and me, we don't like it in our place because it *ain't* our place!' Then he got real quiet and he says, "I had me a Bible once but I gave it to an old man squatting alongside the road so's he could use it to clean himself with!"'

The fire was quiet now, down to its dark red loafs of embers, and the men felt the presence of the dark woods about them.

"I seen him walk right up to a man and shoot him in the face and not even blink about it," said Ed Koger, roused. "I went and asked him about it afterwards and he said he couldn't remember shootin' a man in the face."

"Now listen here," said Jimmy Little, "we was just playing in the haymow before Charley come."

"Yeah, but Jimmy," said Bill Hallar, "how do we know Charley ain't goin' to ride us somewheres and like he did over at Morgan Walker's, change his mind about things and we get caught in *his* ambush. After all, he said there wasn't no right or wrong in all this, didn't he?"

"He won't do that," said Andrew Walker.

"You boys make me puke!" said Jimmy Little, getting to his feet. "If it wasn't for Charley, I tell you we wouldn't be what we are, and you know that! Every pigass boy from Sibley to the High Blues knows about us and wants to join up with us!"

He was even beginning to stomp off into the woods the way Charley Quantrill did.

44

Jimmy Little was right. It all began about a week later when they looked down through the pasture and across the meadow and saw a man riding toward them with a white flag over his head. Ed Koger had already given them the bird signal from the bluff, and they rushed about arming themselves and taking up positions among the trees. The stranger rode slowly but surely toward them, into the dip and up the near side, past the small copse of cottonwoods and across the meadow toward the corral.

"Wait until I give the signal!" said Quantrill, and Jimmy Little passed the word along. They watched him come into the green bowl and head straight for their camp. Quantrill fired once, in warning, and the horseman stopped.

"It's me!" he shouted. "Joe! Joe Vaughan!"

"Vaughan!" said Jim Kelly. "How'n hell did he know where to find us?"

"He's been ridin' with a bunch of bushwhackers over at Fire Prairie," said Bill Haller. "Maybe they found out where we are."

"Throw your rifle down!" shouted Quantrill.

"God Almighty!" said Vaughan, when they helped him down from his horse, "what in hell's a fellow got to do to join up with you boys? You know, I spent the last week lookin' right at you and I didn't even know you was here!"

Ed Koger's brother John came to join them, and Sol Bassham too, and then a tall man with a banjo, Harry Trow, and a sharpshooter by the name of Joe Gilchrist.

Which made thirteen.

And Quantrill went all through it again, and they built a powder cellar into the ground, and procured some wagons and Indian paints. The men were getting bored doing the same routine over and over. "I'm tired of Spybuck," said Bill Hallar, when he had had too many shots of juice. "When are we goin' out into the great big world outside?"

"You don't need to go outside," said Andrew, "when you got a good reputation out there fighting for you."

"That's bullshit!" said Jimmy Little. It had come out of his own mouth, and for a moment it looked as if he wanted to recall

45

the words, but he was like a man already poised to dive. "We ain't offerin' like we should. We should've run down there to Raytown last week, but you said it was too late. And what about old man Liddy? We could've gone over there."

"I guess it's my decision," said Andrew, making his words square and orderly. "I figured there were too many of them at Raytown, and Liddy, well it was just too far."

Jimmy Little looked over at Quantrill to draw off some of his power and charge up his words. "I want to go lookin' for them for a change," he said, his voice breaking under the strain. "The only way you can come up with a good defense is by making a good offense." The words were too hard for his mouth, and the boys knew it was something Quantrill had told him. "If we're goin' to sit here like nice boys and wait until it's safe for nice boys to go out, I say we'll get shit on everytime."

"So," said Andrew, deciding to call his bluff, "what do you propose to do, Jimmy? Go give somebody a good spanking?" He was sewing a stitch on his saddle, pretending merely to make passing comments, but they could tell he was worked up. "I think you forgot one thing. We come up here to do one thing and I think we're doing it goddamn well. We got a reputation for fair play. We don't strike first, we aren't a bunch of border ruffians, cut-throats. We are only protecting our own people. If we were to launch out of here and head for Independence or The Landing, how far do you think we'd get before they cut us off and then beat us into the ground like dogs? Then who'd take care of things down here?"

He paused with the needle in the air and looked hard at Quantrill, who was, as usual, slouched over against a tree some distance from the fire.

"Charley? That's right, isn't it?"

Quantrill adjusted himself and tried to clear his throat. "I don't know, Andrew," he said, neutrally.

"What do you mean, you don't know!" The words were edged with anger. "You're supposed to be a man of knowledge in this. Of course you know I'm right."

Jimmy Little waited, took off his boot and tossed it at

Quantrill. "You ought to answer the man's question!" He laughed, but his mouth was firm. "You're the only one who can tell us when we're ready to ride." Quantrill studied an insect on the ground. "Well? Look at me, I let my fingernails grow . . . I file my teeth sharp every morning!"

"I can ride just the way you showed me, Charley," said Bill Gregg. "I beat Jimmy the other day."

At last Quantrill looked at Andrew Walker, who had gone back to his stitching. "You boys know when you're ready to ride. Don't look at me. But . . . if you ask me, and you asked me . . . I'd say Andrew's right."

"I told you so," said Andrew Walker, thread in his teeth. "You listen to Charley."

"But look what we done to Searcy," said Ed Koger, snarling. "Jimmy strung him up and Johnny put the noose over his head and me, I kicked the chair out from under him. I . . . I didn't feel a goddamn thing!"

"Searcy was a snake," said Quantrill.

"Don't matter."

"It's easy to kill a snake." He slid down the tree and let his hat fall over his eyes. "Anybody can kill a snake. Ed, do you think you could shoot your own brother?"

Ed Koger looked at his brother. "Now, why would I ever want to do a thing like that?"

John Koger jumped to his feet. "Come on, Charley!" he said, barking. "Quit runnin' away from us in words!"

It happened so fast nobody really saw how he did it: Quantrill knocked Ed Koger off balance, kicked his legs out from under him, and fell upon him with his knife hard onto his throat. "Would you kill me now!" he said, growling into his face. "I'm goin' to kill you, you better learn how to kill me." But Koger merely stared up into the madman's face and waited for the game to end. "Shit!" said Quantrill, jumping to his feet and turning to the men around the fire. "If you boys are ready to kill anybody at any time for any reason, then you're ready because whether you want to do it or not, you boys are commissioned to kill other people and to ask no questions, not getting anything out of a

47

Bible or the newspaper, but because it's got to be done . . . when you're ready to do that, then you're ready to ride!''

"Enough of this!" said Andrew Walker, tossing the saddle aside and walking in amongst them. "What is this, some sort of Redleg organization? Who said anything about killing?" He looked Quantrill in the face. "As long as I'm in charge the killing's got to make sense and it's got to be done only when there's nothing else to do."

Quantrill's eyes receded into his head and a small smile played over his lips.

Later he climbed the hill and sat under a tree to read the stars. He didn't know much about the Heavens but he could pick out the Dippers and The Lion, The Bear, The Archer, and so he sat for some time trying to put it all together. Nothing seemed to fit, and he kept going back to Polaris to re-orient himself. The only thing he could make of it was that it resembled The Great Skull which he had found one night along the Sugar River behind his house. He wondered if anyone else had ever discovered it up there, for surely it *was* there, he could see it for himself. It was like everything else, just a jumble of faint lights, accidents in space, but the mind, in its haste to put it all together and make sense out of it and give it a name, the mind had to come up with a pattern, and his pattern was that of a skull. Was he perhaps chosen to see it? Was it a gift? Was it up there for a purpose? To tell him something? They thought of the stars as eternal, as the 'heavenly bodies', as keystones to understanding why certain kinds of people do certain kinds of things. It was all just a dream. Yet . . . there it was, the great skull, the eyes, the mouth, the cold hard jaws. He could see it because it was there.

A week before Christmas (his second in Missouri) they heard that a Yankee patrol had slipped into the southwest corner of the country and captured a boy who had come down from the Sni Hills to visit his family. Andrew's outriders came in later with news that the patrol was coming back to Independence by way of Dr. Lee's Prairie and scouted with Pawnees.

"Wouldn't this be a case when the shooting's got to be done because there ain't nothing else to do?" said Bill Hallar, to nobody in particular.

"These aren't just Jawhawkers," said Andrew Walker.

"I don't see it matters!" said John Hampton.

"John," it would bring out the entire garrison if we interfered."

"We could teach them a lesson!" shouted Jimmy Little.

"Maybe us too," said Hallar.

"Teach! I'm no goddamn school teacher!" But it was too late to retract, the blunder had been made. Quantrill tried to hide his discomfort by dropping his eyes. "Anyway," said Walker, recovering, "maybe they had a good reason to arrest him. And who was he anyway? We don't even know his name." He looked over at Quantrill and knew he needed him badly. "Charley isn't goin' to risk his neck and ours for some unknown boy down from the hills."

The others knew: Andrew Walker had put his neck onto the block and dared Quantrill to lift the axe.

"Charley?" said Bill Hallar, when it had been quiet too long; he went over to him and looked down at him. "You think they had a good reason?"

"Are we jest goin' to set here," growled Jimmy Little, "and let them haul in a boy from Blue Springs?"

Quantrill stared at Walker for a while, lifted the axe and said, "If you boys want to go, you can count me in."

The two of them exchanged a long hard look.

"You'll have to go without me then," said Andrew Walker.

He hid a third of them in the maple trees that hung low over the entrance to Manasseth Gap and took the rest of them along with him below a bridge a hundred yards beyond the entrance. He told them — eleven scared men, their hats pulled low — that they had to look like thirty men when they came at the Yankees, which meant coming up in a steady line, kicking up the dust, keeping up that high steady whine the Osage make, firing at random, saving that last lead for a close-up chest shot. "Whatever you do don't let the Yankee see you're scared because they got a way of laughing at you," he said, "and remember you got to convince them the only way to escape you is to turn and run the other way and you know that's where Bill Hallar and the other boys are."

All they had to do was ride straight into the Yankees and take his word for it that they wouldn't see through it, that they would laugh and stand their ground and watch the little plow-boys bitch and grovel at their feet.

Oh boy.

They hid under the bridge and heard the scouts rumble across the planks and out into the curve that would take them once more out onto the prairie and then somewhere near the bluff the echoes of hoofbeats came to them as the main troop fell into the gap. They watched the barometer in the face, and when, at last, without consulting them, he let loose an insane howl he said he got from Spybuck and pitched himself up the ledge and out onto the road, they gave in to him and became him, screeching like Indians, rushing up into the road in his slipstream, holding their revolvers just above the ears of their mounts, firing once, rushing on, feeling strangely invincible!

It was hard to say what happened. The Yankees crumpled, soldiers fell from their horses, shots were fired into the air, there was for an instant no east north south west up down back forward, only this wall of crazy Indians pouring all over you like a volcano, and even if you had your wits about you and were able to turn your horse and take refuge in flight, why was it suddenly that even the trees behind you were full of men shooting at you?

Six were killed in their saddles.

Some fell into the deep grass, losing their long Henrys, which had been ready to fire, and even in the grass, where they lay, the hysterical mounts were tumbling and sprawling, bleeding, their hooves like blades.

There was no escape.

Six dead, five more dying, ten writhing in agony, their blood collecting below the sand. And the rest of them stood about in the road with their hands in the air, knowing they would surely be killed.

Bill Hallar came cartwheeling down the road and the Little Brothers followed, shouting, "We did it! We killed the sonsabitches!!" The hostage was dragged out of the weeds, and a hurried explanation was given to him by one who was more interested in joining the celebration up on the road.

"Well," said Jimmy Little, when they returned to Hell, "we stripped the bastards and tied up their mounts to haul back to camp, and then Ed Koger and Hallar, they marched the ones that survived on down the road without their boots on, and at the signal we all cut loose and split up into forty different ways . . . and that was the end of it."

Andrew Walker stood beside a horse. He had tied his bedroll behind the saddle, his bags were packed, and he had put a rifle through the sling. He tried to smile at them, but it was forced, and, at last, Quantrill came to him.

"Just go," he said. "Don't make a speech. Don't make no regrets, just go."

Andrew Walker looked around the clearing at the men and then fixed his eyes on Charley Quantrill. "No hard feelings," he said. "I only hope you know what you're doing and you don't let this thing get away from you because if it does, Charley, you'll never be able to get a hold on it again." He paused, tried again to smile, turned to look at the others. "You boys know Charley by now, you know what he can do and what he can't. He can't make your mind up for you, but then, when you got your mind made up, why you go with Charley. Charley, he says no speeches. He don't have anything to say about me and what I do anymore. So let me say this. Don't go looking at Charley for answers to your questions because he hasn't got any because he doesn't trust any questions anyway. There ain't no right 'cause there ain't no wrong, no up because there's no down, nothing forward or backward. There's only the one thing he can do for you and that is get you to do what you know you got to do."

Andrew Walker waited for a minute to see what would happen, and when nothing did, he put one foot in the stirrup.

"That ain't your horse, Andy," said Jimmy Little.

51

"Where's your horse?"

He climbed into the saddle and squared himself, took the reins in his hands. "I'm leaving him for Charley Quantrill," he said, "because I got no use for him anymore. He's a warhorse, you seen it in him. The bastard knows how to run. This here horse," he said, patting his mount, "is more my speed. Gentle horse, no hurry to get anywhere."

He turned and rode out into the field, and they watched him go until at last he was a small white flame dancing in the shadows at the far edge of the horizon.

EIGHT

Captain W. S. Oliver was a man not easily shocked. A veteran of the Iroquois Wars, he had been sent out to Independence because of his stomach, but the incident at Manasseth Gap was more than he could face. He sent a telegram to his superiors in St. Louis that was more than a military request: it was a hysterical demand for immediate action. He insisted that the country be placed under military law and reinforced with ten fully-armed patrols to launch missions deep into the guerrilla stronghold.

He characterized the attack as 'political' in nature and as representative of a sizeable number of Blue Springs people who were 'secessionists'. Whoever it was that had destroyed the patrol had to be apprehended at once and brought to Independence to face firing squads.

The settlers of Blue Springs, however, felt as though angry clouds had gone around but graced them with a mere spring shower. Chronicle and record of the event grew into legend when it reached the dark creek bottoms of the Blues and the high lonely grasses of Lickskillet and Texas Prairie and Six Mile; legend waxed into myth and fancy around the smouldering campfires in the thickets above Sniabar, where the young refugees huddled and waited for good news. To some, however, it was too good to be a yarn, too true to be mere news. It was a chance to escape the lean days and sour food.

"It's time to go back," was like a refrain.

One by one they slipped out of their holes and up onto the Divides.

Black night, slivers of moon, the seeing sound of the owl, and they would slip to the end of the woods and flash across the stubble to the tree behind the barn, around the corner (the road was empty), to the house, slip along till they came to the lamp in the window.

Who's there for Christ sake!

Ab? It's me, Bill. Bill Gregg.

Bill Gregg! Where you been? Last I saw the Bluebellies had you bound onto the tailgate.

With the rest of them, Ab, up White Oak. Listen now, tell me 'bout that raid over at Manasseth.

Manasseth. Don't that beat all! Manjack bastard, what's his name?

Quantrill.

That one come over from Yankeetown to nigger on Morgan Walker that time. Yeah, what you call him, Quantrill. Only he called himself Hart—

I got to find him, Ab. Where can I find him?

Well, I don't rightly know. Nobody knows. Even Andy Walker, he come round here talkin' about it but I couldn't make heads or tails out of it.

You got any ideas where they are?

Well, Lark Skaggs tells me he heard they got some kind of a place up above Lobb's somewheres . . . this side of Hudspeths . . . Otto Hinton, he lives up there, maybe he could set you onto him. Yeah, don't it beat all how them boys . . . Bill? Bill? Now, where in hell . . .

It was like an outer gate and it opened only when you pressed the right key into the lock. If they knew you or your daddy, if they knew you had a right to be angry, if you showed a true desperation and curse when the Yankees came and burned you out because they suspected you of being a secessionist . . . if it was the right combination, they let you through the gate. The second one was more difficult, because it was this gate that took

54

you inside to within walking distance of the hideout.

Psst!

Who's there?

Otto, it's me. Bill Gregg.

Gregg? Bill Gregg? I thought you was . . . well bless my casket, it is Bill Gregg! I was tol' you were up with Ol Shepherd.

I was up with Ol Shepherd.

Paterson's Mill, along in there. You been after them packets and coaches, right? And didn't you boys cut that wire above Baltimore Thomas?

That was me and Davey Pool. Listen, Otto, I want to find Andrew Walker's outfit.

Don't know nothing about it. How you 'spect me to know anything about it?

Ab told me.

Ab Cowherd's got a mouth full of lies, ain't he?

Listen, Otto, I got to find them. I come down out of the hills and left Shepherd all alone . . . I risked my neck getting here . . . now where in hell are they?

Well, I might know somebody who knows about things like that, Bill.

The third gate was the last gate: it might be Bill Hallar or Jimmy Little or Sol Bassham, and they made certain when you entered you knew where you were.

This here's Bill Gregg.

Wasn't you the one whose folks got burnt out by Jennison?

Montgomery.

I see. You was the one who cut that wire over at Sibley?

Baltimore Thomas's, just above the creek. Middle of October. Held up that mail coach at Blue Mills first weekend in November.

I see. You know my brother?

Yes, his name's Johnny. He looks like you.

What do you think, Otto?

Bill Gregg. Everybody knows his folks.

Once inside, it was more like a vault that had to be opened: a series of fine tumblers and sliding cylinders and safety locks.

Ever shot a Colt?

Sure. Navy Dragoon. 1851 model.

You figure how many pickets up at Osage?

Ten, twelve, depending. They set shift about three times a day.

The mail packet leaves Six Mile . . .

Twice a week, Mondays and Wednesdays, around midday. You could pick it off at the gristmill.

No, too many Northern men around it. You got to wait until he gets into the woods near that bluff at ol' man Perkins' place.

Major Tate is Southron man?

Figure so. He lives south of the red bridge, half-mile this side of Big Blue on the Morristown Road. Plank house, but clapboard over them.

How would you get three dozen men across the Line and into Aubry without being seen?

And when the men returned to the confines of Hell in January — only Sol Bassham went missing, having shown himself at Rip Alley's Christmas dance, where Captain Oliver's men arrested him and shipped him off to Illinois for safe-keeping — they found eleven new faces around the fire. "I think," he said, "most of you boys know each other, don't you? Bill Gregg . . . George Todd, no, he's a bricklayer from The Landing . . . Cole Younger, Davey Pool, Cole's brother James, Ol and Georgy Shepherd, Dick Burns, Riley Crawford, who tells me maybe he is only 13 years old but he's got a 26-year-old trigger finger . . . and down from Independence, boys we used for our insiders but say they want to be outriders now, Gabe George and Hop Wood." A jug was passed around. "I might as say right off we're not going to play around with fire any longer. That might've been Andrew Walker's way of doing things, but you boys know it got us nowhere. Now don't go getting me wrong about Andrew, I got respect for him and I hope to call him my friend, but you and me, we

56

hereby make a complete break with him. We're not going to sit around here and wait for something to happen. We sat around long enough. We can't sit around until we get wind of something already gone wrong, we got to spot it before it happens. And it's time for any of you boys who think this is some more child's play to leave because we aren't playing hide-and-seek any more." George Todd leaned away, carving something with his pocket knife, and Bill Gregg chewed his fingernails and spit them into the fire. "It's our turn, they had theirs. We're going into Independence and ring that courthouse bell so loud they can hear it all the way to Lone Jack. And then we're going over into Kansas and collect a few debts." Cole Younger looked as if maybe he had got in over his head. "There's going to be lots of bells ringing, lots of fire, and if you don't want to get burnt, you better ride on out of here tonight when the rest of us are asleep because fresh tomorrow you're all going to be different people." He felt the fire inside of him, and the words carried the combustion. It was a new experience, for it was his custom to chisel words out of the ice he carried about for that purpose. "While you boys been handlin' the little bottoms of sweet things in haymows and dancin' with your ol ladies, me I been workin' for you, me and Bill Gregg here and George Todd. The three of us rode up to Independence in those blue uniforms we got at Manasseth Gap and we got a close look at everything. We met Gabe George and Hop Wood up there . . . where are you boys? . . . there, those two know the inside out of that place and now we all know the inside out. Now listen, we're goin' in there tomorrow and ring that bell so loud everybody in the county will know we ain't about to be bullied about anymore!" He studied their faces: some were surprised, some elated, a few grew shadows across their faces. "Listen to me, boys," he said, dampening his words, "scattered men make scattered targets . . . if you don't show them where you come from they won't know where you're goin' . . . your mount and you is one person . . . you can't be in one place when you're everyplace . . . one bullet goin' where you put it is worth ten that ain't . . ."

Rily Crawford set his jaw and tried to look as if he understood.

They walked Indian-file and led their horses along a path that divided the bronze papaw bushes, crossed Bryant's Branch and along to a slow draw till they saw Bill Gregg in among the trees waiting. "The Noland Road is open," he said. "Younger is up ahead in the woods waiting for us." He whistled like a lark and they heard Younger's mating-call response, slipped across the opening and into the woods, where they tied their mounts and loaded their rifles. Quantrill walked among them, slapping them on the back, encouraging them, and crossed the last trees to the edge of the woods to survey Independence. The small village slept in the first light. He wanted it to be Lawrence: perhaps if he thought of it as Lawrence, imagined that Lane's little white house was among its quiet streets, dreamed that the old man had just risen and was standing at the glass running his blade over his chin, pretended he would rush into the house and jam a gun into his lathered jaw and say, "Gen'lman Jim, I want that reason and I want it now!"

But it wasn't Lawrence. It didn't even look like Lawrence. It was merely a puny wood town in the middle of a prairie crowned with a courthouse now in the hands of the Yankees and bearing their flag (which lay limp in the windless morning) and a small tower with a bell in it. He lifted his eyeglass and trained it at the bell he intended to ring all the way to Lone Jack so that everyone in the country would understand that the Quantrill Company was now in business. But then, that was not his real purpose for being there, and, in his own mind, nothing to do with the exercise. It was to free the prisoners. There were a dozen of them by now, young men dragged from their homes for refusing to kneel before the Yankees: he would take them back to Hell with him and show them how to win the war.

He returned his glass to its case and went to his horse, mounted, and turned to the men. "As soon as we have the courthouse," he reminded them, "Dick, you and your boys will head for the Rock Street jail and Jimmy, off to the east to keep that garrison penned in until you hear me stop pulling on the bell, and then we all scatter to the seven winds." He centred his hat and charged into the prairie, Hallar close behind, the black flag streaming, Bill Gregg and George Todd, Jimmy Little and then all the rest of them in full flight, like a tidal wave of horses that swept toward the unsuspecting vessel.

They quickly surrounded the courthouse, Quantrill leaping into the building, followed by Hallar and the flag, Bill Gregg and George Todd, who penned the guards to their beds. Quantrill and Hallar went up to the second floor and while Hallar pulled down the Yankee flag and ran up the black one, Quantrill gripped the rope of the bell and pulled with all his might. Instead of a clear peal, it came down with a crash, clattered down the roof and fell at the foot of Johnny Hampton's horse, who reared and threw the rider.

But that was only an indication of the trouble to come.

Dick Burns stood on the plank walk and was about to lift the maul that would knock the lock from the door of the jail when he heard gunfire, turned and saw Jimmy Little and his men retreating toward him being pursued by a hundred Yankees. "What in hell!" he said, jumping to his horse. He turned to run and saw Little rushing past him. "Who are those people?"

Little did not stop to talk. "Come in last night!" he shouted. "A whole regiment! Got to warn Charley! Get out of town, Dick!" But it was too late, the first Yankees were clearing the corner of the block and before they could run, Gabe George fell off his horse and died, and Hop Wood went and kneeled in front of him and tried to stem the advance. He emptied his rifle, turned, and took a lead shot in the back of the head.

It was little consolation that their retreat was successful.

The Yankees rode across the Divide for a few days and emptied their rifles at shadows. In frustration they arrested a dozen young men and took them up to the jail at Independence. They got mean with the old folks and burned a couple of barns. Then, at last, the pickets came to Hell and told Quantrill the Yankees appeared to have gone home again and it was safe for all the men to come out of hiding.

"These things happen'," he said when they sat in front of the fire, scraping off what little he had to feed them with. "That

Ohio troop must've come to town after we pulled Hop Wood out of there. Look at it this way," he said, and laughed. "Now you know what it's like. You know you can't make plans. You got to be ready to do what you got to do at the time when it happens."

"I went to his funeral," said Jimmy Little. "They called him a goddamn traitor." It grew silent. "They wouldn't let them bury him in the churchyard, they had to take him out on the open prairie, and then they came out and called him a goddamn traitor. Mrs. Wood cried but they called him a goddamn traitor. To her face! Listen, if he hadn't done what he done, we wouldn't none of us got out alive. We can't make another mistake like that."

"Don't go calling it a mistake!" shouted Quantrill, flashing his anger. "It happened." He dropped his eyes and softened. "It happened."

"You got us in there and you got us out again," said Bill Hallar, soberly. "That's all that counts."

"Hallar's right," said Ed Koger. "It learned us a lesson. Now, let's remember it and head out of here. We're ready to go, all we need is to be told where."

"We'll go anywhere," said Johnny Hampton.

"Would you go clear to Kansas?"

It was a cold rainy March night. Forty of them came up out of the marshes and stood at the road that led to Aubry. He sent pickets north and south and sat in the mist. "Stay close," he said. "I don't want anyone to go off by themselves and miss the fun." They carried small lamps as they moved south until they reached the bluff, spun out to the east and west and came into a small basin of grey grass and the settlement. The eastern horizon was defined, and he could tell by looking into the faces of the new men that they were scared. "Harry," he said to one of them, "nothing's going to happen to you if you just do what you're supposed to do and not go pretending you're some sort of fool." He touched him. "Stay close." The scouts came in from the Ft. Scott Road and reported the countryside was empty from top to bottom.

Urine-coloured sky.

He let them all sit there for awhile. It was good for them: it would let them think about things, harden, work it all out in their heads.

Peach sky, the landscape coming out.

Aubry had come out of a vegetable commune settled by New Yorkers who had come out to practice virtue but found only an indecent sun and tribes of irreverent Pawnees to whom a pumpkin was a pumpkin, instead of private virtue, single solitude and symbol of grace. The pilgrims had gone to their graves by the time the Abolitionists came, not to grow pumpkins, but to make certain that the country stayed in the Union. It had been hard for them too: loneliness, hard nights, Indians, sand . . . and now this.

The sun touched the edge of the sky.

He raised his hand.

The townspeople had done it before: stowed the children under floorboards, sealed the windows and the doors, thrown themselves onto the floor to wait until the bushwhackers or the Indians or the drunken scum were once more out of town, but this time it was different. This time the streets rang with random gunfire, doors were punched in and men dragged into the streets, driven together like cattle and herded into the road before the hotel and made to stand there until the mayor was brought before them. There was also a Union officer, bound and gagged, standing in the doorway to the hotel. A chair was fetched, and the mayor was asked to take a seat.

"Mr. Mayor," said a tall stranger, "my name is Quantrill and these men you see about you are Missouri citizens who are sick and tired of you people coming over there and burning them out of house and home." He turned and addressed the Yankee. "Lt. Randlett," he said, "under terms and conditions of war, I claim you as my prisoner. You will be taken with me and I promise you fair dealing." He went to the edge of the walk and looked down at the fifty men standing in the street. "Men of Aubry," he said, "take a good look at these people from Missouri...

memorize them . . . because if they find you supporting the Jay-hawker raids into Missouri, they'll be back again and then it'll be for blood.'' He turned back to the mayor again. "Mr. Mayor, I want your solemn promise, and I'm going to hold you to it. I want you to promise me that not one man in your town will ever again ride to Missouri without knowing when he gets home again, you're going to arrest him and have him bound over to me for a good old-fashioned hanging!'' The mayor was a short round man with little spectacles and a bad rash around his flabby ears. He was trying very hard to be brave. "Is this your answer, Mr. Mayor?'' The publican's face was red and moist. "You know, it wouldn't take much for me to lift my hand and there wouldn't be but ten men left in Aubry.'' The man on the stool sweated profusely, and he was beginning to tremble. "You know, Mr. Mayor, I just don't understand your line of thinking!''

The man's line of thinking broke from him in a force quite surprising, even to himself. "The people who live in this honest town are civilized people!'' he barked. "They are accustomed to living out their lives under law!''

The mayor turned nervously as if expecting applause, but the crowd in the street observed him as if he had uttered a public indiscretion.

Quantrill leaned over him. "Is *that* your answer?''

The mayor fixed his eyes on the street people.

Quantrill nodded to Bill Gregg, who stood in front of the citizens, and Gregg stuck a rifle into the ear of a dark-eyed and well-dressed man.

"Mr. Mayor!'' said the man, beginning to cry.

"George Mendelsohn!'' said the mayor, severely. "Take it like a man!''

George Mendelsohn lowered his head and swore.

Quantrill smiled and placed his own rifle three inches from the mayor's nose. "Take it like a man, Mr. Mayor!'' he said, smiling discreetly.

Upon consideration, the mayor said, "I will do what you say. Now leave this town in peace.''

62

NINE

He gave Randlett to George Todd after he told the mayor that the hostage would be killed if anyone came after them.

No one came, and after a week they rode back to Hell. Todd brought the Yankee along with him. It looked as if the young man had fallen off his horse: he was red and puffy about the face, his eyes were black.

"The sonofabitch tried to run off," explained Todd, when the pair of them climbed from their horses and stood before Quantrill and Jimmy Little. "I had to teach him a lesson."

Randlett was a small mousy man incapable of lifting a hand against anyone. His hands were tied together and he stared at the ground.

"Looks like he learned it."

Suddenly the Yankee lifted his head and shouted, "I never run off!" Quantrill saw something in his eyes that told him the truth. "This man beat me for no reason whatsoever!"

"Why, you—!" Todd threw himself at the hostage and began to beat him with his fists; Quantrill and Jimmy Little worked to pull them apart, and Quantrill pushed Todd up against the tree.

"Get a hold of yourself!" He stared at something in Todd's face, something uncontrollable, frightening even to him. "What's got into you, George?"

"Goddamn Yankee!"

When he had Randlett alone in his tent, Quantrill waited until the man calmed down before he said it. "What's the story, Randlett?" he said. "I never saw George Todd *that* mad. You must've done something."

Randlett stared at him a while before he could talk. "This man is quite insane," he said, choosing his words carefully. "He attacked me for nothing at all. He tried to kill me. The others stepped in, otherwise he would have succeeded."

Later, when Todd was walking his horse, Quantrill went to him and told him what Randlett had said. The pair of them walked together, and at last Todd turned to him and said, "I told you the truth, Charley. He tried to run away."

"He said he didn't."

"Who you goin' to believe?"

After a while Quantrill turned back. "I'm going to try to ransom Randlett. Maybe we can make a trade."

"Kill him," said Todd. "Don't make no business with the enemy. Don't take no hostages. You don't understand these things, Charley, but I do. Captain Oliver ain't goin' to listen to you. It's kill or be killed and don't you forget it." Quantrill stood watching Todd's face darken as he spoke. "You got to go whole hog from now on. There ain't no turnings in this road, and the quicker you learn that, the quicker we'll ride that last road together. The men are watchin' you, Charley. They're ready to run off on their own unless they see you doin' what they want to see."

"Thanks for the lesson, Todd."

"You listen to me and you won't go wrong."

They went to Liberty and chased the Yankees out of it, swung south again, cut the telegraph lines, and fell upon a stagecoach full of Yankee officers, killed them, fought off a rear guard, vanished into the marshes, where they waited to see whether anyone was interested in their border games. They waited an hour; Quantrill fired his gun, and they all came up one by one out of the trees and gathered around him before a thicket of pawpaw north of Brush Creek, a slow meandering stream that rose in Kansas and fell into Big Blue.

"Maybe Oliver sleeps away the afternoons," he said. "Or maybe he's just plain scared. Let's go have some fun!"

A young boy with an over-and-under stood at the toll bridge. He couldn't have been twelve yet. Todd told him to get out of the way, and when he wouldn't, someone kicked him to the ground. Todd wheeled and shot the boy, but before Quantrill could lecture him, it was too late. Someone rode away from the house on the slope above the river. Now Oliver would know where they were.

A half-hour later, just short of the Pack Train Route, which wound its way out onto the Kansas prairie, they saw a long line of men in blue, swinging in an arc to cut them off. They dove into the bottomland of Big Blue, scattering among the trees, building the Quantrill Noose, waiting.

But the Yankees rode together across the knoll and down into the draw, firing as they went, staying away from the darknesses, and, suddenly, without warning, wheeled back up onto the Divide and rode toward Cave Branch creek.

Perhaps it was a trick.

Quantrill waited.

No one moved.

"I'll go," he said, signalling to Jimmy Little. He slipped off his horse and crept up to the lip of the height: the prairie was empty.

They found Johnny Little hung from his saddle by a leg.

"It went in the front and come out the back," said Jimmy Little, hovering above his brother helplessly. He looked at the blood in the sand. "I don't see nothin' it took along with it, but I sure don't like the looks of Johnny, do you?"

Quantrill knelt beside him and brushed the sand out of his eyes. "Don't you quit on us, Johnny," he said. "We're going to get you to a doctor real fast."

"Ain't no doctors hereabouts!" said Jimmy.

"It hurts, sort of," said the bleeding man.

They ripped off his shirt, and Jack Jarrette came wheeling out of the trees to examine the wound.

"Bill," said Quantrill, "find us a wagon and get Johnny

65

over to Doc Parsons. His place is on the bend north of Kemper's Station. Jack'll go along with him. Make sure he stays put until the doc says he can leave and if you have to, leave a couple boys around to watch over things.''

They rode south with George Todd and Bill Gregg running the forward scouts, staying high on the Divide, unhurried, cautious. The men were tired and hot; they began to let up, their heads fell. He had to get them out of the sun or it would come down to an easy contest if the Yankees showed up again. They came down to Indian Creek as it fell into Big Blue, where the woods thickened and he knew it was dense enough to put everyone into. He sent Joe Vaughan over to have a look and signalled for a halt. The dust cloud blew away and they stood in the glare of the sun. ''Vaughan is down there making sure there isn't a pack of Yankees waiting for us,'' he said. ''We don't want to get too far ahead of Jimmy Little and the boys who took Johnny to the doc.'' He saw Joe Vaughan waving to them, ''Let's go cool off until it's time to head for our lodgings for the night.''

The men slipped from their mounts into the cool deep leafstrewn shadows and sprawled to watch the treetops flutter in the high Kansas wind. Quantrill walked among them until at the edge of the woods he came to a man whittling a stick. A marionette, a toy skeleton, lay sprawled over his knee. A large square man, yet he moved his fingers like delicate tools: they were polished hands, fingernails smooth and glossy, long thin fingers, the vessels large and modelled. As he worked, a child's smile played over his lips. Quantrill lowered himself against a beech tree and watched him wire the smooth stick to the hip of the skeleton.

''So!'' said George Todd. ''Mr. Bones! Mr. Bones!'' He slipped the strings over his fingers and set the feet onto the ground. ''Dear Mr. Bones, the sarabande? The cotillion march?''

''Don't you get tired of making skeletons?''

''Me?'' he smiled, looking across at Quantrill. ''Why, I'm in the business of making skeletons. I'm a master craftsman at

66

it." He finely tuned the femur bones, glanced across at his audience. "Don't give me that look, Charley. I can admit it even if you can't. You know, you've got to give up this idea you're doing a favour for people."

"I never said that." Quantrill leaned back and let his hat fall over his stubbled chin.

"No, but you think it. You and all these goddamn plowboys. Me, I'm not from here. I'm from up in the Red River country. My daddy was in the Royal Navy but he's a fur trader now. Hudson Bay Company. I come down to The Landing to show you people how to build stone walls. I ain't one of you. What in hell does Bill Gregg know about me? Bloodthirsty! Hell, look! I ain't doing anything different. Only thing is, that's where me and you differ, Charley. You don't take this thing serious enough."

"Serious!" Quantrill sat up and tore off his hat. "You know, George, one of these days we're going to part company."

Todd lowered the skeleton. "What are you talkin' about? We just got underway, you and me."

"You got a real mean streak in you I don't like."

He looked shocked. "Says who?" He went back to his work. "Anyways, I notice you always like what I do for you. Otherwise you wouldn't've put me in charge."

"You're not in charge."

Todd looked at him again. Why don't you just tell me what's on your mind instead of beatin' around the bush? Here I throw my fortune in with yours, I give up a good career in masonry and you tell me I got a mean streak in me. That's all you can remember, I got a mean streak in me."

"A real mean streak."

They studied each other for a while, and Todd was the first to break. They both laughed foolishly for a while. "Maybe I'm just tough," he said.

"You got a real mean streak in you." Quantrill watched the subtle manoeuvres to make the leg swing in a human way. "I always figured myself as a dark man, George. I never seen anyone yet who could beat me at darkness."

67

"Darkness?"

"Darkness."

Quantrill picked up his hat and rose to his feet, stood dusting himself off and looking as if he meant to apologize, and then he put the hat on and looked down at the carver.

"You Americans talk funny," said Todd, swinging the toy in front of him like a censer.

The wind had begun to fall off and the light became silvery as he walked out into the open, his hands thrust deep into his pockets. He stared at his feet and thought about George Todd, about his meanness and darkness, and knew the company would be in deep trouble without him because they had come to depend on his perversity and fearlessness.

But the darkness, if that should get loose among the men . . .

He wandered alone, his hat pulled low over his eyes, until he saw a man coming out of the woods toward him. It was Jimmy Little. Had he been out walking so long? It had seemed only minutes since he left George Todd. He watched Jimmy approach with a light buoyant stroll, a good man, Jimmy Little, good *good* man, none of the darkness. Cunning, yes, even devious perhaps, quick to anger, yet when Jimmy rode into the smoke and fire, he rode like a person, not a demon.

"That didn't take you long."

"Johnny's goin' to be fine," he smiled. "Parsons said it was a clean wound, no poison, nothing inside touched. He'll be in bed about a week."

On their walk back to the woods, Quantrill said, "What do you think of Todd, Jimmy?"

"Todd?" He walked a few paces. "What about him?"

"I'm goin' to put him right under me in command."

"What's this 'command'?"

"I mean I'm going to put him in charge while I'm away or . . . if the same thing should happen to me as happened to your brother."

"The men like him. He's easy to drink with."

"But you were here before him, isn't that what you mean?

You and Hallar and Johnny Hampton?''

It always surprised Jimmy when Charley Quantrill had seen through him. The man was like that: he never let you near him but he always seemed to be able to penetrate your defences. "Something like that," he said.

"I want you outside all this, Jimmy. I want you in there beside me. It's a lonely business this, and it's going to get lonelier." They walked for a few minutes. "The boys, this is rough stuff for them, it's going to get rougher. We're on our own out here and nobody telling us how to run things. One of these days it's bound to crack open and somebody's going to want to run things different. You see what I mean by lonely? That's when I'll need you, Jimmy. Somebody the boys can turn to when a decision has got to be made."

After that, they walked back into the woods, their arms behind their backs, eyes lowered. The men had built a fire and were cooking salt pork and boiling a wild onion soup.

"Here's the breakdown," said Little, walking out in front of the men stiff-legged because he felt a little uncomfortable giving orders. "Most of us is goin' down to that little hollow between Wilson's and Wyatt's, you know, where that warm springs is, and a dozen or so will be goin' on with Charley up to the Major's house. You got the cheesecake because Major Tate has said he can put all of you up inside his house for the night."

"I'll pick the men I want to take with me, Jimmy," said Quantrill, a half-tone deeper. "Steve Shores, Jack Jarrette, Perry Hoy, the Rollins brothers, George Shepherd, Buddy Younger, Will Freeman and Dan Williams," and he paused, thinking of an older, more seasoned man to put with the greenhorns, "and Dick Burns, you and George Todd, maybe the pair of you can tuck in the littl'uns."

TEN

Quantrill's party rode under a darkening prairie sky and up a long sweeping rise toward a tall windowlit clapboard house that commanded a height above the divide it sat on. It was an elaborate house with tall shuttered windows, double-storeyed, a long ell leading back to a fieldstone barn whose back pastures fell to the woods along Big Blue Creek. Once the elegant manse had crowned the rise and was reached only by a long leisurely yew-lined carriageway, but now the stageroad bore straight through the gardens. The major had erected a tall picket fence and ornamented it with roses and lilac bushes and small cherry trees to preserve a small measure of privacy.

He was a small pot-bellied man with generous manners, his white beard covered his chest, and when he spread out his hands, you could see the marks from the hand combat in the War of 1812. His wife was a tall severe woman with eyes the colour of pickles. The two of them stood in the door watching the men come out from the pasture and file into the yard like ranch hands, their hats at their knees, deferential, worn, friendly. The Major called them up onto the porch and shook hands with each of them, and his wife nodded slowly as she inspected their hands. They were allowed to wash but had to sit for an hour before retiring because the Major and his wife had set out tea for them and his grandchildren were asked to perform on the spinet. The men sat reverently, but Steve Shores fell asleep and spilled tea onto the China carpet, and Will Freeman farted while Mrs. Tate stood before him with a platter of preserves. After the concert George Todd presented the two children each with a skeleton, and then, one by one, they were all shown to their rooms.

Quantrill had to sleep with George Todd.

The mattress on the bed had subsided, and the two of them first clung valiantly to their heights, back to back, exploring the pockets of horsehair for toe-holds, tugging at the short blanket. In time, however, they surrendered to gravity and ended up butt to buttock, with George Todd stung by a slumber and beginning to snore. Quantrill could not sleep. He fell further into the abyss, toward Todd's sweaty corpulence. The moonlight reached them and played across Todd's latest unfinished work of art, an armless one-legged figure, mere sticks, crucified wood. Quantrill skinnied up to the precipice of the mattress and peered over and into the sleeping faces of the men on the floor, their features still and deathly.

Todd sent out a right to the body and then inch by inch began working his way up out of the pit, and Quantrill shoved one arm up against him and held on. Todd was like a square stone. He had to put his feet against him to keep him from sinking upward. Somewhere in the house a great clock laboured through its twelve numbers and he heard a horse in the road. He took hold of the headboard and placed both feet against Todd's back and began to push. It was a horse in the road.

"George!" he barked.

It was closer now.

"George!"

It turned in at the gate.

"George!" He began to shake him. Footsteps across the porch and coming toward the door. "Wake up, George!"

Pounding on the door.

"Wazzat!" said Todd.

Quantrill had the lamp lit before the man was in the room.

"Bluebellies!" he cried.

It was John Hampton.

"What?"

71

"Bluebellies! Hundreds of them!"

"Hundreds?"

"Hundreds of Bluebellies!"

"Where?"

"Comin' down the road!"

The men jumped out of their beds and began hurriedly to dress.

"Don't make no lights!"

"How many hundreds?"

"Hundreds and hundreds!"

"You drunk, Hampton?" said Todd, calmly.

"These boys know damn well where they're going! They ain't out for no evenin' air!"

"How'd they get past the picket?"

"I don't know, I just looked up and there they were."

"How close are they?"

"By the crossroads I s'pect!"

"Wrong," said Jack Jarrette, tucking in his shirt at the window. "They're coming up the hill right now and they know damn well where they're headed!"

"Sonofabitch!"

"What can we do?" cried Steve Shores. He had his shirt on backward. "What can we do? We've got to get out of here!"

"Let's get out!" said George Shepherd.

"How in hell—"

Perry Hoy only knelt and worded a prayer.

"Let's get to hell out of here!"

"They've gone around behind the barn," said Jarrette, still acting as lookout. "They'll be seeing those horses any time now."

"Somebody better think of something pretty fast," said George Todd, squaring his hat. "This ain't where I want to be."

"Charley?" said Hoy.

"Well?"

"Jesus Christ!"

It had even begun at last to rain.

"Buddy!" he said, quickly. He had no time to think. "You

and Jack and Henry, you boys get your asses downstairs and out to those windows. Steve, you and George Shepherd, over there. Dick, you organize the Tates. Tell them to get down under their beds and wait until I tell them to come out again. Now, you boys at the windows, don't let them see you from the road."

Out in the hallway he met Will Freeman and the rest of them coming up the stairs.

"Everybody just relax," he said, "and think about what you got to do."

"How we goin' to load in the dark?"

"You can't load in the dark," said Todd, coming along down the steps, "you don't deserve to know!"

He was down the steps and into the parlour without knowing he was doing it. "Jack," he said, "cover that window over there by the clock and George, can you take the other side? Keep in touch, keep talking." He slipped to the window and looked out into the road.

It was true, it was all going to happen at once.

The first ones past carried torches that showed it was raining. They walked on past the gate and down the road. Then the foot soldiers came, rank by rank, with long black muskets over their shoulders, their eyes fixed on the swaying shape ahead of them, all moving along like a centipede. More torchbearers, more footmen. Somebody touched him on the shoulder; he turned and found the Major looking past him through the window.

"It's Bluebellies," he said.

"So that's what it is!" said Quantrill.

"Must be a hundred of them." The Major groaned and looked at Quantrill. "These boys you got, Charley, are they seasoned?"

"They will be."

"What is your strategy, your defensive strategy?"

"When you don't know what to do next," said Quantrill, more to himself, "you wait and hope the other man makes a mistake. You ought to know that, Major."

"You can't do that, he might not make a mistake. You've got to have a positive plan."

73

"Alright," said Quantrill, "you go join your family."

An officer stood before the gate and lifted a sabre into the air and the entire apparatus came to a slow halt, turned and faced the house. You could hear the commands being shouted up and down the road, and it sounded like a well-polished army.

"Oh, oh!" said one of the Rollins boys.

The soldiers prepared their muskets and a torchman came and held his flames above the picket fence so that the entire yard was lighted.

"Steady!" whispered Quantrill.

The Yankee officer dismounted, handing his steed to a boy. He pulled off his gloves a finger at a time and strode like a victor toward the house.

"Maybe he's lost," said the Major.

"We should be so lucky."

"He knows what he's doing," said George Todd.

Suddenly the Major stood. He walked across the room toward the door.

"Where you going?" whispered Quantrill.

"Let me talk to him."

"Come back here," he growled. "Always let Bluebelly tell you first what's on his mind."

The officer was close now. Already they could see the two stars on his shoulder and the small eagle crouching over a ribbon. Three men marched alongside the torchman beside the gate, knelt and lifted their muskets to their shoulders as if they would shoot their own officer in the back. Quantrill heard footsteps upon the porch and then a hard knocking at the door. The wind stood high in the trees. Silence. Another announcement. The officer then stomped across the porch to peek into a window. Dick Burns could have kissed him on the cheek, he was that close. The officer returned to the door, rapping loudly. Then he shouted: "Make a light in there!" Quantrill figured by now he would have been able to say he had done his duty and gone away but apparently he was trying to make an impression on his men.

"Hold steady, men," he said again.

The Major crouched again.

"Make a light!" the officer said. "This is Major Pomeroy! Second Kansas! Under command of Colonel Robert Mitchell! Open up in there, Tate! You're under arrest! We know you're harbouring the Bushwhackers! I have papers! You're under arrest!"

It was time, he thought. I have to move now or I'll never move. He got up and walked slowly to the centre of the room and levelled his revolvers at the door. The Major watched him in horror and some of the men at the windows covered their ears.

He fired twice and sprawled once again in the dark below the window.

The response was instantaneous: the windows across the front of the house simply disintegrated and the shot clattered into the rear wall, destroying the protraits and the scenes of stillness and taking along the lamps as well. The smell of coal oil and burning powder was all that was left after the volley.

"Jesus!"

"What'd you do that for?"

"Did you get him?"

The men in the road were lining up against the fence once more and levelling for the second volley.

This time it was only the clatter of lead.

"Get out of here, Major!" said Quantrill.

Suddenly, it was silent.

"It's the house," said the Major, laughing. "They found out it's not just a simple frame house. You know it's all rock and brick underneath all them boards!"

"Pomeroy's creeping back out to the fence!" said Todd. He fired three times. "He's back among them, goddamnit!"

"Coupla them!" said George Shepherd, firing. "I hit one of them!"

"Any sign of activity coming from Wyatt's?"

"All quiet down there."

"That wasn't smart of you!" It was Pomeroy, his voice coming from somewhere. "You might've injured me, Quantrill, but you was lucky! Now listen to me. We stand five hundred men out here, you haven't got a chance! Now if you was to come out one at a time with your hands over your heads, maybe we'd consider it a mistake what you done. You hear me in there?''

He had to stall for time. It wasn't a matter of trying to calculate odds: there weren't any. There was only a space he wanted, a little time to work it all out in his head.

"Listen!'' he shouted backward, below the window, looking back at the faint halfmoon faces watching him. "We got a house full of women and children in here, so take it easy. Don't panic now. You wouldn't want it to get around you had women's and children's blood on your hands, would you?'' It was quiet along the fence. "Besides, you ought to know the rules of war!''

"Let my family go,'' whispered the Major. "Me, I plan to stay with you. This is as good a place and time as any to die in.''

"Johnny,'' he said, motioning to Hampton, "take Major Tate upstairs and gather up his family.'' He waited until the pair of them started up the stairs. "Well, Pomeroy, what are you doing out there? Looking up in your book to find out if there's anything about women's blood in it?''

"The ones who break all the rules are the first to holler 'rules' when they're cornered!''

"Who said anything about cornered?''

After a while Pomeroy said, "Send out the Major and his family one at a time!''

And they went one by one, their hands on their heads out into the yard and straight into the flares and vanished.

Quantrill stumbled back and forth through the dark room, thinking out loud. "We're in a hell of a fix,'' he said. "This one isn't going to come out as clean as we'd like it. We'll get out all right, but . . . now, look, I got all you boys into this thing but I can't promise you I'll get you back out of it. There's five hundred out there. Hallar and Gregg and Jimmy Little can't help us now.''

George Shepherd called down from the top of the stairs. "They're shooting arrows at the roof and they're starting to burn,'' he said. "It's only a matter of time.''

"I'm going to give anybody who wants it a chance to get out of here now,'' he said. It was quiet, he looked around. "There won't be no hard feelings. Take it now or forget it.'' Some of them looked at each other.

"Nobody's chickenshit—"

"Shut up, George!"

Will Freeman stood up and walked toward him, his lips tightly sealed, and then Dan Williams came and stood behind him. Will started to say something.

"Don't apologize," said Quantrill. He looked around the room, waiting for a mass surrender. "Anybody want to join these two? Now or never, what do you say?" The rest of them leaned back into the dark and looked up at the two men standing in the middle of the room.

"Pomeroy!" shouted Quantrill. "Two of my men are surrendering! They're coming out! They'll throw their guns out ahead of them!"

The door was thrown open and the two of them, caught suddenly in the halo of light, blanched. Will Freeman looked back into the darkness to find Quantrill and when he found him he tried on a smile asking forgiveness.

"Git!" said Quantrill, looking down at his boots. "At least maybe you got a chance this way." They threw their revolvers out ahead of them into a small puddle of water and walked out into the yard, blinking, their hands over their heads.

A wall of lead came at them, they stumbled and fell face down into their own blood.

The door was thrown shut. "Bastards!" screamed George Todd. "They shot them down!" Perry Hoy was moaning, and Burns and Hampton opened fire at the fence. "Killed the buggers in cold blood!"

Lightning forked the sky.

"This I'll never forget," said Quantrill, leaping into the window and opening fire. And for some time they fired at the fence, which periodically exploded from the other side with a new volley that flattened against the bricks or against the horsehair plaster behind the men in the windows.

But the roof burned merrily.

"We're all dead!" screamed one of the Rollins.

77

"Goddamn sonsabitches!"

"I got one!"

Someone jumped into the yard and flung an oilsoaked ball of fire into the sitting room: Dick Burns jumped into it and, with his bare hands, flung it back through the window. The flames had eaten his hands, and he went raging back toward the kitchen. "Butter!" he cried, as if waiting for someone to come to his aid.

"There's no way out of this one!"

"Maybe it's time to go with the house!" said Todd, ignoring him. "Better than going out into that bunch of killers the way Williams and Freeman did."

"I'm damn sure of one thing," said Quantrill, quietly, "and that is that we can some of us get out of here, I don't know how many, but it's worth a try. I don't relish George's idea myself. I'm too young to die in a burning house. We got to weigh the chances this house is going to come down at a certain time, where there's too much fire even for the Yankees to look at it. There's something about a burning house that puts people to sleep watching it. They get fixed looking at it. You know what I mean? Besides, maybe this is put here for us to overcome." He wasn't a man given to theory or sentiment, but at the moment, it seemed crucial for him to find the right combination of words to open his mind. "Maybe this is the test, the thing we worked toward. I don't know. There's just the dozen of us and five hundred of them, it don't seem right, but there it is, the chance to see whether when it comes right down to it we're any better than they are." The house was on fire. "I'm goddam sure if we try to get out of here all at once at the right time we could do it. Anyway, what else is there to do?"

A rumbling sound in the attic.

Younger said, "Let's work it all out and then goddamn well do it!"

"I'm for it." said Hampton.

"George?"

Todd laughed.

"Jarrette?"

"This is the moment I been waiting for!" I think I got an

idea. If I could find some kind of coat to wear over your clothes, see? Something that wouldn't burn and then you could put on a mask of some kind—"

"Next time, Jack!" barked Quantrill. "Right now it's this time and it's got to come clean. Run like a goddamn clock. One wrong move and . . ."

"—you could put it over your nose and it would filter out all the smoke—"

"Quiet, Jack!" he said, slipping to the window and peering through it. The Yankees had strung themselves out along the fence and were standing idly about like neighbours over to enquire about the fire and finding it too late to help. He could tell they were convinced that it was all over for the people inside the inferno, that it was only a matter of time before they could go inside and collect the bones and take them back to Independence to show to the disbelievers. The heat must have become intense, because some of them stepped back and shielded their eyes. Strange how, in the house, inside the fire, it was cooler and safer. He saw a number of them lighting cigarettes and smoking, gazing off into the surrounding fields. He would have to depend on them.

"The sonsabitchin' assholes shot down Williams and Freeman!" snarled George Todd, holding his head and staring at the floor.

"Listen, Charley," said John Hampton, shivering, "if you get me out of here, I'll follow you to the end of the world."

"This *is* the end of the world, Johnny."

He knew they would be shocked to find him coming straight out of the fire, unscathed, but then, how long before they recovered and started to shoot? He had to risk it, he had to surprise them, it was all he had left. "On your knees," he said. "Follow me!"

They looked like children at a game, crawling single-file out of the front room, around the rocker, along the hall and through the back door, into the summer kitchen, where they kneeled together in the smoke.

"Load up," said Quantrill, and each of them pulled out his

79

Colt revolvers and loaded. "You got to have words at times like this," he said, quietly, like a man forced to talk over his work. "But the only thing coming to me right now is if you make one mistake in this, you're dead! That don't sound too much like a sermon, does it?"

George Todd stood up and looked out the window toward the side wall. The door gave out into the south walk, which led to the barn. "They got a crazy notion we're coming out the front door!" he said, in a slow thoughtful way. "Maybe because Pomeroy's out there and they think he's the one we got to answer to. There's only a handful out here. We got to get past them and out toward the barn where I don't see nobody!"

"If I don't make it, Charley—" said Hoy.

"Shut up!" said Quantrill. "No time to draw up wills."

"I can get four or five of them myself," said Jarrette, snarling. "You take five, George, and that's it!"

"This is nothin'!" said Dick Burns.

"This is everything, Dick!" said Quantrill, on his knees at the window, the others behind him, waiting. "Everything we ever needed, boys! Now, that goddamn wall is coming down, everything's coming down and we can't wait for it. We got to find the exact minute to get out of here, you follow me? We're coming out like one man when that ceiling comes down . . . we're here and we ain't here! Nobody says, Shit! I can't make it! You can *make* it!" The smoke was in their lungs, their eyes burned. "If you can't do it, if you can't get out of here, then nobody can!" Overhead, somewhere, they heard a ceiling go down, burying its fiery lake among the rich oaken pioneer furnishings. "Fire as we go, left and right and don't stop for nobody!"

"Charley!" said George Todd, paused. "Listen!" They listened: all they could hear was a house coming down at them, folding up like a mountain of fire. "Someone's shooting at them!"

"Who?"

Todd raced back into the sitting room; the rest of them hung their heads, held hands, waiting for the end.

"They've come for us!" screamed Todd. "It's Bill Gregg . . .

Jimmy Little . . . the whole bunch of them, the Bluebellies, they're turning now, running for cover! I can see Pomeroy! I can't hear what he's saying!"

The ribs of the house gave in with a terrible roar and fragments of the ceiling fell onto their heads in a cloud of dust; Todd came low around the corner and dove amongst them.

"They've got something to worry about!"

"It's time to go!" said Quantrill.

The house reeled as if in an earthquake and began to buckle and the dozen of them sprang into the night!

It was an odd turn of fate. Jimmy Rollins skipped high in the air as if stung by a bee, swatted himself, and sprawled onto his back. Seeing him, his brother paused and, looking around saw nothing, felt as if someone had slammed the barndoor onto his nose, saw light everywhere, and, before he fell into the sky, saw his brother's eyes — had he spoken? — then cocked an ear, waited, but heard only the soft silence everywhere.

Odd. Just the two Rollins boys, the others, in the consternation, ran firing in a circle, cleared the barn wall and found themselves followed by a few of them, dropping to their knees and taking aim, but as they ran they could see their own kind looking across a Colt revolver and firing into the wall of Bluebellies which, as it came, like sand on sand, fell smaller and smaller until at last, there was nothing left to shoot at, and Pomeroy himself came and investigated the darkness at the bottom of the hill.

"We've got the two of them anyways!" he said, but there was no disguising his disappointment.

ELEVEN

Heroics. Like so many words, made out of thin air. He didn't believe in heroics. You were a hero when you made a bad move and found you had to pull yourself out of it by your own bootstrap. The men had rallied around him, that was true. Stature, place, these had come to him now. But he was still the same man. He looked at himself in the mirror when he began shaving and wondered who he had become. He had never thought of himself as anything special. He had even tried to destroy what was left of him after his daddy was finished with him, tried to deface the coward he was when Colonel Torrey and Har Beeson had hacked off his piece of land over in Kansas and kicked him out of the house, tried to hide when Mr. Stone told him he wasn't good for anything more than washing dishes and sweeping out fireplaces at the City Hotel in Lawrence . . . and then there was Jim Lane, who sat there grinning at him, fat bastard! Sat there in the hotel in Lawrence and grinned at him like he was some sort of nigger. God, the scum! And Andrew Walker, at least he had found something in him . . . what?

He made himself into something there in front of the mirror: he shaved himself and left a moustache behind, one that stood out like a flag. Why, he was twenty-five years old already. Halfway to fifty, a quarter of the way to one hundred. Middle-aged, he was middle-aged!

At the fire and before the men, George Todd presented him

with a skeleton doll that looked exactly like him, showed his curious large eyes, the thrust of jaw, the forward tilt to the pelvis. Cole Younger looked at it and said, "Why, it looks jest like you, Charley! Ain't there a law against makin' graven images? I heard there was."

"Make me one of them things, George," said Perry Hoy, "because I know who to thank for gettin' out of that one alive!"

"I'll make one looks like you," said Todd, angrily, "unless you shut up!"

"You got yourself out of it, Perry," said Quantrill, fingering his doll.

"You showed us how to do it, Charley," said Jack Jarrette.

A new man, Frank James, came over and looked down at the doll. "Todd could go into the business of Quantrill dolls and make a pile of money," he said. "Why, everybody up in Liberty wants one." James was a tall man who talked slow but dropped his words like lead slugs. "I'm here because of you, Charley. There'll be others, you wait and see."

"I seen him," said John Hampton, after Quantrill had walked off into the trees dangling the doll before him as if it was a dead bird, "seen him in the fire. He was a different man, one I never seen in him when he had just come back from Wilson's Creek that time, him and Walker, remember? I figured he was just another Jayhawker, but then, that time he looked down in the ditch and saw Mrs. Strawder . . . why somethin' just come over him."

Quantrill left him and went to see Andrew Walker.

"I hear you got into some sort of trouble over at Major Tate's," said Andrew, being watched carefully by his wife. "It won't work, you know. You can't just go on killing and killing, Charley. Killing isn't the way Christian men go about their business."

"He's a *hero*, Andrew!" snarled Beth.

"You are a hero, Charley?" said Andrew, scoffing.

"A word made out of thin air," said Quantrill.

Hot air made by the lips, pursed, expulsing the bruised air of the lungs, making a sound and forgetting what it means.

It happened twice again that summer. He was over at Sam Clark's place, there were fifty of them now, more and more of them coming to him, waiting for him to invite them to stay. Sam Clark, yes, he had gone to meet a young man by the name of Frank James, James and his little band of brigands, they had had some fun up around Liberty, and they wanted to get together and help fight the Yankees. He looked up and found Company D of the First Missouri in the hills, and he had to run for cover again, inside the house, since it was right out in the open, and this time it was the end of the road, since it was broad daylight and he had no chance to find a way out of the house and suddenly, all around him, the woods opened up and the Yankees had to run for cover. And he had come out and stood around, when the farmers came out and waved their hats at him.

He should have learned a lesson, but he didn't. He was a teacher, not a student. It wasn't his way to learn anything. This time he was down at Jordy Lowe's, the men and he, riding around and it started to rain, and he put them up inside the house for the night only to find the First Missouri back again, like varmints, following the carrion host . . . and it would have been *so* easy to quit, quit and lay down the arms, come out with their hands over their heads, and hope that they simply wouldn't cut them down like they had at Tate's . . .

But standing here, in the room, feeling the cold wall behind him, listening to the monotonous THUD THUD THUD as the lead splayed across the front of the logwork, his back against them, facing the boys he had got into this corner, standing there he knew all he had left was heroics. He would throw himself into the fire, he didn't care, it was stupid! But he did it, firing at them, knowing they had been put into a strange situation, seeing one of them coming out shooting when they had already made up their minds this was it, Quantrill was finished . . . and out he would come, zigzag, zigzag! He had these sixshooters, the Colts, and all they had was the old muzzleloaders and the primer caps.

And at Jordy Lowe's, with Frank James with him, they had the advantage of that strange man's nasty ways, and the two of them came out, James and Quantrill, the pair of them, drawing

84

fire and exposing positions, and the rest of them following, but Joe Gilchrist fell that time, the Irish lad seriously hurt, and a couple of them fell into the Yankees' hands. Perry Hoy became a prisoner.

Tenth of July and they were at Lotspeich's back acre when they told him a pack of Yankees had seen them and were coming along the road.

"We can't run away," said Quantrill.

"Why should we run?" said Jimmy Little, at his side.

"Let's not play around inside houses again," said George Todd. He looked over at Bill Gregg as if they shared some sort of secret about houses. "We always get burned at it!"

"Buddy," said Quantrill to Younger, "you take your boys up there, load up, and just stand around in the yard like you didn't know nothing about nothing! I'll take George and the rest of them with me along the road and hide in those trees and they'll come on down the lane because it's narrow, it'll break their momentum, don't you see? and once they're inside it and heading in for the yard, we'll open up on 'em from the sides!"

They came, broke their stride, and Quantrill's men killed fifteen of them. Captain Kehoe fell from his saddle and Quantrill went over to him and shot him in the chest. The Younger brothers were at the end of the lane with the gate open, and fifteen good Yankee mounts with fifteen St. Louis saddles on them flew into the yard. Quantrill watched the remaining Yankees rushing back across the road and into a small woods, and he pulled his men together. "They're mad!" he said. "And there's still eighty or more of them comin' after us so let's get to hell out of here . . . back down to the ravines, boys!"

They took up positions and waited.

The Yankees came around the barn, swords in the air, screaming for blood, but there was little they could do, what with the trees and shrubs; Quantrill could see their horses running free and he realized they had taken up positions among the rocks and it was going to be hand-to-hand combat from here on out. Quite by accident he turned and saw them above him. "What in hell!" he said, saw Todd below a man. "George! Above you!"

Suddenly, they were overpowered, and Yankees were everywhere.

Quantrill struck one of them with an oak club as he fell from a tree beside him. The man dropped his sword, stared at him angrily, seemed to miss a step as he staggered and fell onto his face. Quantrill took his sword and buried it into his back. To his left John Hampton was down on one knee reloading when a hatless Bluebelly came at him with a bowie knife, and as he struggled to step to one side, Hampton lodged a foot between two rocks and the man fell onto him and slit his throat.

"John!" he shouted and was about to charge the Bluebelly when another stepped in between them and he was faced with the two of them. He lifted his rifle, but the Yankee was too fast for him: he leaped across the opening and struck him, pinning him to the rock, and, as he held him by the throat, the Yankee raised his arm and Quantrill could see the blade spark in the sunlight. There was a shot, the man trembled, a look came over his face, something about Death, the unfairness of it all, and he fell backward, his legs thrashing about, then still, his hands reaching for the wound, finding it, as if to verify it, the arms fluttered in the knowledge and fell to his sides.

Above him stood George Todd laughing.

What he couldn't see was the Bluebelly under the rock, crawling up toward Todd's feet.

"Do something for me once!" shouted Todd.

"All right!" said Quantrill and fired. The Bluebelly leaped into space, threw his knife at the ground, and fell into a pile of arms and legs, twitched and expired. They went over to him and heard him mumbling something about 'kingdom come', but it was too late for him to finish it.

When it was over, Quantrill laid twenty-six men on the ground and left them for Independence, and then he saddled six of his own dead onto horses and called everyone together. "Boys," he said, "we lost Johnny Hampton and Jimmy Kelly, Ed Koger, most of you knew them. They been with me for a long time . . . and then there's Dick Chiles and Otto Hinton and Bill Carr, they're gone. We'll take them along and put 'em in the ground. There's a number of you boys cut and wounded too.

86

We'll see to that."

"Look at yourself," said Frank James.

He thought it was sweat he walked in, but looking down realized it was blood leaking out around his sole.

"You'll never catch Quantrill," said the cable. It was sent to the headquarters in St. Louis. "He maintains no headquarters nor camp, his patterns erratic. The partisans in the district support and protect him. They supply him with food and fighters. The only way to prevent him from continuing to mount guerrilla action would be to deprive him of this support and then burn off the prairie."

Too radical, said the new commander of the federal forces in Missouri, Brigadier General John M. Schofield, but at the same time he commissioned Lt. Daniel David, who had on several occasions penetrated Confederate lines along the Mississippi, to go to Blue Springs as a spy and find more about the guerrillas.

David lost no time, arriving at a farmhouse near Lobb's Church in mid-July and asking where he might find Quantrill. He got as far as Hell, where he found five men and one Union prisoner who seemed pleased to remain in his little house, and when he put the question to them, he was told that Quantrill was over in another county. Quite by accident he found a man who led him to a campfire, around which fifty men sat outfitted in Union Blues. "Are you certain?" he said, and when the farmer nodded, he broke his neck and rode quickly back to Independence.

"If Quantrill can ride as a Union patrol," he told Captain Oliver, "then I can ride as a crew of bushwhackers! I want fifty men, Captain, and I want them dressed in nankeen trousers, Quaker coats, guard boots, floppy black hats with red ostrich feathers, and I want them now!"

Quantrill heard about Lt. David's plans and sent for George Todd. The two of them rode off alone together and went down to a woods and took off their clothes for a swim. The water was cool, they were refreshed, and afterward, lying in the sun, Quantrill said, "I been watching you close, George, real close." Todd hadn't shaved for a week, he looked meaner than ever. "I saw the way you handled yourself over at Lotspeich's when we had those Yankees in the rocks with us."

"Get to the point, Charley," he said, letting the sun play over him. "I ain't much of a talker. I just want to know what's on your mind." Todd had a face cold and square and grey as a tombstone. "I got no time for all you Yankees always tryin' to find some reason to do what you know you got to do."

"Somebody named David, Lt. Daniel David," he said. "A spy, I guess. Putting together an outfit that looks like bushwhackers. Coming down some day soon and trying to join up with us." He laughed, closed his eyes and for a moment thought of himself as resting alongside a creek with a boyhood friend. "I want you to make sure we know when he's coming."

"Simple," said Todd. "While I'm up there, I'll have a quick look around. I think it's time we knew what they're up to at Independence."

As usual, Jack Jarrette was fooling with something. He had been repairing George Shepherd's Army Colt when he announced to everyone he was going to build a gun that would fire twelve shots instead of six. He spent the afternoon drawing pictures of it, and that's as far as he got. Once they were pulling down telegraph wires and he said he'd take them back with him to camp and string them low in the grass and then rig it so that, when the Yankees came, he could raise it quickly and trip their mounts. When anyone complained that he was slacking off, he'd say, "You're against science, ain't you?" He loved horses more than any other living thing and always talked to them when shoeing or tending them. The horses always seemed to know what he was saying. "Why stop at twelve shots," he said, "why not, say, twenty-four or . . . ."

Once as they prepared an ambush down behind the Wells and Starr Mill, Jarrette mounted his horse and rode back to camp, leaving the rest of them to finish the work, and when they all returned, they found him at the forge constructing something out of long iron bars. He scarcely looked up when they rode in, or when, later, Quantrill came to him and said, "You bolted, Jack. You run out in the middle of things."

"You can drag this thing, you see?" he said, more to himself. "They'll never see your tracks that way. One guy rides behind the rest of them dragging this broom."

"You ran, Jack."

"She'll just scatter the dust behind the trace, and it'll toss off the scent too."

"Jarrette!"

He looked up, surprised to find someone standing there.

"You ran."

"You against science?"

"I'm against running."

"You're against science."

Or the time something got loose among the horses. It wasn't the Thrush, Jarette could *smell* the Thrush before it began; it wasn't Strangles, they had had a run of Strangles, and Jarrette ran it to the ground before they lost all their horses to it; flus, viruses of all kinds, vectors, he was more than a good horse doctor, he was a scientist of horses. "This time," he said, "I'm stumped. I figured it was that load of bad hay we got from Moore, but that wasn't it." They had fevers and loss of appetite, droopy lips, some of them walking into trees or falling into creeks. "It must be the mosquitoes, Charley," he said. "Yes, I know, we'll be in a hell of a way if we have to do some riding." He spent the night with the herd, talking to them, feeling them, swatting them from time to time; you could hear him in the middle of the night addressing them.

It took him a week, but he cured them all the same. He went into The Landing and returned with what he called 'the syrup', and like a wise parent, he made the herd go to bed and not move around for three days, and by the end of the week they had got better. Jarrette's chief occupation, besides dreaming, was company farrier, and he had tools both historic and useful, arranged in a scientific way in backpacks, which he hung from the sway of two mules he called, respectively, 'Back' and 'Front', or, collectively, 'the foundry'. So far as Quantrill could tell, the mules never slept or maybe it was that neither of them was ever fully awake. They could be tethered together for two or three days in the middle of some creek bottom, never eating, scarcely moving a nostril. Jarrette could have been miles off at the time, and yet they would stand in that immobile semi-somnolence, waiting for his return.

"What was it?" asked George Todd. "Some kind of sleeping sickness?"

"I don't know," said Jarrette. "I never did find out. It was in Chinese. I don't speak Chinese."

"Chinese?"

"Sure. The mules told me. Mules speak Chinese, you know."

"No, we didn't!" laughed Ed Koger, a tall man not usually given to laughter.

"Well, what did they say then?"

"I don't know but it worked."

Later, Todd said, "Charley, you got to get rid of Jack. He's crazy."

"I don't give a damn if he's crazy. Look how he cured that run of sickness."

"Next thing he'll start on the pair of us. Hell, if I ever get a cold, I'll be damned if I'll go to him."

Horses were all they had, and if it hadn't been for Jack Jarrette, they wouldn't even have had them.

Todd took his assignment seriously. He went to Hell and talked to Lt. Randlett, who had turned pale and forgetful because he never left his little house in the trees. He was writing poetry now, and when Todd told him he wanted his help, Randlett turned him down. The Canadian was able to convince him, however, that if he accompanied him to Independence and told them that Todd was defecting and had stolen Randlett out of hiding, that Randlett could help Quantrill more than sitting in the woods writing poetry. The two of them rode into Independence, and Randlett convinced Colonel Buel that Todd was a turncoat and was prepared to assist the authorities in whatever way he could to destroy Quantrill.

90

"Well," said the Colonel, "this couldn't have come at a better time, Mr. Todd. I think we have a little plan that we could use your help on." But David looked him over skeptically and shook his head. "Lieutenant David," said the Colonel, "I have spoken to this man. He hates Quantrill with a passion."

"I have been waiting for a chance to kill him," said Todd, narrowing his eyes and breathing deeply. "I was second in command, you know. I realize now he cannot win, there is no hope. I would prefer to be thrown in jail or hanged, if need be. Yes, I have made a mistake. I am from the Red River Valley settlement, I shouldn't even be here. I don't know how I got here. Please send me away."

"David?"

Within the week, however, George Todd had thoroughly convinced the young officer that he was sincere, that all the information he offered on the operation of the guerillas was valid. "I want you to lead me to him," said Lt. David. "I want you in front of the men, disguised of course so Quantrill will not know you . . . and then, if there is any trouble, you will be the first to be shot."

It wasn't long before Todd's note reached Quantrill, who called the men together and told them for the first time about Lt. David's plans. He sent Bill Gregg into the Divide south of Blue Springs along with thirty men, established twenty in the woods at the top of the hill where the trail comes down through the trees past the lookout, left ten men in the camp to make appropriate sounds, and detailed John Koger and Johnny Little, now nearly recovered, to get out front to meet the wolves in sheep clothing and escort them into the trap.

Something went wrong.

Perhaps it was the sun, caught in the mirror of a gun barrel, the snort or fart of a horse in the high grass; perhaps it had been worked out ahead of time without Todd's knowledge. No one knew. Riding three abreast, David's men came down the draw smiling and chatting with Johnny Little and John Koger, when, without warning, three of the Yankees snapped out their Colt revolvers and shot their escorts at point-blank range.

Todd was too fast for them. His horse reared, Todd slipping around on the back side of him, rushing away toward the distant grass. Suddenly, all the Yankees opened up on the surrounding woods and one of them caught Todd in the shoulder and sent him sprawling out in the open.

"Cover Todd!" shouted Quantrill, jumping to his horse and firing at the rank of Yankees closest to him. It appeared, however, that Lt. David was not about to stay around to take advantage of his surprise move. After his men had emptied their revolvers into the trees, they swung around and fled up over the draw and north along the Divide toward the Independence Road.

"Let them go! Let them go!" Quantrill sprinted toward the downed Todd. "Take care of Johnny and Koger! Jarrette! Get over here!" He fell beside Todd and ripped his shirt for him, inspected the wound in the shoulder. Blood surged from him, his teeth clenched, he stared back at Quantrill.

"What happened?"

"I don't know, Charley . . . I . . . where's Koger?"

Jarrette rode over to them and threw his little black bag to the ground and fell alongside Quantrill.

"They're dead," said Jarrette. "Both are dead."

TWELVE

They moved down behind John Moore's farm into a thicket along Little Cedar Creek, entered only single-file and below two bluffs Quantrill used for his sentry posts. Once inside the woods (a level place of bushes and low trees, thick-thumbed beech, oak, willow) you would have to follow the creek until you found the opening and the path that would take you to Quantrill's tents. At one end of the clearing Jarrette installed his foundry and hospital, and at the other, Ike Hall built his kitchen below a canvas roof and in front of a small house for provisions.

It was good. If you knew the right questions, you might, in time, come to the gates and, providing you knew the password ("Bat 'em boys over the left eye!") you were admitted into the compound. So, late in July of 1862, two men said the right things and turned in along the creek until they met another man, who took them along the path to Jimmy Little, waiting beside the fire.

"Leave your weapons in your saddlebags," he said, "and come with me."

Colonels Upton Hayes and John Hughes.

Confederate States Army.

They presented a letter from General Thomas Hindman of the Mississippi Command, introducing the pair of them as emissaries, conveying the regards of the Southern States and deputizing them to commission Quantrill as Captain of the Confederate States Army.

"Captain?" said Quantrill, as if he smelled foul meat. "What is the real purpose of your visit, gentlemen?" They smiled awkwardly. "I don't believe they would send two high officers a thousand miles to deliver a letter."

"May we sit?"

"Please. It is my custom, however, to stand."

An awkwardness was visible and inexplicable. "Your efforts on behalf of our struggle for independence from the oppressor have not gone unnoticed, sir," said Colonel Hughes, who found a frog in his voice. "You have many admirers at our headquarter regiment in Cross Hollows. Colonel Joe Selby is one. You *do* know him?" Quantrill tried to smile. "One could say you are all the talk down there, Captain Quantrill." It was the first time he heard the words: they frightened him. "When you go to winter quarters, you are invited to visit Colonel Selby."

Colonel Upton Hayes tried to break the tension. "You have asked us the real reason for our visit," he said, looking back at Jimmy Little, who leaned against the pole at the flap. He smiled at Little. "We are under orders to scout for recruits for a winter offensive in Tennessee."

The cards were on the table, but Quantrill was not easy. "My men are occupied at the moment, sir," he said.

"Of course," said Hughes, "but we were informed that you might help us to find those men whom you find unworthy of your own company, yet—"

"I don't know where to find them. They come to me when they want me."

The following morning the two officers told Quantrill's men that under the terms of the Partisan Ranger Act, which gave officers the right to commission others on the battlefield, their leader had been made a captain in the Confederate States Army. Colonel Hughes gave Quantrill a piece of paper, saluted him, and, after the new officer sat, made a startling announcement: "Captain Quantrill," said Hughes, "has recommended two men for the position of lieutenant in your company, and I shall ask you to step forward at this time. The names are . . . George Todd and Bill Gregg."

That night Bill Hallar came to his tent, his face long and white, a wistful line about his eyes. "I should've come to you first," he said, "but there wasn't no time. I had to meet them before they went off on their hunting expedition."

"Them?"

"Those two Confederates."

Quantrill gave at first as if he were shocked, and Hallar sat on a stool. "Why, I was in this company even before you was." His eyes grew bright. "And I risked my goddamn neck for you and that Walker too, many a time." He was trying to get a fang into his words. "You seem to have forgotten a lot of your old friends, maybe it's time you started to give an account for what you have done."

"You come for an explanation?" said Quantrill, distancing himself. "Winning is everything," he announced, "losing is nothing."

"That's bullshit!"

"Bill, when I come over there that day with Andrew Walker, you boys were talking about an eye for an eye." Quantrill had been struck, he limped back and forth in front of the table like a lawyer. "You boys hadn't no idea where this thing was headed for, just a little gunplay, shooting them from your bedroom windows only when it's too late, when they're in your yard. It don't work that way no more, Billy, and that's why I made Todd and Gregg lieutenants because for them it just ain't an eye for an eye, those boys know how to blind a man." He had gone too far; he leaned forward, smiled, and then sank onto a stool opposite Bill Hallar. "Besides, that's the Confederacy, Bill, Todd and Gregg are lieutenants in the Confederacy. You and me, we're still fighting for Blue Springs."

Hallar did not look convinced.

"Things have changed," he said. "It don't have anything to do with blindin' or anything like that. It's George Todd, Charley. He's made the difference."

"Todd?"

"Him and his boys. He's bringin' in people I don't want to

associate with, people don't give a damn about Blue Springs or Missouri . . . they're in this only for the blood.''

"Todd?" Quantrill tried to laugh, but it had to be staged, and he knew he had made a fool of himself. "Harmless fool, carves wood all day, making toys for the children.''

"You seen him at work. He don't know when to quit.''

"But don't you see, Bill, I made him a lieutenant so's he had a little responsibility. It's responsibility that takes the boy out of the man, you know that. You know, I don't like running this outfit at all. I'm not a natural leader, you know that. This is an army belongs to everybody, Bill.''

Hallar stood and settled his hat onto his head. "I don't want to ambush you into saying somethin' you might have to take back some day, so I'm leavin'.'' He thrust out his hand. "Say I'm one of Blue Spring's boys who graduated from Charley Quantrill's school and has gone out into the world knowin' just about everything there is to know about fightin' a war.

Hallar wasn't the only recruit: by the end of the first week in August the two officers from Cross Hollow had four hundred boys in the creek below Stanley's, and Colonel Hughes rode over to tell Quantrill he was pleased with the take. He had a confession to make. They had four hundred men of all ages, two hundred horses and one hundred and twenty Kentucky rifles, which would mean an unequal conflict against any Yankee patrols along the way to Arkansas. "I can't ask you to take me down there, Captain,'' he said, "but maybe I could ask you to find me some horses and a few Navy Colt revolvers.''

Quantrill gazed at him in that oriental way, his eyes deep in his head, a samurai's confident smile pursed on his lips, about to utter an aphorism that would disguise any concern about the world where loss is always present. "You have four hundred men, Mr. Hughes,'' he said. "I have one hundred, but I have three hundred horses and three hundred new Colt Navys still in their boxes from Connecticut.'' He said no more, receded once again, waiting for the young officer to draw a quick conclusion to his offer.

"I accept," he said. "What do you want to do?"

"You have a recruit named Bill Hallar, a friend of mine. I always promised him Independence, but I never had enough men to do it. Last time I was there, I made a serious mistake and had to run for cover."

They sewed all their blankets together and hung them from a flagpole on top of Mt. Bowler. You couldn't say they weren't warned about what was about to happen. Still, it was disconcerting to be advised during a meeting in the Southern Bank Building that someone had seen a huge flag flying from the guerrilla hideout deep in the Divides. Colonel Buel was taken up to the roof, and someone gave him a pair of glasses. "My God!" he said, thoughtfully, his eyes fixed, "it's some kind of a black flag. Something on it."

"How did they get it up?"

"It's on Bowler."

"It isn't white, that's for sure."

"But what's it supposed to mean?"

"Insult," said Buel.

What they didn't see were the four hundred seventy-five men gathered in the dark down below John Moore's barn pouring lead and greasing guns, eating for two days, going over their plans. Quantrill would lead the charge, Hayes and Hughes to take their four hundred boys and old men around east of town and pen in the Yankees, Quantrill to circle on into the centre of town, take the command headquarters and free the prisoners, get back some of the Blue Springs boys, destroy the offices of the Yankee Warlord. A lesson in punishment, a body blow.

Fifteen new men had joined him at the end of July. "Seventy-five," said Jimmy Little. "Todd, I don't know where he finds these people." Darkness, thought Quantrill, gathered by numbers. "I'm sending them out to George to learn how to handle them new Colt pistols, and Bill Gregg is riding with them, showing them how to fade. We got old lady Slaughter makin' us those nankeens, and Chiles shot down a stagecoach full of guard

97

boots, fifty of them! Blunt, he went over to Westport and brought home a bunch of Quaker coats and Kossuth hats." But Little knew when he saw it in Quantrill's eyes: uniforms don't make soldiers, they just tell which side you're on.

He had to have something to bind them all together, something like a loyalty oath or pledge of allegiance, something which, when said, made you feel small and insignificant. He went to his tent, stayed for two days, and emerged, halfmad and hungry, and called all the men to the meadow, where he made them all kneel before him among the bird songs and repeat his words after him.

"The purpose of war," he began, "is to kill! God Himself made this Honourable in the Defence of Principles, for did He not cast Lucifer out of Heaven and relegate the rebellious angels to the Shades of Hell?" Maybe it was too wordy, he thought. "The Love of Life cannot be measured but under two conditions: one is when our surroundings are happy and our attachments numerous; the other is when our liberties are subjugated and peace destroyed, and everything we hold dear is torn from us." The words were sung. "In the name of God and the Devil, then, one to punish, the other to reward, and by the Powers of Light and Darkness, good and evil, here under the black arch of Heaven's Avenging Angel, I pledge and concentrate my heart and my brain and my body and my limbs. I swear by all the powers of Hell and Heaven to devote my life to obedience to my superior officers . . ." and he paused at that, ". . . that in fighting those whose serpent tails have winnowed the fair fields and possessions of our allies and sympathizers, I will show no mercy . . ."

He liked to do it at night, with the fierce anger of the firelight to punctuate and heighten his words.

". . . my brain, my body, my limbs, never to forsake a comrade and I will defend and sustain Quantrill's Company with all my might and defend it with my blood . . ."

He looked like a man possessed.

Todd watched the proceedings from the safety of a tree and put away his toy to go find Jack Jarrette. He found him bent double over the glow of his most recent contraption; sparks from the makeshift forge flew into the night or fizzled and spiralled to the ground.

"We got a name for that kind of talk back home," groused Todd.

"What?" Jarrette did not want to be disturbed.

"Politics. This man's becoming a politician, Jack. You're going to have to construct a chariot for him one of these days."

Jarrette swivelled his head around and looked at Todd. "The pot and the kettle," he grumbled. "I'm surprised you ain't over there swinging the Christians into the lion's pit."

Jarrette stared at the embers as if he saw something. Todd sat watching him, hearing that high flat nasal Ohio voice winging through the trees, like an owl. "The purpose of war is to kill!" he said, laughing to himself. "The purpose of war is to ride a chariot."

"Go carve a skeleton, George."

"Lucifer! Rebellious Angels! Christ!" said Todd, shoving his hands into his pockets and kicking at the stones. "What in hell is he talkin' about? Goddamn it! He don't know a goddamn thing about it!" He stumbled off into the dark and Jarrette could hear him throwing stones at the water.

". . . before violating a single clause or pledge of this obligation," he sang, "I will pray an avenging God and an unmerciful Devil to tear out my heart!" He made the appropriate gesture, tearing out his heart, roasting it, etc. "Tear out and roast it over my brains scattered over the Earth . . . that my body be ripped apart and my bowels torn out and fed to carrion birds! That each of my limbs be broken with stones and cut off by inches . . ." The younger ones stumbled over the words, and he always made them repeat them loud and clear. ". . . that they may be fed to the foulest birds of the air . . . and lastly may my Soul be led into torment and stiffened by the fumes of Very Hell . . . and may this punishment be meted out to me throughout all Eternity . . . in the Name of God Almighty and of the Devil Himself . . . Amen!!"

The Amen often shattered the night. And the ensuing

silence deafened them. Afterwards, he walked among them and looked deep into their eyes so he could tell them he had seen their soul. "Name is Boon Schull but they call me Press...Lark Skaggs, I eat Yankees!...Kit Dalton, one of Daltons...Woot Hill, sister's been killed by one of them..."

It was Sunday, just before the ride into Independence, and, as he worked his way around the fire after the Oath, he looked down to find his hand full of black fingers.

"What are you doing here?" he said.

"I'm in a rut," said the Black man.

"What's your name?"

"John Noland."

"What's a nigger like you doin' out here on a dark night?"

"You tryin' to say you don't take niggers?"

Someone laughed out loud.

"I got nothin' personal against 'em."

"Well, Whitefolks, what are you tryin' to say then?"

"I think you got your colours mixed up."

"I ain't studyin' no colours," he said, stiffening. "I been round the world, been a tobacco slave, been bought and sold, been set free, went to Orleans and up to Memphis and so far it's the same ever'wheres. I know Whitefolks 'round here don't like niggers mixin' in with 'em but it's all in they heads. I can do what they do and shinkshanks! do it better! Why I can hit anythin' movin' betwixt my eyebeams... I takes me one bath whether I needs it or not . . . and I speak English because someone wrote her down on my tongue. Now what in hell's wrong with all that? It's 'bout time Whitefolks started to takin' niggers serious because one of these days there's goin' to be a hell of lot more of them around than there is nowadays!"

"We don't want no wise-ass niggers," said a man somewhere behind Quantrill.

"You hearin' me, Colonel Quantrill?"

"I hear you."

"No niggers or I go!" came the shout.

Quantrill turned around, saw an unfamiliar face flickering at him. "What's your name?" he barked.

"Slim Whitsett."

"What are you trying to say?"

He stepped closer, the venom glistening upon his lips. "We come into this war to put them niggers into they places . . . and I'll be damned if I'm goin' into this thing fightin' alongside a goddamn coon!"

Quantrill turned back to look at John Noland, who, in turn, stared at him.

"Take this Slim Whatsit and show him his horse!" said Quantrill.

"Goddamn niggerlovers!"

Quantrill scarcely moved as the man was led to a horse and put on top of it while he foamed at the mouth. John Noland fixed him with his eyes. "I don't ride as nobody's packhorse either, Colonel. I ain't goin' to take shit off'n anybody. If I got to ride as hard as the rest of them, I got to take none of their shit! I taken enough shit off'n those Whitefolks in Lawrence!"

It was John Noland who laid the first hammer to the county jail on Main Street. Quantrill stood behind a wall watching him break from an alleyway and claw at the wall as the fire burst around him from inside the jail and from the courthouse, and then he and Dick Burns pulled the door and shot the three guards, one two three! A few minutes later he cannonballed from the jail, firing at two men positioned at him from across the street, dragging a huge ball and chain, and ran to an Independence saloon and tossed the whole works through the window, following it inside.

"He's a drunkard!" said Quantrill.

He watched Noland jump back through the window, and before he was twenty feet away, an explosion broke out all the windows in the place.

"He's against drinking!"

Noland returned to the jail and came out dragging two dazed prisoners.

"What's he doing now?" asked Jimmy Little.

"He's freeing the whiteman!"

Quantrill shook his head. He had too much to do to keep an

101

eye on Noland. At dawn, he had driven the four hundred and seventy-five of them across the prairie until they split up, Hayes and Hughes moving off east toward the garrison campground and Quantrill into the courthouse square. Buel had been suitably surprised, but thoughtfully had sealed himself inside. By nine, Buel surrendered, and Quantrill went into the building and began to pull things off shelves and burn papers. Todd came running to tell him the bad news. Colonel Hughes had been killed in the attack on the campground, Colonel Hayes shot in the foot, ten men were dead, and the Yankees had refused to lie down and surrender. It was not going smoothly at all.

Quantrill met John Noland in front of the courthouse. "The Yankees are fighting a war to set you free, John," he said. "It appears to me you aren't pulling your own weight!"

"I'm doin' my share by you!"

"I'm not fighting this one over you!"

John Noland stared at Quantrill and shook his head sadly. "Don't you worry none 'bout me," he said. "I'm runnin' things my own way. I don't need Whitefolks tellin' me what to do!"

Quantrill told Noland, however, to take four men with him and go inside to hold down Buel and his staff while he led an attack aganst the Yankee garrison. Then he gathered up his troops and rode around to the north and came down upon the campground, thereby pinning the Yankees in between the crossfire. It was all over in an hour. They found thirty dead Yankees on the ground and sixty wounded, hands in the air, requiring medical attention. Quantrill gave them none. He lined them up against the wall and Morgan Mattox drove a wagon through to the arsenal to load Yankee weapons into it. He told Dave Pool to march the Yankees out onto Six Mile Road until they got to Gregg's Corners, where he was to let them free. He made a small speech, told them never to show their faces in Independence again or he would return again, next time not merely to parole them, but to kill them one by one.

Once the Yankees were gone, he instructed his own men to raid the powderhouse and truck off all the weapons and powder they could put their hands on. "Nobody touches a hair on a citizen's head!" he screamed. "Quantrill is not a beast! We came to Independence to free them from the yoke of the Yankees!" He went back to the courthouse, sat in Buel's chair, and had the Colonel stand before him. "This is my declaration of war, Buel," he said, quietly. "Independence belongs to the citizens of Jackson County, not to the Union Army. Go back to St. Louis with your soldiers. If I catch you here again, I shall hang you like a common criminal."

Buel stood looking past him as if he could neither see nor hear him.

This time it was a triumphal march down through the Divides. People came out of their hiding places and stood along the road waving to them. They gathered below Bowler's Point around the flagpole, where Quantrill bade farewell to Colonel Hayes, all bandages and blood. Hallar stood before him, his eyes wet, and shook his hand.

"I'll never forget it!" he said.

Quantrill rode his men off into the woods and saw Hallar waving to him.

General Schofield paced back and forth before the window in St. Louis, glancing through it as if he could see all the way to Independence. "We shall not tolerate this blood-thirsty outlaw any longer!" he said, spitting at the glass. "I am sending Lieutenant David back to Independence with the instructions to destroy Quantrill and this time I shall give him enough men to do it!" The other men in the room had never seen the general so angry. He had already broken one riding crop and was starting on another."I'm sending some artillery along. There must be a military solution to this problem!"

As an insult, he went to his desk and wrote out an order to have Perry Hoy hanged by the neck until dead.

"And outside the goddamn walls!" he barked. "Let the buzzards take the sonofabitch!"

Word of the hanging reached the bottomland, and Quantrill roused his men out of their anger, sending them up one early September morning and into the sleeping town of Olathe, Kansas.

It was a simple matter to drag everyone out of their houses and into the streets before the bank. Quantrill told them about Perry Hoy and said it was his policy to kill ten men for every one of his. He asked for volunteers, and when none were forthcoming, he stepped in amongst them and touched the strongest of them. George Todd collected them and took his men out into a field, where he lined them up and, before the eyes of the townsmen, executed them. They looted the supply stores and hauled the loot across the line and into the shadows of the High Blues. Jimmy Little hid the goods and burned the wagons, and the rest of them hightailed it for the darkest holes they could find.

David's men were everywhere. The roads were full of the sounds of patrols. Houses and barns were searched and burned, suspicious people hauled by wagons to Independence for further questioning.

They sat in the dark places watching the leaves fall about them.

"We can't stay here," said George Todd.

"We can't go up there yet," said Quantrill.

"Every goddamn leaf in the country is coming off," said Cole Younger. "We ain't got no hidin' places nowhere."

"Maybe we should take Colonel Hayes' invitation and head for Cross Hollows."

"We need a vacation."

"Nights are getting cold," said Jimmy Little. "We'll be building fires to keep warm. Christ, even the Yankees know where there's smoke, there's fire, and where there's fire, there's bushwhackers!"

They looked at Quantrill.

"I hear you," he said. "I'd like just one more crack at David." Then he smiled. "Well, it's harvest time, there's bound to be a harvest moon. Let's go down south and celebrate."

THIRTEEN

The company passed the dark rainblown days of winter on picket duty at Cross Hollows. Colonel Joe Selby told everyone they were 'Knights of the Bush' and made certain that they bivouacked with him on the hill. He invited them to his tents, where Quantrill entertained Shelby's junior officers with tales from the High Blues. His own men were impressed, perhaps even surprised that their exploits came out looking like high adventure. Shelby had to confess that the senior officers were not so enthusiastic and that, indeed, some had gone so far as to call them 'murderers' and 'assassins'. Quantrill's commission, he admitted, was meant for the border country and carried no advantage at Cross Hollows.

Quantrill was directed to take the matter up with General Tom Hindman. The General, however, seemed unimpressed by his little speech, smiled like a good parent, and indicated Quantrill should take a seat. He himself, he said, was not well, sat on his cot with his feet in a tub of hot water and a blanket about his shoulders. He looked like he had been underwater for three days. "I got in dutch the first time I recommended you for a commission," he wheezed. "I'm not going out on a limb for you. You got to understand, they don't see things the way Colonel Selby sees them. They told me I should just throw you into the brig." He tried to smile as if to retract his confession, but he could tell by the hard look on the young man's face that he was not interested in retractions. "There's nothing you can do."

"Who's above you?"

"The President , . . Jeff Davis."

He went back to his company and told them they were mere roomers and boarders at Cross Hollows. George Todd blew his top, and Jimmy Little said they ought to go back to Missouri; several men agreed, and they elected George Todd and Jimmy Little to take them because Quantrill told them he was going to Richmond to see Jeff Davis about his commission. Bill Gregg was chosen to captain those who wanted to remain at Cross Hollows and chase deserters and drunks. Quantrill asked Andy Blunt to accompany him to Richmond to represent the company, and they went together to see Hindman.

"Permission requested to visit Richmond," said Quantrill. The General examined him as if he were looking at a madman, but he gave his permission anyway.

It took the two of them twelve days to get to Virginia because everywhere they went, they were asked to tell their story to officers who wanted something to cheer about for a change. It was no surprise to them when they arrived at Richmond to be met by an officer from the War Department who told them that their letter had arrived and that the President planned to decorate them at a ceremony the next afternoon at a downtown hotel, where they would be guests at a state dinner and dance and that all the belles of Richmond would be on hand to show him the latest steps.

There were twenty others in line the following day, officers and men from various combat garrisons to be decorated by the President. They stood at attention until Davis pinned the gold medal on them and shook their hands and then moved off down the line. Quantrill tried to read his upside down, then rightside up, but it still didn't make sense. It was a splendid meal and afterward, though he stood behind a palm tree, he was fetched several times onto the dance floor by women. Afterwards, he went to Andy Blunt and said, "I met Davis's adjutant and he's making me an appointment to see the President tomorrow."

"You got your speech all memorized?"

106

"Since I was a boy, Andy."

It was nearly noon when he was led into Jeff Davis's room, and as he stepped through the door, the President rose from a blue and gold chair before the fire, smiled broadly, and indicated a chair beside him. "Well!" he said, "it is a pleasure, Captain Quantrill."

"Your Honour," he said. "I want to thank—"

"Do sit down."

"I should say before we start I didn't come all this way to Richmond just to get that medal."

Davis sat and laid a hand on his arm.

"I came to make a request."

Davis then turned and rang a small handbell. Someone came out of the shadows as if he was riding on an overhead rail. He stopped at a worn spot on the carpet and closed his eyes. His hands were folded together as in prayer, and, swaying to some unheard music, he muttered something Quantrill could not hear, some rubric, formula, the subtle invocation of high society. Quantrill's eyes fed on the rich brocades as the President spoke with his servant.

"Jeremiah, bring the Captain and myself some of that brandy you think so highly of . . . you remember what it was?"

"Your Excellency, it is Napoleon Brandy. That is the kind you spoke of with General Bragg, I believe. It was a gift of the English ambassador."

"You're sure?"

"Indeed."

"Well, fetch it then."

Jeremiah spun upon the bearings of his heels and was whisked off into the dark.

"Now, you say you have a request?"

"Yessir."

"Well?" The President waited.

"You see—"

Jeremiah wheeled about with a bottle in his hand, dislodged the cork and wrapped a towel about the neck; he levelled up two glasses on a silver platter and brought them over. The President

107

and the Border Ruffian nodded to each other, touched rims, and drank as Jeremiah spun out of the room.

"Very good. Now, this request."

"Respecting your honour."

"And?"

"Well. . ."

"Get on with it, young man. I am not accustomed to waste my days sitting in my rooms drinking with people who do not know what they came to ask me for. What is it?"

The room was full of mirrors, and he could see himself from several angles.

"You may have heard that we fight a different kind of war out along the border."

"Yes," he said, neutrally.

"Quite a vicious kind of war."

"Yes, yes."

It suddenly struck him how far away was Missouri: it was as if he were a visitor to another land, and yet he remembered the pleasant rooms at the Walker house.

"We probably fight in ways you might find difficult to accept."

"That surely must rank as understatement of the day," said the President, pensively watching the fire. "There are men at this moment in my Cabinet saying I should have nothing to do with bushwhackers. If there are too many of them, why then I am finished. No, Captain Quantrill, you thoroughly misunderstand the power of a government in a democracy such as ours. It is a totalitarianism of little people . . . the presidency is but a paper tiger."

"Who's at the helm, sir?"

"There is no helm. You cannot make any proper analogy to this government. It is only an office. It is not an army . . . not a dramatic play . . . not even a vision given to a poet. It is not a philosophy either, not even a set of rules and regulations. It is but a bargain struck between a few men lucky enough to have escaped the luckless many and who wish to remain in office merely because there is nothing beyond it."

He broke his cynicism by a cruel laugh.

"It was not wise for me to meet with you this morning, Captain Quantrill."

"Is it a crime to defeat the enemy, sir?"

He laughed again, this time at the young man's naiveté. "You are a Western man; we are all Eastern. There is no South, only an East and a West, and they have little in common. The West is quite incomprehensible to us. I mean to say, we have all read about your dark exploits, Captain, and perhaps in secret we all admire your pluck. But this is the 'fabled East', don't you see? Our romances are all about business. A mere shuffling of paper. What you have done in Missouri reads like an adventure."

"But I came to talk about real things."

"You came to ask something of me. Now what is it?"

"Colonel John Hughes commissioned me and my men last summer under terms provided by the Partisan Ranger Act—"

"That was the brain-child of General Hindman. I have never been fond of that particular piece of legislation and as you know General Hindman has come under attack for his commission of guerrillas in Missouri."

"I have come all the way from Missouri to ask you to legitimize our commissions and to honour our successful campaigns in that part of the country as efforts of the Confederate States."

He fixed his eyes upon the President and refused to move them, even when the old man tried to outstare him. "You aren't serious."

"I *am* serious, sir. I've never been more serious. Unless I have some kind of sanction for my activities in Missouri, you will not be able to count on them in the future."

They watched each other for a moment.

"I trust this simply implies some sort of blackmail."

"Not at all, Your Excellency. Without legitimate status, we shall not be able to withstand attempts on the part of the Mississippi Departments to interfere with us."

"No," said the President. "I cannot give recognition to

109

your operations, Captain Quantrill."

"Then do not call me Captain, for I am none."

"I don't think you understand. There is *fundamental* opposition to you throughout the commonwealth, both in government and throughout the military. We have new friends in Europe, our armies in the field have won signal victories. But it is far from over, this war. Mr. Lincoln is a ruthless man, a tyrant over his generals and government. But in the Southland all men are big men. I am merely a servant. I have none of Mr. Lincoln's charisma, but even if I had it, I should have to live with Southern men. No, I cannot sanction bushwhacking. It is something that must proceed without my official blessing. I can only say that, from now on, I shall not stand in your way. I shall perhaps waver and lose action through studied neglect, but just as I cannot sponsor, neither will I impede your work . . . not because I am a voyeur of bloody deeds, but because in my own mind I realize that you are a soldier with a deep-seated wish to prevent the vicious raids carried into Missouri by the Abolitionists of Kansas, and that is bravery, if not nobility."

Another glass of brandy appeared.

"So long as I am President of the Confederacy, you shall have my promise never to interfere with your operations along the border. Perhaps after the war, if we are victorious, there shall be time to recognize your efforts for what they are."

"I see."

"That doesn't strike you as a bargain."

"Allow me to reflect, Mr. President, that you do not sound like a man who wants to win this conflict. I may even go so far as to say you seem content with the prospects of losing it."

"Losing it?"

"Yessir."

"But tell me, Captain, just how do you propose to win it then?"

"As we have been doing all along: living close to the earth and under it if we can find a passageway. Breaking all the rules of war because by rules the Northern armies are surely going to win; raiding towns and holding hostages to get what we want . . . by taking ten Bluebellies for every one of our own, and by making them come to us . . . so to commit mistakes because they do not know the hills. By enforcing and preserving the natural friendship of the peoples who live in the country . . . by guerrilla practice.''

"The only legitimate guerrilla practice is, as you know, cavalry encirclement.''

"The South will win, Mr. President, only if you make them come for you. You will never win in Pennsylvania. Not against Grant and McLellan. But if they try to come on down through the Shenandoah and the Blue Ridge . . . or into the Ozarks or the Tidewater regions, any number of Southern homelands, why then you could win the war by guerrilla strategy.''

"*We* are not a President of guerrillas!'' At that the President stood. "In this present conflict *we* are leader of a civilized government.''

"Then,'' said Quantrill, joining him above the table, "I shall needs return to Missouri without your good will.''

"At least, Captain, you shall ride without my condemnation.''

"What I do from now on is continue to do what I have successfully done in the past.'' The President's eye grew cold. "It is the only way I know. Unless you dig in now, Mr. President, the Union will mount a long and powerful scissor action that will cut the forces of the Confederacy off and the blockade will be complete. I'm afraid you are on a losing course when you entertain the Bluebelly at his own rules of war.'' He polished off the last of his wine and set the glass on the bright table. "Your only heroes will become villains . . . Mosby and Morgan and Stonewall Jackson, Ashby and—''

"Quantrill,'' said the President.

"—dispatch well-trained and secret agents deep into northern cities with coordinated efforts that will destroy the machines of war . . . encourage draft riots, hold up banks and trains . . . destroy the will of the enemy to carry out the war. In short, Your Excellency, translate what we have been doing in the prairies to the streets of the city. Why not send a man to

111

Washington with the express purpose of shooting President Lincoln?

"Shoot? Lincoln?" The President of the Confederacy found the idea quite appalling. "Are we going about now shooting presidents?"

"Well . . . " He bit his lip.

"Well?"

"These are desperate moments," he said, "and they invite desperate acts."

Davis seemed for a moment unable to focus his eyes. "Yes . . . indeed," he said, rising and walking to a desk; he took something from the blotter and returned with it in his hand, which trembled as he held it before him. "It has been a . . . good talk, Captain Quantrill." He gathered himself and placed a hand onto the guerrilla's shoulder. "Let us have no more talk about assassination. In this envelope you will find a patent from me that allows you all the necessary powder and ball you need, and saddles, horses, revolvers or rifles, if that is what you want. It is a confidential letter and should be burnt once you have finished with it. Do you understand?"

Quantrill took the envelope. "I appreciate your sincerity," he said, "but no thanks. We get our supplies from Union depots and coaches. They are of much higher quality, sir."

When he was back at the barracks, Andy watched him pull off his boots distractedly.

"How did you find the President?" he said, idly.

"I didn't. They led me to him."

"Is that supposed to be funny?"

"Andy. I want to go home right now."

"Home? That's the first time I ever heard anyone call a war 'home'."

He took his men into a tent when he returned and told them what Jefferson Davis had said. They were bitter, sad, some angry and abusive. "Let's go to Missouri," someone said. "At least the Yankees appreciate us!"

"We can't go back yet," said Bill Gregg. He had put on

weight sitting around the fires and spoke listlessly. "The trees are still bare, the woods empty. No place to hide. You read Jimmy Little's letter. The Yankees are back in Independence, hundreds of them, and the Redlegs are running loose." He shoved the letter at Quantrill. "Read it for yourself. He says there ain't so much as a woodbox full of wood between Bowler's Point and Six Mile. We'd be sittin' ducks if we went up there now."

"Besides," added Cole Younger, rounder than anyone had ever seen him, "we're detailed to ride out with Joe Selby as scouts on that raid down the river. We won't get back until February."

Quantrill stayed at Cross Hollows, standing in the mud as the men moved out into the rainy valley. And when they returned, they found a letter from him saying he had gone back to the High Blues to make sure that Todd and Little had everything ready for them when they came back in late April. One of Joe Shelby's men told them that he had slipped out in the middle of the night without telling anyone farewell, including General Tom Hindman.

FOURTEEN

He would be ignored, not discouraged: ignored. Jim Lane had ignored him, ignored the truth of the matter that he was the best niggering man he had, the best niggering man in Lawrence, Kansas. Even John Dean ignored his wheelwork, when he worked in his shop. Ignoring him had become a fine art. Mr. Stone had come to him at the City Hotel and told him the hearths had never been so clean and then proceeded to ignore him. He had never been a true son of Lawrence, always the outsider, the outrider, the forgotten man. "Told you not to run around with that heathen Jake Herd," Lane had told him in private. "People are talking, I got a reputable outfit here and I don't want no gamblers and whoremongers working for me." He had a woman in Lawrence, that was true; but she was a fine woman, Lucy Stone. Her father owned the hotel, and she was afraid of him, afraid that someone might discover that she was talking to him. Lawrence was a proper town, with proper people in it, the right kind, the ones who sang songs together and went to church together. "I want my men in church next Sunday," said Lane, and he went, stood there toe to toe with all the others, and when he went to the door afterwards the minister refused to shake his hand. Mayor Collamore stood there beside him, watching him, making sure that the minister ignored him when he came out.

But now that had all changed. He had found men who believed in him, trusted him, fought hard and won, not only the battle, but the war. It was war now, and they couldn't ignore him in the war. They even had to go so far as to invite him to a ceremony, where they gave him a medal and let him dance with the finest belles of Richmond. One of them had followed him around the dance floor, waiting for him to ask her for another dance. He had become a proper gentleman, a Southron man, decorated, fired in the cauldron of war, yet when he asked the President for an end to being ignored, when he requested that his work be sanctified and respected, the man merely decided to ignore him. That was it: he was caught in the door, halfway inside, halfway out, a trapped man, seen but ignored, respected in private or in public, but not in both. He was expected to do the dirty work: steal niggers out of plantations, grease the axles, sweep the fireplaces, fight the Redlegs and the Yankees.

What did it all mean, he wondered? Somewhere, deep in the mill, the ultimate wheel turned . . . yes, if only he could see that wheel, perhaps he could understand why he was ignored by men of property and place.

He thought again of going West.

Nirvana, El Dorado, Eureka, the wide trackless Pacific Ocean, the sand and warm winds, the tall trees, fish so thick you could walk on them, those foggy islands the niggers sang about, lost in the fringes of the west coast, Canada, where gold nuggets the size of acorns lay amidst the pebbles of the Fraser River. He would go to Canada and live in the green mountains and stake his claim and get rich. He would rescue his mother from her rooming house and set her up as a grand lady of the Fraser River so that nobody could ever ignore him again. He would have the gentlemen in to tea and tell them long stories about the war in Missouri and Kansas, about how he had organized the best outfit in the war.

Jeff Davis had told him to go back to Missouri and stay out of sight. Very well, he was a reasonable man, a practical man, a practical abolitionist if he had to be, a practical slaver if that is what it came down to being. Yet, he was not drawn to slavery, another idea that bound and silenced him; he was not taken with the idea that one man enslaved another. He had been a slave all

115

his life. He would be different with his own men, charge them with hate and anger and forge them into an efficient fighting machine. Tempered steel. He would teach them a technique which would drive like a wedge through the ranks of the bluebellies. That was not slavery, but freedom in harness. Todd was different, a cynic. He stood back and the emptiness oozed from him, infected all who came near. The power of Todd's scorn could open up the earth, engulf them all, their dreams, their plans.

I've seen the effect Todd has on them, all the purpose, the tautness, gone out of them. Let him loose on them for two days and it wouldn't be war anymore, but mere killing.

I am not a killer.

I do what has to be done in war. Sides are drawn, aim is taken. Choose which end of the gunsights you want to view it from. The craft is there to be learned, perfected. Sometimes it surprises me how good I am. Todd's not like that, not like that at all, except maybe his death dolls. He's different. Something inside him refuses to acknowledge the pattern in it, something deep, a deep, dark wheel turning so slow, moaning, driving him on to nowhere in particular.

I am not a killer. I am not like Todd, I am not like that.

Quantrill shifted his weight and tried to redirect his thoughts. At times it seemed clear that Todd, or what he represented, was the real adversary, not Yankees, not slavery at all. He was not fighting Jeff Davis, or the Confederates; he was fighting to hold back the darkness. Todd, always near at hand like a loaded revolver, harmless in itself but a trial nonetheless. Well, he would learn to use that gun, point it in the right direction, use it to win his own war.

It was a cold still February morning when he rode stiffly into Blue Springs, two stores, a few sandblown houses, an inn. The streets were empty. There wasn't a horse or a wagon to be seen anywhere. He rode through it and out the other side without anyone coming to see who it was, turned off from the Independence Road and followed a trail along the edge of the divide, coming up behind Andrew Walker's barn. He didn't like the eerie silences. There were no cattle anywhere. It was as if

116

some great hand had fallen out of the sky and plucked up all the living creatures and carried them off.

He slipped through the garden, foul with weeds, and over to the house.

He edged to a window and peered inside.

Four people.

They sat at a table piled high with dishes and the remains of a meal. They were in deep conversation, tilting toward each other as if whispering. An old man, all bundled in black, sat at one end drumming his fingers on the table. It was Robert King, the neighbour of Morgan Walker, an old dried-up man, fierce, with hollow eyes. Andrew Walker sat beside him, listening, playing with a half-empty glass of water. He looked tired, broken. Beth, his wife, sat across from him and studied him, her small white face hidden in a mass of greying hair. But who was the other woman? A beautiful girl, very young, swathed like the old man, in black clothing. She had piled her rich cinnamon-coloured hair high on her head, beneath a red hat with an ostrich feather in it.

He knocked at the window.

The women screamed and ran out of the room, the old man simply rose and stared, and Andrew leaped for a rifle settled beside the door.

"It's me!" he shouted. "Quantrill!"

"Charley!" said Andrew, breaking into laughter.

He set the gun down and ran outside. The two of them embraced each other, and Andrew led Quantrill into the house, locking the door from the inside. Beth merely acknowledged his presence, watching him as if he were a wild animal loose in her house. Robert King stood and marked his entrance with a slight crooked smile on his bone-white lips.

"You remember Mr. King?" said Andrew.

"I remember him," said Robert King. "The man who has saved us from Jim Lane." He had a spidery voice, harsh and dark-vowelled. "Right now Jim Lane is king and the Yankees are everywhere. I don't see he has made any difference here. All he's done is caused more trouble."

Andrew ignored him and motioned toward the young

117

woman in the doorway. "Do you recall the young girl who danced for you that night my father took you up to meet the Kings?"

"I'll never forget."

"Kate," said Andrew, "this is Charley Quantrill."

She merely curtsied to him, but it was a genuine good-natured smile that shone on her face.

"Her name is Sarah Catherine!" barked Mr. King. "We do not allow the word 'Kate' in our house. It is the name of a whore."

"But my name *is* Kate," said the girl, stepping into the room. She had deep blue eyes that flashed when she moved, and when she spoke he could hear something of the slow wheeling waters of the Little Blue in her words. "My sisters and me," she said, "we danced Scottish reels for you when you came."

"You've grown up to be a fine woman," said Quantrill.

"My brother Jasper has told us marvellous stories about you. He says you're a very brave man."

"Your brother Jasper is a fool!" snarled Robert King.

"Jasper King is in jail up in Independence," explained Andrew Walker, quietly, trying to persuade the old man into silence by relaying the gist of the story to his friend. "The Yankees came and took him up there last month and some say he has been transferred to Kansas Landing where they've been putting them because it's safer there."

"I told them I needed Jasper to help me on the farm," said Mr. King, "but they came anyway and took him. Why he had a clean slate! I have never supported these bushwhackers," he said, nodding toward Quantrill, "and I never will and still they came and took him away!"

"And the only one left is me," said Kate. "I can ride and shoot better than Jasper or any of my older sisters but my father says it's unladylike to do anything except ride side-saddle!"

Afterward, in the wake of King's angry departure, Quantrill explained the reasons for his return, and Andrew Walker told him that the Yankees had taken over Independence and installed large garrison under the command of a devil named Colonel William Penick, who had hand-picked a whole outfit of local

118

boys and named them the Fifth Missouri State Military Cavalry.
"First thing he did," said Andrew as they walked the prairie
toward the creek, "was to come straight down to Blue Springs
since somebody must've told him that Quantrill and Company
had gone south for the winter . . . and they had names, Charley,
and they came looking for them. They hung ol' Sam Ramberlin
from the haymow rafter and then they shot John Sanders and
Jep Crawford . . . and then Jim Lane sent in his boys and of
course Penick works in close harmony with the Jayhawkers."

"So this time it's Jayhawkers and Bluebellies."

"Worse than that, Charley. They reorganized the Department of Missouri. Schofield is back in St. Louis, says the
rumour, and he's put a man named Ewing in charge of a new
military district, the District of the Border, and he's got 2500
men up there in Kansas Landing just to make sure you don't try
anything stupid like going over to Shawneetown or Paolo or
Lawrence . . . and he's been reinforced by a general by the name
of Blunt, James Blunt, who got the job because he's an abolitionist and a particular hater of one Charley Quantrill . . . and of
course Blunt has put together a system of patrols along the
Border all the way from Westport down to Trading Post just so
you won't get by Blunt if you get by Ewing."

"And who is this Ewing?"

"They say he's building a stockade up at Kansas Landing
big enough to hold every man, woman and child, not to mention
every cow, horse, pig and chicken in Jackson County!"

They sat at the creek and watched the lively spring waters
and the melting frost.

"And what do you hear of George Todd and Jimmy
Little?"

Andrew looked at him for a moment and said, "Why I
thought they were with you at Cross Hollows."

So that was it, he thought: Todd was waiting for him to
return. Keeping the store, so to speak, waiting for the customers
to come. The following day he left Andrew and Beth and rode
down behind Moore's until he reached the ridge where he always

kept the pickets. There was no smoke anywhere, perhaps Todd and Little had taken the men up to the Sniabar until spring, when he was meant to return for them. He turned to follow the path that would lead him into the campsite, when he heard a voice.

"Halt!"

He looked around, saw no one.

"Throw them revolvers to the ground one at a time and don't make no moves you'd be sorry about!"

He didn't recognize the voice.

"Mothertown!" he cried, searching for the man. "Mothertown! Mothertown! That's the code!"

Someone fired at him, the lead ricochetting off a rock behind him.

"You heard me! Drop them guns!"

"You're dead if you don't!" said another man.

He unbuckled his belt and dropped it to the ground.

"Now get down off that goddamn horse and walk this way with your goddamn hands over your head!"

He dismounted but refused to lift his hands. "You know who I am!" he shouted, angrily. "Now, where's George Todd!"

It was too late. He only sensed the shadow, looked up in time to see a falling man who landed deep into his shoulders with heavy boots, stunning him, collapsing heavily to the ground . . . but he had his wits about him: he jumped quickly to his feet and went for his gunbelt only to see the whirl of motion behind him and feel the sudden shaft of darkness.

He woke in pain.

It was like a man sitting on his head, his spurs driven deep just behind the ears. He saw a face above him, a familiar face, coming down over the edge of the deep dark hole he lay in.

"I didn't expect you home until the end of March," said Todd. His face hurt, pinched together, a dark ridge just above the eyes where the light broke. "You said you wasn't coming until then."

"I gave . . . the password," he said; the action of speaking was like a nail in the head.

"Yes, I know," he said, running a hand through his large brutal beard, "but well, things have got a lot worse since we left, Charley, a lot worse."

"This is . . . my own camp."

"Sorry about that."

Quantrill sat up on his shoulders, drove away the pain. "What in hell have you done to my tent?" It was a mess: dirty linen piled high, the canvas burnt, papers thrown into the sand. "You moved . . . into my tent!"

"Well, I—"

Quantrill examined his wrists where the twine had cut them. "Look at my goddamn wrists, George!"

"Damn it, Charley," said Todd, standing. "How many times I got to say I'm sorry?"

"Get out of my tent!" he said. It was too loud, it drove the pain deep inside his skull. "I'm . . . tired. I want to sleep."

During the night he heard women's voices. He dressed and tried to walk, but fell against a tree and finally surrendered to his pain and fell back into bed again, hearing a high-pitched laugh and someone running out into the stream and throwing himself into it. He would have to talk to George Todd about that in the morning . . . things had fallen apart, Todd was playing around when he ought to have been up on the roads killing Yankees.

But in the morning, even before he was up, Todd came to the cot with a tray of cheese and apples, two squares of cheese and a glass of milk.

"The new men want to meet you," said Todd, placing the tray on the bed. Quantrill refused to eat. "Look, Charley, it's all my fault. Don't blame the men."

"I want the men who jumped me."

"They were only doing their duty."

"I want them, George. Bring them to me."

Todd stood at the door.

"Goddamn it, George!" he said, trying to get up, and, in so doing, upset the tray, which clattered to the floor and broke the milk pitcher. Todd jumped at him and pinned him to the bed,

121

but it was perhaps only the pain that held him there, not Todd. He sat back and looked at Todd from the pleasures of the pillow. "If you don't bring them to me, then the whole goddamn bunch of them will have to leave."

Todd brought two men into the tent and lined them up in front of the bed. Quantrill sat on his pillow and studied their faces: they were bad men, narrow, red eyes, slits for mouths, long ugly black beards, filthy clothing. Their jaws worked slowly and strands of tobacco stained their lips.

"George," said Quantrill, his eyes fixed on the two men, shifting back and forth as one might flick a sabre, "tell these men who I am."

Todd seemed confused.

"Tell them my name!"

"Charley Quantrill," he said, quietly.

"Tell them your name." Todd only squinted at him. "Your goddamn name! Do you remember it?"

"George Todd," he said, clicking his teeth.

"And what are their names?"

One of them started to smile. "My name," he said, "is Bill Ander—"

"I didn't ask you!" he barked, turning to Todd. "What's this man's name?"

"Bill Anderson," said Todd. Quantrill flicked his eyes at the other man. "Arch Clements."

It was a while before Quantrill spoke, and when he did, the pain left and he found the words as easy to grip as if they were revolvers. "Anderson and Clements," he said, "you remember the name is Quantrill . . . and Quantrill is in charge of a man by the name of George Todd . . . and if you aim to stay in this camp, you will have to remember which one is which one."

He waited to see if either had anything to say, and when it appeared they had nothing to say (they reminded him of the students in Mendota whom he caught trying to burn down the school outhouse when they had locked two girls inside), he dismissed them. He fixed his eyes on George Todd for a moment and then patted the bed at his side; Todd came and sat on it.

"George," he said, "I heard women's voices last night. I want them out of here today. In case you forgot, this is an army post."

The women were not to be seen anywhere as George Todd led him through the camp to meet the new men, and as they walked, Todd began to adopt a military posture as men stood before the two of them.

"Sammy Wade," Todd would say, "this here's Captain Quantrill," and instead of shaking hands, Quantrill would salute. "Him and the Trow boys were the ones that went down to Indian Camp and hounded the Bluebelly patrol that cut down Trow's uncle, remember?"

Quantrill examined the fine-shot eyes, the fangs that flashed in the fire. "Yeah," he said, "you strung a couple of them up, didn't you?"

"Bobby hung 'em up," said Wade, "me, I jes' used 'em for gun practice!"

"And," said Todd, "this is Clell Miller."

Miller was an animal: he had a long cruel nose and a pair of cruel eyes. There was not much in the way of light in his face, and he was built like a large claw, his arms hanging loose from his shoulders and his hands loose from the arms, his fingers long and fixed with an outsized nail.

"Miller killed a Redleg and got one of them new Colt cylinder rifles off'n him and he can hit five ducks with five shots."

"Let's hope he knows there's more needed than mere marksmanship," said Quantrill, thrusting his words at Miller. "It takes brains to ride with Quantrill . . . does he have any?"

"Brains?" said Miller, snarling. "I *eat* brains. I knock a little hole in the one end and then I suck out the juice . . . and then I hang the whole thing up to dry. If you leave a little brain in it to dry out," he cackled, looking about at his audience, "you can use it as a gourd 'cause it makes a little noise, don't you know?"

"Miller likes a little scalpin' party now and then," whispered George Todd.

"There's no work here for a man like this," said Quantrill.

123

They stared at each other for some time, and then Miller looked down at his heels. "Unless he does what he's told to do."

"Oh, he's very good at that," said Todd.

And so he worked around the first fire they had built since Christmas, and Quantrill met Boon Schull and Ambrose Maxwell and Jig Robb, Lark Skaggs, Frank Dalton (a close-mouthed man with a loud clock in his shirt), Hiram Guess, Clark Hockinsmith, Ed Hink.

"Ed's our priest," said Todd. "He's got the spirit in him and he can talk in tongues. Why the one night he even fetched up the Devil out of the mud!"

Hink had the look of a defrocked and strung-out man. He was a mild-figured creature, with a soft, red face, with liquour-puffed eyes and a wealth of grey flesh about the mouth, and he clung to a large, well-thumbed Holy Bible with ribbons running out of its back pages. He seemed to tremble slightly, and his eyes appeared to float freely in his head.

"But can he shoot?"

"Shoot?" muttered Hink. "I can knock the weather vane off the top of Lobb Church. I hit St. Peter in the head from the woods just behind Antioch Church. And you know how I done it? By prayer, that's right. I got God right there inside that little trigger finger, Charley."

"*Captain* Quantrill."

Later, when he was alone with Todd in his tent, he shook his head. "These new men, George," he said, "what hospital did you raid to get them?"

"You don't like them, Charley?"

"It isn't whether I like them or not—"

"They each of them lost a family member one way or another, either to the Redlegs or to the Bluebellies and they want revenge."

"Revenge isn't what we're looking for, George. I don't like the look in their eyes. Something like darkness."

"Darkness?"

"Darkness."

FIFTEEN

There were times that spring when the sky over Blue Springs seemed constructed of glass. You could ride out into the prairie and find yourself among constellations of wildflowers and star clusters of clover. He remembered the story his mother had told him, how the sun and the earth had been lovers once but had had a falling out, so that now the sun took revenge by alternately burning and freezing. But here...now...he felt like the offspring of an empassioned embrace. The insistent sun, the urgent earth, the undulant wildflowers, the soft green hills and deep arcades, the long draws of pussywillow and lady slipper, the dense thicket where he heard the round songs of the creeks as they bore off the winter.

It seemed all harmony and wholeness, a burning away of definition and distinction.

He remembered Canal Dover and its formation of upright white clapboard houses with tall polished windows and plain red stoops. It was a cold town, a conspiracy of Methodists and Lutherans who preyed upon each other during the week and sought redemption from the sky on Sundays. It had never seemed like 'home', nor, for that matter, had any of the innumerable watering holes across Indiana and Illinois as he moved out to Kansas, a traveller and temporary social problem, a dangerous and alien man observed in silence while he sat cross-legged before them in church halls and school buildings. They seemed bent on exposing his innermost thoughts, to see if he bore any newfangled ideas long with him. He learned to see himself as a man of mystery. Disguise became an art. He became an expert at holding several names at the same time, trying to remember which designated his profession as a schoolteacher and which as a man who rode through the night burning schoolhouses. It made him feel good just to be able to reinvent himself and to alter his composition merely by changing his name.

Sometimes, however, he forgot just who he was, and it worried him.

This morning, lying amidst the clover and flower, he was a man without a name, without a definition. Without a place to go, without a thing to do. My God! he was free, free. He could do what he wanted to do, let the darkness of men blow away in the warm winds of spring. He jumped suddenly to his feet and called Charley, mounted and rode off without a direction in his mind.

Yes, he was free.

He went down a slow hill and through the hollow and was approaching a copse of oak and cottonwood when he saw someone ride out of the bushes and sit watching him approach.

He thought about Andrew Walker.

Whoever it was, he seemed to have been waiting for him to ride that way.

Still . . .

Suddenly the strange man pulled out a gun and pointed it at him.

He fired once over his head.

Quantrill drew up and waited.

The shot had been deliberately high. If the man had wanted to kill him, he could have.

He aimed again and fired. Closer this time.

Quantrill had four Colt revolvers with him, two in the saddle and two in his belt: he pulled out one and pointed it at his assailant, returned the greeting high above the man's head.

At which, suddenly, the man jammed his gun into his belt and rode up out of the draw and out onto the open prairie. That didn't seem to make much sense, for if he had wanted to escape, he would've ridden down into the woods.

It was curiosity that drew him after the stranger. He gathered momentum, noting the two hundred yards between them. Yet, this was no average rider! He tried to close the gap between them, holding fast to Charley's rolling back and surprised that the horse had more speed than usual. Still there was someone out there ahead of him more skilful than himself because even at this pace the man was pulling away. It seemed as if rider and horse had become one and floated free of the earth and sky, disembodied, defying gravity.

On they raced across the serpentine meadows, down a slow draw and out across the high field and then up the bluff, across the tableland and the road and into a small woods and out the other side until they came to the delicate grazing lands of Oak Creek, and he was still far behind.

They seemed to own the very earth since nobody challenged them.

He now moved closer. Suddenly, the horseman leaped sideways into an oak woods that thickened as it ran toward the creek, and when he reached the woods, he reined in. He saw a path winding off down through the trees toward the bottomland and jumped from his horse, tossed the bridle up over Charley's head, tied it and ran around to swat him on the rump. He knew exactly what his master required, fled off across the field until he reached a small woods and vanished. In the meanwhile Quantrill ran to a large tree near the opening into the woods and began climbing it. He found a comfortable perch in a crotch halfway up, pulled out his revolver and pointed it at the path below.

He was not about to be ambushed by anyone — ambush was *his* stock-in-trade.

In time he heard someone coming up through the trees. He waited, holding the trunk between him and the rider, watching the man ride below him on the path. He was a thin, tall man wearing a black hat tied tightly to his head . . . and when he reached the opening, he drew to a halt and peered out into the prairie.

It was curiosity that made him press the moment to its conclusion. "If you move once," he shouted, "you're dead! I can kill you or your horse, it don't matter much to me!"

The rider turned quickly in his saddle and searched the trees. He had a revolver at his side.

"Throw that gun into the bushes . . . and then climb off your horse and walk toward me . . . and quickly! Put your hands on top of your head!"

The rider reached for his gun.

"One false move and I shoot!"

"Please! Don't shoot!" The gun was tossed away.

Quantrill waited for a moment before dropping his gun. The rider pulled off the floppy black hat and ruffled her hair, her long wonderful hair, which fell clear to her waist.

He dropped his feet down through the crotch of the tree and let himself fall, miscalculated the distance and struck the ground at an angle.

The pain surged up his left leg.

The girl on the horse saw him and uttered a small cry, leaped from her saddle, sprang to his side. He lay on his back looking up at her, holding his ankle, and she seemed to be trying to say something to him without words.

"You!" he said.

Her face hardened, and she went to her horse and mounted, leaving him without a word. He lay for a while watching her vanish and crawled into the bushes to retrieve the revolver she had thrown away. It was a Colt Navy pistol with a scene of a naval battle etched onto its cylinder and appeared never to have been discharged before.

He whistled for Charley.

Before mounting, he stuffed the gun into his saddlebag. Very well, if she would not offer an explanation he would have to go and demand one. He rode up and out over the main divide toward a collection of weathered structures, tilting in various

128

attitudes, trailing long vines and bare branches, the house tall and bare-windowed, the shakes falling like leaves, and the weathered barn, swaybacked, if not capsizing, and the scattered but equally neglected pig pens and chicken coops and horse sheds. They seemed to darken the landscape along the ridge and contrast with the stately structures of the Walker Farm in the distance. The ancient weatherstricken house provided a peculiar setting for the lovely young girl who sat in the large wicker chair on the front porch.

He stopped when he reached the house and took off his hat. They observed each other for a while and then he reached into his saddlebag.

"I think this belongs to you, Miss Kate."

She said nothing. She did not even bother to look at what he held in his hand.

He was about to question her when the screen door opened and a man shrouded in dark garments stepped onto the porch. The door complained on its hinges and snapped shut behind him and into the face of a woman who peered out of the interior as one who had been conversing with ghosts.

"Mr. King," he said, nodding. "Mrs. King." He lowered the gun and smiled. "I come over to have a word with Miss Kate. I was wondering if maybe I had your permission." Robert King did not answer. He came to the edge of the porch and looked up and down the road with worried eyes. "It's all right, Mr. King," he said. "I already made sure there wasn't anybody to see me ride in to your place. I'm pretty good at coming and going without anybody seeing me do it."

"So I'm told," said the old man, watching him slip the gun back into his saddlebag.

"What are you doing with that gun?"

Quantrill thought to disguise the truth and was heartened to hear Kate King do it for him. "Mr. Quantrill," she said, "found it in the woods. He was only showing it to me."

"Has this young man," asked Mr. King, growing sterner even as he approached the side of his daughter and leaning over to her, "given you any expectations, Sarah Catherine?"

129

The girl seemed to be making up her mind,

"Well?"

"No," said Quantrill. "It was quite by chance that I passed this way." He looked at Kate. "I was on my way to Sibley . . . when I found this gun in the bushes and I thought perhaps it might belong to her father."

"What on earth would I want with a thing like that!" said Mr. King, coming to the edge of the porch. He was wrapped in black, and, although it was already a warm day, was dressed for mid-winter. "It is just a trick. I know what is going on down there in the woods, Mr. Quantrill. You're just bad medicine, you're worse than the malady! What do you want with us? I don't want you coming 'round here. What do you think they would do if they caught you coming 'round here?"

"They won't catch me coming 'round here."

"We can't take that chance."

The next time they met he said, "Where did you get that gun?"

"I found it," she said. But she knew he was able to see through it. "I shot a Yankee," she finally admitted. "He was all by himself . . . maybe a picket, I don't know. I made sure he was alone. He tried to outrun me but couldn't. My brother Jasper gave me the gun before he escaped into the hills."

Then he took to waiting for her in the woods down behind the barn. When she arrived, they would ride without talking along the creek until they came to a sunspeckled clearing where the birds chattered and moved behind the leaves. Quantrill and Kate King would dismount and stroll alongside the creek and say the same things to each other they said the last time they met.

"You shouldn't come. He don't want me seeing you. Besides, it's risky."

"I like risks."

"Me too."

"Why did you shoot at me?"

"I told you already."

"I want to hear it again."

"You don't believe me."

"I believe you. I just want to hear it again."

"I wanted to see if I could get away with it."

"Are you satisfied now?"

"I told you I was. Now, go away. I have to get back to the house. They think you're an evil man."

Toward the end of February she brought him into the house and sat him down on a horsehair sofa that smelled of urine and coffee. Her mother sat in a trance on the opposite side of the room, watching him, half expecting at any moment he might spring at her. She had dark crooked eyes, glassy, as if she might be blind, and a thin withered mouth that moved only by proverbs. "Those who live by the sword," she said, "shall surely die by the sword." Kate's sister Marion stood at her mother's shoulder like a keeper, smiling secretly at him. And, from time to time, he caught a glimpse of Kate's small brother, who ran around chasing chickens and hitting cats with a broom. Kate's father wore a black gown that looked like a shroud. He spoke in a monologue.

"We come to depend on young Kate, Malinda and me. Marion's too young and Sam's still a boy. Martha, she up and got married on us and Jasper's tucked his tail 'twixt his legs and run off. Her mother can't keep up with the chores around the place. You can see that. Her mind's about gone." He appeared to believe that his own was intact. "Why, if word got out that one of our children had taken up with a bushwhacker . . ." He seemed to envision the ensuing torture, to feel the sharp knives that would be thrust into him, and began to pace about the room, pursued by phantoms. "When we came out from Illinois to the Divide, we came with dreams of fulfillment . . . but you see the result of our mistakes. The winds have robbed us of our harvest, the rains our land, the sun our minds . . . no, what you ask . . . it is out of the question."

"We . . . my men and I, we will take care of you," said Quantrill. "Don't you worry none."

"The sting of death is sin," mumbled Malinda King, "and

131

the power of sin is the law.'' Quantrill observed her as if he were listening. ''Make no friendship with a man given to anger, nor go with a wrathful man, lest you learn his ways and entangle yourself in a snare.''

What he was doing, he said to himself, he was doing for them, and yet they turned their backs on him. He looked at Kate, who sat smiling at him as if her mother were proving a point to him.

''If you take our daughter from us,'' said Mr. King, leaning into his face, ''you take our only means of support. Why, you'll have to steal her from us, just as you do all the young men and women of this county!''

''Lie not in wait as a wicked man against the dwelling of the righteous. Do no violence to his home, for a righteous man falls seven times and rises again but the wicked are overthrown by calamity.''

Kate walked as far as the creek with him. He liked the way she walked: it was no 'woman's walk', as one who might be out of her path when it came to walking with men through meadows, but, instead, she moved as if it were *her* meadow, *her* woods, *her* waters. She was thin, that was true, but strong, not like his mother, who used to pitch him headfirst into bed and then stomp on him with her foot, lifting it so's he could see the long white lacy undergarments that shrouded the world of women in a ruffle of laundry. No, the few times he had touched her, felt her body against his, he had found a lean strength, a toughness that was hidden in the satiny white surface. She took one step at a time, that woman.

''A body can find anything it wants in the Bible,'' she snarled.

She wore a yellow cotton gown, tight about her waist, with a black belt and diamond brooch in the middle of it. It was most likely glass, but on her, it was diamonds, and the nosegay she had pinned to her blouse was more than mere wildflower, it was made out of flowers not even he had ever seen in the deepest of creek bottoms. Her eyes were large and moved slowly, with surety, and she never dropped her glance when it seemed she should.

"Charley," she said. "I want to know how you feel about me."

She pursed her lips, looked deeply into him, tilted her nose up to him and waited.

He had to invent another lie. With women he had to lie because they always worked their way in so close that there was no elbow room for him, and if it came to hate, he needed his hands. Yet the thought of hitting a woman made him shudder and he became sick with the thought. If it was love. "I guess I like you all right," he said, tightening the reins on the horse, his back to her. "I like you a lot." Love made him weak, confused, and although he had often felt himself tighten when with women in the bars in Lawrence, he avoided them when he had come to a decision. Once he had gone so far as to touch Lucy Stone in her father's hotel storage room but she had fled from him and never looked at him again. Besides, this was something new, something he had never felt before, deeper than the others, more confusing. So lying helped; it put off the need to tell her the truth.

"Is that it? Like?"

"Yes," he said, climbing onto Charley.

"I see," she said at the ground. "Well, I s'pose it's better than...nothing."

"Darn right," he said, settling his hat. "I can't stand the rest of the people in the world."

He rode away without looking back at her.

SIXTEEN

She made the flag out of black cotton. There were rolls and rolls of it in the attic, all shades of black. Her mother bought the fabric at Slaughter's by the roll because her father insisted that everything be done up in black. The flag had to be seen from the pole Cole Younger had erected at Bowler's Point above Dr. Lee's Prairie clear across the Divides to the courthouse in Independence, and so she made it seven by thirteen feet, black. George Todd said it needed a skull and crossbones, but Quantrill told Kate whatever she put on it, it was *not* to be a sign of death. So she cut up the red velvet dress he liked, made letters out of it, and sewed them into the word QUANTRILL, which, when it whipped in the wind often said QUILL or QUAIL or just plain ILL.

He showed it to the men the night they returned from Cross Hollows, laid it out before them at the bonfire, and fetched Kate King out from behind Jimmy Little and took her to the fire with him. "Our own Betsy Ross," he said, and they smiled and some of them clapped. She didn't play the woman to them, and she wasn't dressed like one either, strode about before the fire in men's britches and boots and matched them look for look. Yet she didn't try to be 'hard' with them, and you could tell they knew it. "Now, you all know Kate King, don't you? I never mince my words when I'm talking to you boys, and you know that. And so when I say the company owes Miss King respect at all times, I think I know you boys and you'll give it to her."

George Todd came to the fire with a skeleton dangling from strings attached to a stick.

"I'm sorry," she said, stepping back, "but I don't want one of them."

"Oh, but everybody gets one whether they want it or not."

She recovered and made her face into a small flower. "When I became a man," she smiled, "I put away childish things."

"Childish?" He laughed. "These ain't childish. Why, these're works of art. They belong in a church somewheres. Up above the altar."

Quantrill watched her exchange looks with George Todd and was pleased when Todd limped back into the shadows with his skeleton dangling against his knee. "Men," he said, to turn their minds away from the woman standing at the fire and the puppeteer falling back into his shadows, "we're all back together and that's good because I got plans for all of you." Kate ambled over to Todd and sat beside him, but the man refused to look at her. "We'll pick out one of Penick's little patrols, the ones he thinks so highly about, and ambush the hell out of them! And then we'll find another and another until he knows it ain't safe to run patrols down to Blue Springs anymore." He walked back and forth, weaving his words with his hands. "And when we get some elbow room, we can start making our own moves. This is *our* summer. I don't want to go down south and play picket duty for the Grey Army any more than you do. We mean to own this country and if you do your part, we'll be able to winter among our own people." Someone cheered. "Now, we got three new camps to hide in. Hell ain't safe now that Independence knows where it is. George Todd and his boys worked hard getting these camps ready. One is over at Russell's Mill, down behind Dupee's . . . one not too far from here, down behind John Moore's place . . . and one west of here, down by Indian Camp. These are pretty hard to see even in the daylight and there's good lookouts. I'm putting George Todd and his boys down behind Moore's, Bill Gregg over at Indian Camp, and the Younger Brothers over at Dupee's." Cole Younger put his arms around his brother and the

135

others smiled. "Me," said Quantrill, "I'll be around, I'll be everywhere at once. I got things to work out in my own mind. I need to find a way into Independence and into Kansas Landing and scare the bejezus out of them!"

Jarrette made him a chariot after all. It looked more like a pony cart by the time he rolled it out of his little shop. "Quiet," said Jarrette, proudly, "real quiet, this. You see, I put leather rims on it so's the pair of you could ride around the country without anybody hearing you." He put Kate into it and rode out into the night to try it out. They came out above Dillingham's along the creek, across the gravel, and you could scarcely hear it move. He held the team with his left hand and Kate with his right. She tilted into his shoulder and closed her eyes, and when he tried conversation, she merely mumbled incoherently.

"I want to see if I can get across the border with fifty men on horseback," he said to himself. "If I can get fifty across why can't I get a hundred? It would be sort of a dry run, don't you see?" The sky retained a touch of yellow. "Once inside, why we'd go as far as we could before they caught us, and then we'd turn around and try to get back across the border and down into the creeks before they found us." No, the light came from the earth, not the sky. She moved deeper into him and ran one of her arms inside his shirt against his skin. "Why, if I could do that," he said, "I could do anything, go anywhere, do anything I liked. I could go clear to Washington, Kate. Why the country wouldn't be safe."

"Just take me home," whispered Kate.

"You had enough of George Todd for one night?"

He looked at the glowing light.

"He's waiting his turn," she said.

"Turn?"

"He's like a sharp knife. You have to be careful when you use him."

It was a fire.

"What's that fire over there?" he said.

136

She sat up and looked across the prairie. They rode on leather wheels, the truth dawning on them, neither of them wishing to give it credence by saying it, trusting that a new angle would not make it so.

But it was so.

"Oh God, Charley, hurry!"

Both the house and the barn were pillars of flame by the time they reached the knoll behind the road, where they paused to get their bearings on the Yankees that had gathered in the front yard, some fifty or more of them, merely standing around watching the fire. The night was freighted with the sounds of dissolution, of explosions and collapsing walls, as the roofs fell inward among the highly polished black-scarved housewares, roaring as it went.

"Charley!" she screamed. "They've got my father tied to a tree! See there!"

"Where's the rest of your family?"

Even by the bright light they could find no sign of her mother or brother and sister.

"I've got to get help!" he said, springing back into the wagon. "You stay here, Kate. Don't try to go down there and help. There's nothing you can do until I come back with the men."

"Hurry, Charley!" she said, throwing herself to the ground and watching him disappear into the night.

It took them a half-hour to ride across the Divide to the King ranch and when they got there they found mere smouldering altars of ash and no sign of anyone on the place. He raced up to the knoll and called her name, but there was nobody there. They sent out search parties along the roads north and south, they roused people from their sleep, but to no avail. The King family had disappeared from sight.

The following week his heart was not in it. He told George Todd to organize the trial run into Kansas and went up to In-dependence with Jimmy Little to try to solve the disappearance of Kate King. It took them four days of hard riding (and sometimes dangerous riding) to follow all the rumours to their sources: someone has seen the Kings being taken to Independence on the night of the fire, others said that Robert King had been given the ultimatum, either that he take his family to a jail in Kansas Landing or that he leave Missouri for good. Once Jimmy Little heard that someone had seen them on a road in White Oak Woods, surrounded by a Yankee patrol escorting them southward, but after two days and innumerable meetings, they found little substance to it, and went home again.

Kate had vanished.

Jimmy Little went with him into the hollow down behind Dupee's where they gave the code. "Stonewall Jackson!" shouted Quantrill, and the picket took them to Bill Gregg's tent. They ate brown bread and potato soup while Gregg walked about them nervously.

"You didn't find them?" he said.

"No. My guess is they're gone to Arkansas and Kate with them."

"So," said Gregg, leaning into their faces with a scowl, "you two goin' down there lookin' for her?" Bill Gregg wore his hair long, and when he leaned forward, it fell across his shoulders. He had large green eyes that flashed in the lamplight, a scar down his left cheek from a fight in a tavern, and when he talked, you could see he was missing some key teeth in his mouth. He was a large man, strong as Todd, not quite so fast, and at times he was inclined toward a belly. He had bad breath from smoking cigarettes. "Yaeger goes over to Kansas and it's up to Todd to get him inside and out."

"Something's on your mind."

Todd paced back and forth. "I know you told Todd to put this one together, Charley, but I think you made a mistake in leaving it up to him." He looked over at the pair of them emptying their bowls. "Now I don't mean to say you haven't had good reasons not to have—"

"Get to it, Bill," said Quantrill.

"It's hard to know," he said, moving again. The lamp on

138

the table cast the shadows against the tent larger than life. "Nobody knows what Todd told Yaeger before he left. Nobody knew Dick Yaeger, not really. He wasn't one of your boys, Charley. Todd brought him in while we were down south, and so he must've known what was on Yaeger's mind when he went."

"Known what?" Quantrill drank the coffee cup dry.

"He must've known it would be hard to keep Anderson and Clements close."

"You know, Bill, you have to learn to describe everything the way it is."

"I'm trying!" said Gregg, snarling.

"Maybe he even wanted it that way."

"So what did they do, Anderson and Clements?"

Bill Gregg pulled up a chair and sat across from them, leaned forward and set his jaw. "Now listen to me, the two of you," he said. "This is between the three of us, all right? I don't trust Todd. That's right."

"Bill," said Quantrill, quickly, "if you're going to say anything against Todd I'll want him here to listen to it."

Bill Gregg looked at Jimmy Little.

"All right," he said, leaning back, relaxing, "I won't say anything you don't already know about him, Charley. Todd's got ideas, you know that." He paused, waiting to see whether he hadn't stepped over the line. "He's just standing there waiting for you to trip and fall on your face. He knows you got a woman now. That fire couldn't't've come at a better time. It's only a matter of waiting for you to trip and fall on your face."

"Bill," said Quantrill, leaning closer, "tell me what happened on Yaeger's ride?"

"Straight?"

"Straight."

"Anderson and Clements brought home a couple dozen scalps."

The three of them went to the camp below Moore's where Todd's men were busy unloading a wagon of supplies they had 'found' on the road to Blue Springs. George Todd saw them and came running, and, shortly, there was a large fire and the mash was passed around so that Yaeger could once again explain how he had breached the border without incident and got clear to Council Grove before he had run into any opposition — a posse of one hundred farmers down from Lawrence — and how he had outrun them clear to the border and down into the woods, where they lay and picked off the Bluebellies as they came down the draw.

Amidst the songs and drinking Quantrill went to George Todd, who worked over a large skull, and asked him to find Anderson and Clements and bring them to his tent. He took Little and Gregg with him along the winding path through the papaw and up a cottonwood hill to a yellow tent that had been pegged a trifle higher than any other.

"I want to handle this, fellows," he said, taking a chair and placing it behind the table in the centre of the tent. Bill Gregg lit a cigarette, and Jimmy Little took off his shoes and lay back against a bedroll half-asleep. In time Todd brought Bill Anderson and Archie Clements into the tent, left them at the table and went to the bed, sat and pulled out his little knife. They stood before Quantrill like a pair of bad schoolboys, and it was painfully obvious that things would not tumble down right when Anderson came forward and leaned down to stare at Quantrill.

"You wanted to see us," he said.

Anderson had close-set arch-blue eyes, a long thick nose and tight lips which were tentacled with a black moustache. His small chin sported a thick beard, which he had manicured and waxed, and his ears flared like bugles.

"That's right."

Anderson lit a cigarette, drew the smoke deep into his lungs and let it seep out of his mouth and nose; he passed the butt along to Archie Clements, who stood silently behind him.

"Get rid of those scalps, Anderson."

Clements laughed. "Why," said Anderson, slyly, a faint smile breaking his lips, "you wasn't s'posed to know 'bout them scalps, Charley. They was s'posed to be a birthday present. Ain't you got a birthday comin' up? It was jest a little surprise."

140

He dropped his voice. "I don't get surprises." The men along the walls of the tent watched the pair of them, waiting for blood. "I *give* surprises, Anderson, I don't get them."

Todd was busy carving away on the bed, little chips hitting the sides of the tent.

"You don't?" said Anderson, smoking again. Clements crept a little closer toward the table.

"No I don't!" he said, trying to hold tight. "Now you get rid of those scalps, you and your Navaho there and if I ever catch the pair of you doing that again—"

"Then if you don't get surprises," said Anderson, heaving one of his buttocks onto the table, "you already heard about Jimmy Vaughan." Quantrill hadn't, but he held his face as a mask. "You know Penick come down yesterday and took him off the farm because he was Joe Vaughan's brother. The one that rides with Quantrill." Quantrill waited, feeling his anger rise. "And since you don't get these surprises like everyone else, you already knew about the new general orders come out of St. Louis that says it's all right just to go down into the county and burn everybody out who has any boy that might've rode with Quantrill." Quantrill turned to look at Jimmy Little, but his face was as empty as everyone else's. "Now, what they do is, you see, they take everybody on up to Independence and say to them, you got two things you can do, you can get to hell out of Missouri or you can go live in that jail we're building over at The Landing. Why, you know it all, don't you, Charley? All about how The Landing is full of Bluebellies now, bigger than Lawrence, they call it 'Kansas City', not 'Missouri City', because it's part of Kansas, ain't it? Ain't all of Jackson County part of Kansas? That's where they're going to build that dandy new prison and they're going to make it big enough to store everybody in it who knows anybody who rides with Quantrill." Anderson stopped and inhaled his cigarette fumes again, a smile playing around his lips. Clements leaned in close and sneered at him, his mouth working but nothing coming out of it. "But then," said Anderson, sleeving his words with smoke, "that don't come as a surprise because you don't get surprises."

"Goddamn you, Anderson!" said Bill Gregg, coming out of the corner, his hands balled into fists.

Quantrill held him back, his eyes fixed. "Where did you hear all that?" he said.

"Well?" said Anderson. "*I'm* surprised. Maybe you don't get surprises, but I do. Well, well! Anyway, if you don't want our scalps for your birthday, maybe we can give you this," he said, holding out his hand to Clements, who pulled a newspaper out of his shirt and passed it across the table. Quantrill observed the paper in Clements' hand. "Go ahead, Charley, open it. It's a new paper they're printin' up at Kansas City. It's all about that new general order and how they're gonna have to get rid of you by killin' everybody in the county first." He stepped back and collided with Clements, who stood aside. "Now, that don't come as a surprise, does it?"

Anderson looked at them, his chin thrust as a challenge, turned and fled, carrying Arch Clements in his wake. Todd could contain himself no longer, cursed and heaved the wood skull after Anderson: it thunked the side of the tent, slid to the ground, rolled under the flap and down the path, careening off rocks as it gained momentum and striking the back of Anderson's leg. He growled at it and kicked it high into the air, and when it hit the ground it rolled into the fire.

Todd said, "You let him get away with it, you'll regret it, Charley. He made a goddamn fool out of you!"

Quantrill rose slowly and leaned forward on his spread fingers. "It would make you real happy to see me wheel out of here right now and shoot Anderson in the back right before the eyes of the men . . . but I'm not going to give you that satisfaction."

It was difficult to know whether Todd understood or was beside himself in anger. "It would teach him a lesson," he snarled, "and the men too! They'd know who was up in the saddle. They don't know who's up in the saddle."

"I'll handle this my own way."

"Handle!" Todd laughed, "You're into something here that's way over your head. Me. I understand all this, I can see

142

what's happening. I come down from the Red River country, I seen what's happening up there, I seen it happening here too. I can see more than you can. Take it from me. Anderson's goin' to cause you a lot of trouble 'less you take him in hand.''

Quantrill was silent for a moment; he looked at Little and Gregg. "Relax, George, relax," he said. "As long as it's my problem, I don't think you have to be afraid of him."

"What are you sayin'?"

"I mean," he said, looking at Gregg, "if I ever lose control over Anderson, the rest of you are going to have to learn to live with him. Anderson's going to have to be broken; I'll have to break him."

"Not before the men though," said Todd. "You was the one that said it."

"You know you think you got everything figured out just 'cause you come down from Canada. You got it all measured from a mason's point of view, all straight lines and everything. Well, you don't know anything about me, George, and you don't know anything about Anderson."

He was asleep when the picket brought the message to his tent. He shook himself and lit the lamp, found an envelope with her writing on it. "I have returned from Arkansas," he read. "My father is in a hospital and my mother and sister have taken rooms in the town. I shall wait for you down at Dillingham's hunting cabin, you know where that is." He paced in his tent long enough, and went down to Jimmy Little and took him out behind the tents in the trees, showed him the note and waited until he had finished reading it before he said it.

"I have to go, Jimmy."

"It will only make it harder coming back."

"I'll be fine," said Quantrill, ready to run, "don't worry about me."

"I'm not worried about you."

He wanted to say more but he let the darkness give Quantrill enough time to see what he meant.

"I'll be at Joe Dillingham's cabin in case you need me," he

said, patting Little on the back. "Keep George Todd away from Anderson."

"Two of a kind."

The cabin lay back among the midsummer cottonwood and scrub oak and couldn't be seen from the road, but he knew it was there because Joe Dillingham showed it to him when he was looking about for good hideouts. It was in the wrong place for the Company because the narrow draw that led in was also the only way out, but it was right for Kate King because now she could keep an eye on the road and know when he was coming.

She didn't bother to light a lamp. She ran across the grass and leaped into the creek when she heard him coming. "Charley!" she cried, wading to him. The moon was high and made halos of light where she scattered the water. When she reached him, he leaned down and lifted her high into the saddle. "My father is barely alive," she said. "They shot him in front of my mother. Made her watch while they held the gun to his head." They rode to the house and dismounted. "They wouldn't listen to him, even when he told them you had kidnapped me and locked me away somewhere."

They went into the cabin and stood together in the window looking out at the moonlight.

"Poor girl," said Quantrill.

"And then they went and burned the house and the barn. They left the cattle all inside. Some of them took my sister down to the creek and the rest of them stood watching the fire." She paused, and turned away from him.

"And then what happened?"

"Nothing."

"Nothing?"

"After a while, I heard her crying, Marion, and well, I couldn't sit by without helping her! And so I ran down into the woods toward her voice. There were . . . twelve of them and they . . ." She dropped her head and seemed to be fighting away the tears. "There was nothing I could do." She turned slowly, held to his arms. "They put both us girls afterward into a wagon and

144

drove everyone to Independence—''

"Kate," he said, interrupting, "did they—?"

"—and made us go into a room in the courthouse which had nothing in it but a floor and we spent the night there."

"Kate."

"The next day we were loaded into an old farm wagon smelling of manure and vermin and they drove us out of the county."

"Kate."

She looked into his eyes. "There was nothing I could do," she said, breathlessly. "It happened so fast I didn't feel a thing."

"But they . . ." He couldn't say it.

"Yes," she said.

"You know their names?"

"They didn't have any. I never saw them again afterward. I never really saw them the first time. Maybe it never happened."

She left him. She opened the door and walked out into the night, and he could see her down by the water, sitting on a rock.

"It never happened," he said, touching her.

"Yes," she said, looking up. "Yes it did."

"It happened," he said, trying not to feel anything. "It happened so fast you didn't feel a thing."

"Not a thing."

"Maybe it never happened."

She got to her feet. "Does it matter?"

"Depends," he said, sitting down. She stood before him as one condemned, waiting for his sentence. "My daddy used to say all the rules in the world come from a few people who want you in your place." He breathed in deeply and closed his eyes. "And my mother," he said, snapping them open as if he had just seen her face, "said the rules were there to keep people from getting hurt."

She hadn't been able to follow his argument. "I mean," she said, leaning forward, "does it matter . . . as far as you're concerned."

He looked at her as if he saw her for the first time. "Where's your horse?" he said.

145

"In the corral."

"I'll saddle him while you get out of those wet clothes."

"Are we going somewhere?"

"Oh," he said, jumping to his feet as if he had forgot something, "be sure to wear something fitting for the occasion."

She watched him walk toward the corral.

"I'm too young to get married."

He lowered the bar and walked to the mare.

She followed Quantrill into the corral. "And anyway," she said, her voice roughened. "what makes you think I want to marry you?" He busied himself with the halter. "Charley, you have to make plans. You have to publish the bans and you have to go get someone for the bridesmaid . . . and you have to have a witness." He tightened the halter. "The one thing you can't go without is the minister."

Then he led the horse out onto the path and she followed him.

"I know where there's a minister," he said.

"I need my parent's consent," she said. "I'm only fifteen, you know."

"Your parents are sick and besides they aren't even in this country."

She pulled the halter out of his hands and thrust herself in between Charley Quantrill and the horse. "Why do you want to marry me anyway?" she said, her eyes narrowed. "You don't just marry people you like; there'd be a whole lot more marriages than there are now." He didn't seem to understand. "Charley," she said, angrily, "not once have I ever even heard you say you love me!"

"For Christ's sake, Kate!" he said, turning away from her accusations. "I've only known you for one month!"

"That's what I mean!" she screamed. Her voice echoed back and forth along the canyon. "You don't just marry someone you met a month ago unless it's for some kind of reason."

He looked deeply into her eyes as if confessing a deep secret. "I never have done a thing in my life that I didn't want to do . . . leastways since I left my mother's house."

146

"That doesn't seem like a reason to me." She swung her head so that her hair flew out like a pair of wings, and she walked away from him, suddenly stopped and buried her face in her hands. He led the horse to her and stood for a while behind her. "All I want," she sobbed, "is a good reason for marrying a man I've only known for one month."

"I don't have a good reason," he said, apologetically. "And right now I can't come up with a bad reason either." Kate's mount nibbled playfully at her shoulder. "I can't tell you what's happening to me, Kate. I've had trouble breathing lately. I haven't got my breathing straight since the day we met and you tried to shoot me." It was less a confession than a search for a set of words he himself could understand. "I fall off my horse all the time, in between nightmares. I don't even have good nightmares anymore." He touched her arm and his voice dropped. "Kate, it doesn't take me a year or two sitting around some parlour peeking up your skirts to know it's you I want."

She turned slowly. "You're marrying me because of what the Yankees did."

"I don't give a damn about the Yankees. If I gave it as a reason, I'd be telling a lie, and coming from a confirmed liar, you'll have to believe me."

But Mr. Cobb wouldn't marry them. He told them he had quit the church when the church walked out on him. "They come to me," he said, in a low voice as if counting the numbers on a safe combination, "and told me I had to baptize this black baby, and I said I wouldn't." He stood beside the sputtering Coleman lamp, casting a nervous glance backward from time to time at a small toothless woman peering out of a bedroom door. "Why, I ain't even celebrated a communion in ten years. I ain't a churchman at all."

"I don't believe you heard me when I told you who was going to get married in your house," said the young man who stood with one hand on the butt of a revolver and the other on the shoulder of a beautiful long-haired girl who smiled at him. "I said, 'Quantrill'. I said, 'Mr. and Mrs. William Clarke Quantrill.'"

147

"Quantrill!" The woman in the door squealed and pulled the door closed.

"You must have a Bible somewheres around your house," said Quantrill, while the minister, adjusting his spectacles, stared at the sixgun and the belt studded with cartridges.

"Fella doesn't need a Bible," said Mr. Cobb, nervously. "He has to have a proper set of papers and of course a witness." He turned and buried himself in the hindquarters of the house, exchanging words with his wife, and at last emerging with papers and a wife, suitably dressed for the occasion, and they stood there, arm in arm, while Mr. Cobb browsed through the Bible, muttering homilies and imprecations, and at last dropping the book and staring at them. "I guess that's enough, I now pronounce you man and wife." He looked at Kate, took a step closer. "How old are you, Mrs. Quantrill?"

"Twenty-two," she said.

"Ummmph!" he said, turned and filled in the papers in a hand indecipherable.

Outside, Quantrill kissed her and said, "It doesn't matter what he said in there, it's all just hocus pocus."

"Why did we do it then?"

It seemed to strike him as a question beneath his contempt, but, seeing the look on her face, he realized she had asked him a question and he had to answer it. He scratched the back of his head and helped her into the saddle. "Kate," he said, "I told you I don't care what happened there in that ditch. I only know that from here on in nobody can say we didn't do the right thing."

She waited until he was on his horse. "You poor man," she said, "you don't even know it when you speak out of both sides of your mouth at the same time."

"What do you mean?" He seemed hurt.

She laughed and set the pace, and soon they were stretched and flying to see who could reach Joe Dillingham's little house first.

Kate insisted he wait outside until she was in bed. He went to the creek and stripped, lowered himself into the cool waters and

148

let the current play over him, watched the moon through the trees and waited until he heard her calling his name. He stood in the front room watching the moth hurl itself against the glass as if devoutly wishing its own demise. The room had the peculiar odours of men without women, of skunk oil for chills, of pipe tobacco in jars, of spilled liquour, and the walls were showpieces of twelve and fourteen-point hornracks and a calendar stopped at December of 1861. He laid his gunbelt on the table and prepared his pants and shirt, in case he needed to get into them fast.

He left the door ajar, making the room yellow: he wanted to see what she looked like, but he didn't want to see too much. It wasn't as if he had never seen a woman before — they were always in the rooms at the City Hotel in Lawrence, always watching him, especially when he had come in during a bath — it was as if he had never really looked at a woman before. She had pulled the covers up to her chin and was staring at him like one who was about to play a joke on him. He sat on the edge of the bed.

"Don't look so scared," she said, smiling. "I'm not going to bite."

He lifted the sheets and looked down at her bare flesh. It was no fifteen-year-old child he found, but the body of a woman twice her age, yet without the final rounding that comes. The hips were narrow, the outline of the pelvis clear, and when she raised one leg, he could see the rare flesh on the inside curve of her thigh. "Kate," he said, "you're the most beautiful woman in the world . . . this and the next one too."

"That's true," she smiled.

"I can't believe this is happening to me," he said, settling beside her.

"Believe!" she said. "Just this once!"

He reached for her and heard the horse coming down the trail. It didn't stop when it came to the creek, but charged through as if it wasn't even there.

Someone was shouting.

Kate sank back into the bed and drew the covers up to her shoulders.

149

"Charley!"

It was as if he had made a mistake somewhere and caused her to turn to stone.

"Charley!"

The man was running toward the door.

"Charley! It's me! Jimmy! Something's happened! You've got to come to the camp!"

Stone.

SEVENTEEN

They had come to the Vandiver farm only minutes before Quantrill arrived: the barn was a pyre, the house gutted, the furniture piled and flaming in the yard, and tied to the butternut tree, back to back, the Vandivers, who told them that the Yankees had come for Susan because she was first cousin to Cole Younger, and that was all. Old man Vandiver, in his hysteria, tried to recall the words that were cast at him as they drove his daughter away, bound and gagged, in a wagon, something about 'all Quantrill's women...' And on they raced through the night, exchanging shots with the rear guard all the way to The Blue Cut, where they ran into George Todd's boys, who had come down from Westport with the news.

"Armenia Gilvey," said Cole Younger, "my cousin, yes, she's gone. They took her down to the creek and pulled her clothes off her and beat her, threw her into a wagon and took her to Independence."

"My sister Charity," said John McCorkle, a tall man, broken by events. "They come for her at noon. She ain't what you call a beauty. They just put her in the wagon and hauled her up to Independence like common cattle. Somebody else went over to Hickman Mills and took Nannie Harris, she's my sister-in-law."

"Then there's the two Munday girls."

"Mrs. Grey."

"Josie and Mary and Jennie," said Bill Anderson, sitting atop his horse as if he had fallen onto it from a great height. "Goddamn sonsabitches come down and hauled 'em off in a cart and the bastards along the road come out and threw horseshit at them!"

There was a slight mist falling, and they stood around in the sand above the creek in a semi-circle, staring at something that seemed buried in the middle of the prairie. "I'm sorry," Quantrill said, looking at Younger, McCorkle and Anderson. "They come down to the darkness too, taking away our women."

"Yours is next!" barked Anderson, but when he saw the look on Quantrill's face, he turned away.

McCorkle broke the ensuing silence. "I been told," he said, hollowly, "that they're puttin' all of them into an old house up at The Landing, sort of a make-shift hoosegow, since they don't seem to have built a proper prison yet."

Anderson woke up. "There's a hundred of us," he said, snarling. "I say we go up there right now, before it gets light, clean those Yankee bastards out of there and bring those women home!"

Todd rode around the circle so that he would be opposite Quantrill, but not next to Anderson. "This has got to be worked out first," he said. "I know The Landing, you can trust me to get you in there if you know where the house is."

"I agree," said John McCorkle, after a suitable pause. "It may be too late if we wait for tomorrow."

"I'm ready!" said Cole Younger, and his brother James seconded it with a vile curse.

Quantrill had a way of climbing up and standing in his saddle, which he did now, looking up at the rain. "The worst thing," he said, "is to go off in heat. That's just the way they want it. We go in there now, they'll have a nice little snare laid out for us. Why do you think they took all the women in the first place if it wasn't to bring us in there?"

"So we sit!" shouted Anderson.

"Let me think!"

"Let the man think!" shouted Anderson, riding around to

face the circle of horsemen. "You heard him, boys, he wants to think."

"Listen to Anderson," said George Todd. "You know we've got to go in there tonight!"

"I'm goin' in there," said Anderson, determinedly, "if I have to go in there all by myself. Maybe he don't have no women in there, but I do and I'm goin' in there, it don't matter none what Charley says or what Charley doesn't say!"

There didn't seem any way to counter these words, and so Quantrill stood, looking as if he had been dealt a poor hand.

"Now, I'm going in there and you're all invited to come along and help me!"

He turned his mount, and, as he passed Quantrill, the men saw the explosion before they knew where it had come from, and Anderson's horse stumbled and fell to the ground, snorting and spinning, its hooves in the air. Anderson sprawled and came to his feet, spitting blood.

"If you take one more step in the direction of The Landing," said Quantrill, but a tentative sound came out of the words, "you will have to deal with me. This is Quantrill and Company, Anderson, it ain't Anderson and Company. You took the oath just the same as everybody else here and if you think that oath don't mean anything, you take one more step and we'll see what it means." Anderson held his head. "Buddy," he said to Cole Younger, "I'm putting you in charge of this hothead and I'll hold you responsible for his actions." The others seemed impressed: they stood watching him, waiting. "Now, the rest of you, go on back to camp! I got some thinking to do and you ain't any help."

When everyone had left him, he rode back along the road until he came to the path that led past the picket and down to the cabin, hidden amidst the trees like a secret treasure.

He went into the cabin and found her where he had left her, lying on the bed and waiting for him. He undressed and went to her, without words, taking only what she wanted to give him — which was more than anyone had ever given him before.

In the morning he told her about the round-up of Quantrill women. "I'll have to take you along with me," he said. "It isn't safe any longer."

"The men," she said, "what will they say?"

"I don't give a damn what they say."

They ate breakfast and went along the creek listening to the birds and feeling the warm sun on their shoulders. "I know it's a trap," he said as they walked. "All they want is for us to come charging into The Landing and that would be the end of Quantrill and Company.

He could tell she was thinking. She wasn't content to be a beautiful woman. "You always said you wanted to go back to Lawrence and force Jim Lane to give you a good reason why he let you go." She stopped and held him before her. "Maybe it's time to go get that reason."

"There's two armies between us and Lawrence."

"Todd sent that man Yaeger over to Council Grove, Kansas. They got over there and back again. Didn't that prove you could do it?"

"There were only a couple dozen of them. I'd never make it with less than four hundred men."

"Well, go get them!"

The Landing was growing. It was no longer a sad collection of sod houses: it was a symbol of the new commercial presence in western Missouri, a fencepost in the perimeter of Yankee territory, a depot for eastern entrepreneurs, who knew that there was money to be made in the far west once hostilities ceased. They laid streets and lanes and alleys in all directions and began to build stores and houses, gave the people carriages to go everywhere. Brave new sheds and warehouses rose along the river bank, and when the new houses got in the way, they were demolished so that more sheds and warehouses could rise, or, as it was more common to do, merely abandoned and left to fall by themselves.

This is the way it was with the old houses along Grand Avenue — as it was consecrated — where they wanted to erect the large storage buildings. One by one, the houses fell, until at the end, but one remained, property of an old woman who wouldn't budge. She died, and her house was put on the market for one day. The government liked the property: they wanted to construct a battery at that point to protect the proud new settlement from the likes of Quantrill. Until the proper building materials arrived, however, there seemed nothing they could do with the house but use it for a temporary stockade. People were pouring in from the county, claiming it was no longer safe for them to be caught in the crossfire, and some of them turned out to be Quantrill's people, and so they were thrown into the old house.

They put fifty of them into a house built to hold five people. There were only six rooms; that meant nine to a room. The man who built the bars over the windows and installed locks on the doors said that they shouldn't allow so many people into that house at any one time, but the authorities laughed and sent him on his way. This was war, dammit! and these weren't real people anyway, they were Quantrill bitches, they deserved far less than they got anyway. To hell with them! The guards who occupied what was once a sitting room discovered two of the bitches trying to escape and herded them all into one room upstairs, would have left them there too but for the sound of wood splintering, and so the prisoners were led back to their own rooms and chained to their beds.

Quantrill told George Todd to send two men into town to find out what was happening at the house. It would be a difficult assignment, what with the pickets stopping everyone coming into town to see whether they had the proper papers on them. Todd picked Frank James and black John Noland, furnished them with papers, and sent them on their way.

"I know that town like the back of my hand," said Noland. "When you're black, why the Whitefolks, they don't see you."

"I got friends at The Landing," said James. "See you in a day or so."

When the pair of them returned, Frank James went to see Quantrill. "It would be suicide to ride in there right now, Charley," he said, looking at Noland. "You agree, John?"

"They know you're too smart to ride at that house," said Noland. "They got every which angle covered and there's six hundred of them."

"They got that house under their sights day and night."

"They just hope you break down and try it."

Quantrill sat watching an ant cross the floor of his tent. It was lost and had to cover the same ground several times before it ended up where it had started.

"No weaknesses?"

"None's I could see," said Noland.

Quantrill got up and walked around in a circle, his chin in his hand. "You had any trouble getting in or out, boys?" They shook their heads, "You go on back in there and keep an eye on things and let me know the minute they let down their guard."

The days lengthened, and Quantrill stood around. He had the look of a man who had lost the power to move. Anderson watched him wherever he stood, jumped when he moved.

Late one afternoon Frank James and John Noland rode quickly into camp, dismounted and sprinted across the open ground toward Quantrill's tent. It was like wildfire: soon every man was out of his tent and running toward Noland and James.

Quantrill came out and stood watching them approach.

"They've dropped their guard!"

"No, Charley," said Frank James, out of breath. "You'll never believe me, not in a million years!"

"Listen to him!" barked John Noland, clinging to the shoulder of Frank James.

"I'm listening!"

The men were listening too, crowded in around them and staring at the two men.

"Well," said James, looking around, "this is it. The house . . . just . . . collapsed. It fell inside out. Just . . . buckled."

"They must've had all of them in one room on the upper floor," said John Noland. "We heard it, didn't see it, but you could hear it!"

James stared at Bill Anderson. "Your sister," he said, "she's lost both her legs."

"Legs!"

"Your cousins are both dead."

"Jesus Christ Almighty!" he screamed at the trees.

"And so is Nannie Harris and Mrs. Grey. And the rest of them they hauled off in ambulances."

The men simply stood staring at Quantrill as if James had announced sentence upon them. Anderson ran around the camp firing at trees and screaming at Clements. John McCorkle told him he was going home. He said, "You know the Yankees are waiting for you." McCorkle got on his horse and rode away, and the others followed him, all but George Todd and Jimmy Little, who went to their tents.

When he got up the next morning and screwed his Kossuth hat to his ears and announced he was going for a ride, Kate saddled her horse and shadowed him until he turned again for the cabin. He continued withdrawn and dark and took to staring at the creek. The night of the second day, they met at the door, and he said. "There were four men at the door and I went to the top of the stairs. I didn't know any of them but my daddy did. He told my mother to go to the kitchen and wait but they said they wanted her to hear it as well." His eyes were deep in his head as he spoke. "They went into the library and closed the door and I slipped down to it. They asked my father why he had done it. My mother began to cry. He told them he was headmaster and was in charge of school money, and one of them said he found $100 missing and another said he had gone to Cincinnati and talked to the men who had received $100 to print a small book on tinsmithing. My daddy was always down in the cellar playing with tin. He made tin scoops and tin candlesticks and things like that." The words were hollowed out by his voice. "My daddy went to his desk and began pulling the drawers out one by one and then I heard the men coming toward the door and I ran upstairs again and hid. They went running out of the house and my daddy right after them, dragging my mother with one arm and pointing an old pistol out in front of him. I screamed and screamed. Then, suddenly, there was a terrible explosion and the

157

hallway was full of smoke and my mother crying and me running down the steps and out where I could see my daddy standing stock-still pointing that gun out in front of him like he was afraid to lower it because it might go off, and my mother was shouting, 'You killed him! You killed him!' and I looked down at the ground and saw one of the men laying there with blood coming out of him.'' He began to tremble slightly, and she held him. ''The man lived,'' he said, as if it were the moral of the story, ''but my daddy died. Gradually. I hated him because he made my mother right. She always told him to do what they told him to and when he didn't . . . it was just a little thing, a little book on tinsmithing . . .'' He looked down at her, and she snuggled into him. ''I never told anybody that story before. I don't know why I told you.''

They went inside and she stood before him. ''The men are gone, but they'll be back,'' she said, running her hands over his shirt. ''They'll want you to say something to them. You . . . you can't avoid it, can you? You've got to go. It's in the cards, in the stars, you have to go.''

''Lawrence?'' he said, as if he knew. She merely smiled. ''The boys are in no shape for a long ride.''

''You said you had to ask Jim Lane something.''

''I know the answer. I'm not interested in the question any more.''

''Any day now they'll come. It's only a matter of time. You can't be everywhere at once. They'll begin farm by farm until there's nobody left and then they'll know they can come right down and scoop you out of your holes.''

''So I should send three hundred men to certain death because if I don't they'll come down here and throw everyone in jail? Why shouldn't they come down *while* we're over in Lawrence and that way they'd have just about everybody?''

''They mustn't know you've left until you're ready to come again.''

He bit his thumb vacantly. ''We could be there by dawn,'' he said, ''and home again the next day.''

''You'll never get across the border with three hundred men

without them seeing you.''

"No, that's no problem.''

"Once you're inside, you have to worry about them seeing you going toward Lawrence. They might be a little suspicious of three hundred armed men bearing down on Lawrence in the middle of the night.''

"No,'' he laughed, "I know George Todd and Bill Gregg, Kate. If either of them had been at Troy, the Greeks wouldn't have had to go to all the work of building that wood horse.''

"Then what's stopping you?''

Quantrill smiled. "They haven't asked me yet.''

Jimmy Little arrived the following morning and stood sheepishly in the door. He wore a green Quaker coat and a floral slouch hat, brown nankeen trousers tucked into his guardboots. "You can see I'm dressed and ready to ride,'' he said. "So's all the rest of them, they're all over at Russell's Mill and told Bill Anderson to eat his own bullets. They want you to come over and tell them what you got in mind to show the Yankees we ain't goin' to take this one laying down.''

"Now they asked you,'' smiled Kate.

McCorkle was there, and so was James and Cole Younger, Andy Blunt, Jarrette, Dave Pool, Dick Burns, Anderson, Chiles, Foss Key, Boy Greenwood, Clements. Bill Gregg sat manicuring his fingers, half watching Todd's little marionette show, dangling a toy skeleton before two small children and talking funny. Cole Younger walked around with his brother. "I know,'' he said to Quantrill, "I'm puttin' on pounds and pounds. Comes from sittin' there eatin' and eatin' corn fritters and maple sugar hot-cakes.''

"I see you got a new gold tooth,'' he laughed. "You'll have to keep that mouth of yours shut when we're riding or they'll think we're carrying a live bank.''

Frank James came forward with his arm around a boy. "Charley,'' he grinned proudly, "I want you to meet my little brother.'' The boy was small, tough, had a face that should have belonged to a much older person. "I had to bring him along.

159

He's gettin' into too much at home. I figured I'd have to bring Jesse back to the straight and narrow, bein' his older brother and all. He's only thirteen, but you wouldn't know it.''

"Which one of you shoots straighter?"

"Me," said Jesse James. "Frank, he's cross-eyed."

"What can you hit? Rattlers?"

"Men," said the boy, "twice't my age too." He crossed his arms and sprang upon a branch, hung there rocking back and forth.

"What you got against old men?"

"Nothin'. I ain't much on age. I can shoot them my own age too."

Quantrill looked at Frank in hopes he could discover whether the boy was being serious. "Why ain't you in school, Jesse?"

"We ain't got a teacher. He's dead."

Quantrill fought away his curiosity. "So you figure on going into shooting all the time?"

"Jesse's got a bad streak in him," said Frank, "but then . . . what they done to Dr. Samuels, you know, it jest set right on him. Me, I got over it somewhat, but Jesse, well, he's the boy, you know, he never quite got over it."

Jesse's eyes were steady on Quantrill. He looked like a doll, rather than a human being, but a doll some clown at the depot had fiddled with to play a black trick on somebody — he had put in two eyes and one nose and one mouth with twenty-six teeth (so far), two ears, just as he had done a zillion times before, but this time he dropped a snake inside the head and sewed it up again before it could get out. As a consequence, if the light was right, you could get a glimpse of it now and then in an eye or in a word or a gesture of defiance.

"He runs a little band of bad boys, Charley," said Frank. "They cause no end of trouble."

"You run that little band, do you, Jesse?"

Jesse nodded smartly.

"Well, Jesse," said Quantrill, "I run this one."

He stared down the snake for a minute or two, and then

160

turned to the boys who had gathered about him. "Maybe the rest of you forgot about that too. I get a feeling once in a while you need a little reminding about who *is* running this little band of bad boys. I figured this time, coming back from Arkansas, maybe we could go back to the way we were. Small tight little group working together. Maybe there just ought to be a hundred Quantrills running around the country, not just one of them. You all got your own grudges and I got mine. But we used to find common ground. Now we find Bill Anderson and McCorkle and Younger, you boys wanting to run in there and kill the ones who kill women in prisons. Well, you aren't going to run in anywhere unless you work it all out ahead of time. That's where I come in, boys. It's only natural we should work this one out together and decide what to do and then do it . . . as a company, not as a whole lot of angry people takin' it on themselves to solve everything."

"Quit beatin' around the bush, Charley," said Bill Anderson.

"You got to beat around the bush if you're ever goin' to find the bastard hiding inside it."

"Get to the point!"

"That *is* the point."

Anderson was not about to be shouldered aside. "C'mon Charley, this ain't no time to stand around talkin' like a school teacher. I say we go straight into The Landing and shoot everything we see!"

"What about it, Charley?" echoed Cole Younger. "And come home by the way of Independence and clean that pack of Union men out of there."

"Too easy," said Quantrill. "Besides, that's what they want us to do . . . it's what they're expecting. You got to be subtle, that's what I'm here for, to be subtle."

"Another bullshit word," growled Arch Clements.

"Listen to me," said Quantrill, climbing to his feet and looking directly into the face of thirty men, all watching him, waiting to see whether now he might ask them to put their tails once again between their legs and head into the bush. "I told you this was the summer of victory . . . it wasn't an idle threat. We

161

been running long enough . . . they think they got us in a noose. They think they got us as long as they keep us right here in the county . . . they got the idea to cut us off from the outside and then starve us out . . . they'll come any time now and start cleaning off the farms and the plantations and dragging people into The Landing and throwing them into the stockade . . . and once they secure an open prairie, they plan to ride in here and clean us out." He had to convince Anderson, who wanted blood, and Bill Gregg, who wanted a military exercise. The rest of the men stood in between those two men. "Listen to me now, it's time to move. The only way we can move is . . . clean *through* them! That's right, clean through them! Go clean through them and take what we want and bring it home with us! And we can do it! We can do it, boys! We can show the Yankee it just won't wash, coming down here and carting off our women and children and putting them behind fences or in houses that fall down on them!"

They merely looked at him as if they hadn't understood.

"What are you saying, Charley?" said Frank James.

"I'm saying Lawrence, Frank."

"Lawrence," said James, not comprehending yet.

"Lawrence."

They figured the first time he hadn't meant to say it, but saying it twice now, it surely was a deliberate mistake. Lawrence? Lawrence Kansas? Yankeetown? Jim Lane's Yankeetown? The fortress, the citadel, the strongbox?

"Did you say Lawrence?" said George Todd.

"You sent Yaeger out to Council Grove, remember? That proved it could be done."

"Not Lawrence though."

"Why not?"

"There's a couple thousand Bluebellies between us and Yankeetown," said Cole Younger,

"Yaeger didn't prove you could drag a couple hundred horsemen across a border that's been sealed off ever since it happened," said Gregg. "And that's what you'll need, a couple hundred men."

"What are we goin' to do when we get there?" said Jack

Jarrette.

"We'll figure something out."

"Smart-assed answer, Charley!" spat Anderson, his eyes mere slits of light. "Answer the question!"

Quantrill smiled "Avenge the deaths of Josie and Mary and Jennie and Mrs. Grey and Nannie Harris and the ruination of the women of Blue Springs!"

"We been sayin' for over a year now that we're comin' for a visit," said Jack Jarrette, feeling stronger suddenly. "I imagine they're kinda disappointed in a way. More than likely they're bored. Maybe they give up on us. They prob'ly wouldn't even believe you if you was to say you had made up your mind to come at last."

"Jack," said Quantrill, blowing on the flame, "you're the one sits around the campfires all the time shootin' off your mouth about what it's going to be like in the future and how there won't be two armies out in a field somewheres shooting at each other. Well," he turned away and looked out over them, "then I say we get the future over and done with right now."

It was quiet for a long time, the fire snapping away like music, Quantrill waiting, watching them. It was Missouri, like the man said; these people had to be shown.

"Now, I'll tell you what I've come up with, me and Bill Gregg and the others who have thought this through a couple times." He had been through it a hundred times in his own mind, but now, facing the men, he knew that he had to find hard words for a soft dream, real men had to ride on ghostly steeds.

EIGHTEEN

It couldn't be done, shouldn't, was too damn far off, too big, too many men along the border, too much of a risk. Paola or Aubry was one thing, Lawrence was another. "All we got to do," Quantrill said, "is figure out how to ride a couple hundred men clean past those patrols without getting caught, and across fifty miles of open prairie without being seen, slip into an armed camp of 2,000 abolitionists with guns under their pillows, do what we got to do, and then turn right around and charge back through five, six hundred Union soldiers without losing our shirts." They were the ones doing the thinking now: they watched each other as bathers waiting to see who would take the first step. The only sound was the call of the creatures of the night, their still and hollow voices reminding them how lonely they all were.

Bill Gregg stood, knowing it was up to him to make the first motions. "I say we take a vote on it," he said, scratching his chin. "There's no point in wastin' time on this thing. Me? I say, if we're going, let's go and get the damn thing over with."

Quantrill searched their faces for answers. "George?" he said, knowing the men had to hear from him.

He looked up from his whittle. "I'd say it was in the bag," he said.

"Anderson?"

"I don't like the smell of it."

"Frank?"

"I want to see more of it before I make up my feeble mind, but if you're asking me whether I go along with you to see if it could work, I'd say let's get right down to it."

"Jesse? You can't vote up in Liberty but down here in the haymow we don't look up anybody's age."

"I always wanted to shoot somebody in Lawrence."

"Jimmy?"

"If we was to pull it off, why the war'd be over!"

"Burns?"

"My folks' piano is settin' in Jim Lane's parlour."

"Buddy?"

"I'd go for my ol' man, Charley. If he was here, why he'd be jumpin' up and down!"

"Andy Blunt?"

"Only thing is...there wouldn't be no afterwards. We'd be finished."

"Leavenworth...St. Jo," said Quantrill.

"St. Louis," added Jarrette. "The world is flat. How'd you boys like to be squattin' in the hills above Washington? Think of the fun you could have once you got inside that capitol buildin'."

"Clements?"

"It won't work," said Arch Clements. "I don't plan on comin' home empty-handed and there's no way you could get a piano past General Ewing."

And so he polled all of them. It was worth a try. Quantrill would have to sit down with Bill Gregg and the others and work it all out, start to finish; somebody would go over to Lawrence ahead of time to make sure it wasn't a bomb likely to go off once they were on the inside. They'd have to wear Union blues in case they ran up against anyone inside Kansas, and, of course, everybody needed well-shod horses and good guns.

Afterwards, Quantrill took George Todd to one side.

"What about Anderson and his shadow?" he said. "I didn't like their looks."

"Those boys wouldn't miss the party for anything."

"No, but I wouldn't want them to spoil the fun either."

He laid his maps out across the kitchen table. Kate brought him a cup of coffee and cornbread with jam on her way to bed. Just before dawn she woke from a dream in which she saw horses falling off a cliff, spinning like autumn leaves. She smelled coal oil, saw the thin wedge of light under the door, rose and opened the door. He sat hunched over the table, staring at a map as if listening to something it was saying.

"I dreamt about horses falling over a cliff," she said, stumbling across the room. He was so busy with his maps he had not seen the lamp smoke. The glass was black with soot. "Come to bed, Charley," she said, trimming it back.

"I'm not sleepy," he said. His eyes were red and sweat ran down his face.

"You slept only three hours last night."

"No time to sleep now, Kate."

She yawned and lowered herself into a chair across from him. She watched him and said, "I changed my mind. I want to go along with you to Lawrence." He merely looked at her face as if he hadn't heard. "I suppose you'll say you want me to wait here till you return."

"I want you to wait here until I return."

"You think I'd get in the way."

"You'd get in the way."

"Not if I stayed out of the way. You could give me something do do. I could run picket. I could see to the ladies. Anything."

"No," he said, dropping his eyes again to the maps.

"So that's the way it's going to be." She suddenly felt wide awake. "Always in the way. I'm always in the way."

He ignored her.

"And what about afterwards? Where will you go? I suppose—"

"No!" he said, anger flooding over him. He turned his eyes up to look at her, recanted. "No," he said, softer. He turned back to the maps, to the distances and calculations, the mystic

166

markings, lines to a play he knew so well he could say all the parts himself. He would burn the maps in the morning, since their message had been inscribed in his brain. He looked at her again: she sat like a schoolgirl who had been chastised, a thumb in her mouth. He was suddenly struck by her youth and innocence. "No," he said again.

"Well, I guess I'll go back to bed," she said and sailed away, leaving him with his well-thumbed maps. Kate had a deep earthy scent that drew him into the dark with her. "Let me tell you about my dream," she said.

"No,' he said, kissing her on the mouth.

Kate was the first to see it.

The wind flicked one of the corners as if to draw their attention as they rode past. She went to the tree and noted that it had been newly fixed to the bark. It read 'General Order No. 1' in large letters.

"What's it say?" said Quantrill.

"Officers," she read, "will arrest and send to the district provost-marshall for punishment all men (and all women not heads of families) who wilfully aid and encourage guerrillas, with written statement of name and residence of said persons and proof against them. They will discriminate as carefully as possible between those who were compelled, by threats or fears, to aid the rebels, and those who aid from disloyal motive. The wives and children of known guerrillas, also heads of families and those wilfully engaged in aiding the guerrillas, will be notified by such officers to remove out of this district and the state of Missouri forthwith. If they fail to remove promptly, they will be sent by such officers, under escort, to Kansas City for shipment south."

She looked like a woman who had just read her own death warrant, but she knew, as well, that it was much worse, it was the death warrant for everyone in the county. She ripped it in shreds and scattered the scraps into the wind.

"That don't help," he said. "Those notices are everywhere."

She was alone. He had left someone in the trees behind the cabin to keep an eye on the road that led down into the creek. She lay in bed listening to the clock strike the hours until she heard someone ride past the house. She was quiet, trying to interpret the moves as belonging to Quantrill. The horse was being tied to a tree instead of taken into the corral, that wasn't good. She slipped out of bed and picked up the loaded Colt he left on the nightstand, opened the bedroom door and stood just behind it, pointing the gun at the front room door. Whoever it was walked slowly around the corner of the house as if testing it. She began to tremble. Where was the man in the tree? Then the door swung open. "Kate?"

"I could have killed you," she said.

He lit the lamp with cruel abandon and disregard for the woman trembling in the doorway.

"Friday," he said, pulling his hat off his head and letting it fall to the floor. "Everyone's got until Friday. Saturday they come looking for you. If you're still in your home, they'll shoot when they see you." She came to him. "The only ones that can stay are the ones that sign the paper and even that isn't for sure. All the farmland will be sold to the Yankees who stay behind."

"There's no time for Lawrence," she said. "You'll have to stay."

"It's too late. We have to go."

"But you can't! They'll just come in here, nobody'll be safe!"

She turned away, went to the window and looked through it. He went to her, stood behind her and spoke to her image in the glass. "I'll be leaving some men behind to make sure nothing happens to you and anybody else who wants to come down here and stay."

"That's not good enough."

"It'll have to be."

She turned and glared at him. "So you leave us to face the Yankees with a couple of men who aren't good enough to ride all the way to Lawrence."

"Kate," he said calmly, "if we are successful over at

168

Lawrence, the Yankees in Independence will be too busy going off to Kansas to come down and enforce that order, don't you see?''

''And if you're not?''

It was yellow in the east when he rode up to the barn that looked down at struggling little Blackwater Creek. Fifteen men waited inside, and Captain Perdee was there warning them not to smoke in his hayloft. Quantrill dismounted, walked into the barn and went up the steps toward the lamplight. The silent men sat around watching him come up, his head, shoulders, arms, trunk, a leg and then another, as if he were being born out of the darkness in the lower barn. He stood for a moment listening to the only sound, the hiss of the small lamp on the floor, exchanging long looks with the men.

He went to them, one at a time, said the name as if it were some sort of oath. ''Cole . . . George . . . Bill . . . Jimmy,'' yet he said, ''Clements . . . Anderson.'' They did not smile, ''Charley'' was all they said. He felt good about a hayloft. It was comfortable, quiet, sweet-smelling, the men could lounge about without worrying about someone sneaking in on them.

''You got something to tell us, Fletcher?'' he said to a man who was tall and gaunt like an undertaker. ''Mr. Taylor,'' said Quantrill, addressing the men, ''has just come back from Lawrence with a little story to tell.''

Fletcher Taylor told them about his room in the Eldridge House and how he had posed as a horse dealer from Kentucky. ''I had a thousand dollars in Yankee money,'' he said, slowly, ''and I scattered it around the room so's when Mayor Collamore come in he could see it. Him and Jim Lane, they're interested in war horses, they give me a dollar a head, five on delivery.'' He lifted his spectral eyes and smiled. ''I spent a week there looking under rugs and into closets. Gen'lmen, Lawrence is open, there ain't no soldiers to speak of, and most of them is across the river with only a small ferry that could lose its line very easily.'' He turned to face Quantrill. ''Your little story was laughed at, Charley. They think there ain't nobody in the world big enough

169

to make it all the way to Lawrence and do any damage. Now, the other thing is the streets. They're all straight and wide and open, we won't have no trouble ridin' around town at all.''

When Fletcher Taylor finished talking, he folded together his dark, thick-veined hands and fell back into the hay. Quantrill nodded and smiled at him, turned and tacked a large map of Lawrence against the wall. He stood in front of it with a stick in his hand. ''By five o'clock next Friday morning, the twenty-first of August, you will be standing on the top of Mt. Oread with all Lawrence at your feet.'' He was surprised at the resolution that burned in their faces. He had expected fear, perhaps bewilderment, but they sat at his feet like a class of students who wanted to learn precisely what he had to teach them. ''I will send a couple of scouts down into the village on foot. The rest of us will wait until we get their flags . . . and then we ride.'' He turned, and with his stick drew out his instructions. ''We will all swing back out east and down this long hill in three companies, Todd's, Gregg's and mine . . . along here until we reach Lee Street, where we split up, Todd taking his boys up through Berkeley Street toward the two Yankee campsites . . . that's right, two. One for Whites and one for Blacks. Equal sure, but separate anyway. We ride straight through them and shoot them in their tents. They'll probably be asleep anyway. Some of Todd's boys will stay behind and finish off the wounded, and the rest of us are rolling down Massachusetts! At Henry, Buddy, you take your boys and slip behind the Eldridge Hotel. . . and Jimmy, you go straight into the Johnson House, where the Yankee leaders are billeted. . . and the rest of us make straight for the bank . . . the Eldridge Hotel! That's where the money is. Frank, you take your boys into the courthouse, and cover the hotel from that angle. Shepherd, your men go into the Journal Building. That way we'll have that hotel completely surrounded. We'll demand Jim Lane come out and stand in the street.'' He turned to face them, his face hard, teeth clenched. ''Now I want you to let me go to him. I got a question I want to ask him. And when I get it, I kill him.'' His eyes flared. ''That's your signal, boys,'' he cried. ''To the four corners of the world! Each of you has a certain section of the

170

town to take care of. You'll be given a list of names. I want them executed on the spot. Do only what you're told to do and do it fast. We got no time to waste on games." He looked at Frank James. "Now, Frank, you take some men and go down to the river bank and cut those ferry lines. That'll keep the Yankees on that side of town on the other side of the river." He went to Jimmy Little and laid a hand on his shoulder. "You got a special assignment, Jimmy. I want you to take your boys over to Jim Lane's house, just in case we don't find him at the Eldridge. Hold him in the house till I get there. Remember, I got a question I want to ask him."

He went back to the map and faced the rest of the men.

"Now, I want you to listen to me real good. Me, I'm in charge of this operation. I may not be the smartest man you know, but I'm smart enough to know if you don't do exactly like you're told, we won't get to Lawrence, and even if we do, we won't get home again. No fooling with women! That's the law! No scalping! no ruining women! no shooting the few high ranking people we're bringing home as hostages! Now listen to me, from the minute we ride into Lawrence until the minute we leave, only three hours has gone past."

"Three?"

"Four and we're all dead."

"No time."

"I know that town," said Quantrill, "like I know the grain on the handle of my Navy Colt."

"Charley thinks he can turn Lawrence into a cinderbox in three hours!" sneered Bill Anderson, on his knees beside the sanchion.

"Who said anything about a cinderbox?"

"So what are we doin' there, whorin' and drinkin'?"

Quantrill stared at him. "Our objective," he said, staying his anger, "is to capture and burn the Eldridge Hotel, capitol building of the Yankees, take prisoners of Governor Robinson and Mayor Collamore and anyone else we might find in those war rooms in the hotel and bring them back to Blue Springs for ransom."

171

"That don't sound like a whole lot of fun," growled Arch Clements.

"Everybody in Lawrence is guilty of murder!" screamed Anderson. "Everybody dies! No prisoners! One hundred Yankees for every one of them women that died up at The Landing."

Calmly. "We haven't got the time."

"Two hundred people can shoot an awful lot of people in three hours," said Jesse James.

"Nobody dies who isn't on our list."

Cole Younger stood up to talk. "Charley," he said, quietly, "it ain't like the good ol' days when there was just the few of us. You got way over two hundred men now, some still comin' in. You and me, we don't know who they are. Lots of boys with hard grudges. It ain't like a real war with us, you know that. You can tell someone what to do but most of us, well, we're on our own, the way it's always been. You can't go around with a little list in your hand and checkin' on everybody. By the time you find they ain't there, you got a bullet in your backside."

"You got your orders, Buddy," said Quantrill, taking a step toward him. His voice was full of all the silence he could get into it, the words hollow and ghostly, as if it all came from a source deep inside. "If anybody steps out of line, you have my permission to kill him."

"Even our own men?"

"Especially if it's one of ours. The great white father over in Richmond thinks we're all Indians out here. I want to prove him wrong, that's all. I want him, and all the rest of those people sitting in their offices making big decisions, to realize what we're doing out here we're doing on our own, we don't need him at all, because we can win our own wars and win them like civilized soldiers in a civilized war."

"Civilized!" said Andy Blunt. "Who gives a good goddamn! We're trying to save our own neck!"

He paused, looked around at them as a teacher might when it was apparent the class refused to finish the assignment. "I picked out a task each one of you could do and I told you how I

172

wanted it done. Now, if you don't want to do it, just say so, and I'll call it a day and go home and wait for them to come and get me.''

They sweated out the silence.

"You give everybody something to do, Charley," said Bill Anderson. "I seem to got missed out."

"I want you up on top of Mount Oread keeping your eyes peeled for a sign along the roads that the Yankees are coming. You and your friend Clements."

She was waiting for him when he came out of the barn. At first he thought merely to climb onto his horse and ride off with the rest of them to the staging field near Lone Jack, but he considered the risks she had taken to get there, the long ride, her commitment. She stood silently in the trees, motionless, watching him. She would have remained there even if he had turned his back to her, would have watched him ride away and not so much as lifted an arm. He went to her, and they stood wordlessly for a moment.

At last she said. "You're going then?"

"They accepted my terms, Kate. We'll be back on Saturday."

She didn't appear comforted by his words.

"I want to ride with you. I won't be in the way, I promise. I want to be beside you at your time of great triumph."

He touched her on the cheek with his hand. "No," he said. "I want a good reason to make it home safely."

"So that's it. I stand and wait until you need me."

"Something like that, Kate," he said, touching her again and then turning away.

Andy Blunt took twenty men out onto the roads so that the Yankees could see them if they looked and left word Quantrill was heading for Pleasant Hill. Once out of sight, Blunt slipped down into a ravine and followed it west toward the rendezvous at Lone Jack. There were more men than Quantrill expected, nearly three hundred when he arrived, and word was brought that

173

another one hundred waited to join them at the Potter Farm, a company of recruits commanded by one Colonel John Holt, who were underway for Arkansas when they heard of the raid on Lawrence. Another fifty waited in the High Blues, and that would make four hundred fifty men for the ride to Lawrence. He kept Anderson and Clements close to hand and sent Bill Gregg and George Todd out with pickets to make certain nobody surprised him when he came to the border. They rode silently across Shawnee Trace and saw, to the north, the horrible black funnels of smoke as the Yankees began their systematic burning and looting north along the Missouri River. Quantrill's mind wavered, he thought of Kate and her sad words. Perhaps it *was* true. But it was not the time to dwell on Kate, she didn't count, not now. Nothing counted but Lawrence, Kansas. He would tell the men once they reached their night camp in the High Blues just where they were bound and what they had to do when they got there, and he would instruct his officers in front of the men to make sure that everyone did only what he was supposed to do. They were shaving close. But what about Anderson and Clements and the dark shadows that followed that pair? As he rode, he looked over and saw Anderson's pack moving along, outfitted in Union uniforms, looking merely dedicated to remaining upright on their mounts. He had had words with Anderson at the last moment and had to tell him if anyone stayed back at the camp, he would have to submit to an armed guard, and so Anderson decided to go along to the 'party', as George Todd had put it.

At nightfall over four hundred men rode in along the creek bottoms towards Mouse Creek and Lumpkins Fork and the High Blues swampland. They were met by pickets and escorted down inside to the campfires, where another fifty men stood around smoking and waiting for them. When they had all rested and eaten their last meal before the ride, he brought Charley into the middle of the ring and stood in the saddle to tell them they were going to Lawrence, Kansas, in order to burn it down and draw the heat off the extermination of the Blue Springs farmers, told them they would cross the border south of Aubry and swing

174

northwest across the prairie past Gardiner toward Lawrence.

Some of them prayed, some drank, and he circulated among them and listened to their private fears, persuading them that they were doing things right. "They won't forget what you did for them," he would say. "Your name is written in the record whether you make it or not, so it doesn't matter which . . . or does it? I'd like it if you were to be with me when we come back, so stay out of trouble over there . . do what you're supposed to do, remember the names are on the list, you know who they are . . . stay away from them if they aren't on the list." Some of them in Holt's troop were just boys like Jesse James, thirteen, fourteen, too young to shave, pimples on their faces. They were mad, they were scared, a little crazed, hungry even. He could do nothing about their fears, but he could measure their anger and their frustrations by his own. "You might not have wanted to do the same thing your fathers done a few years ago but it looks like you got little choice in the matter. There's no getting away from this, it's got to be done right. You know what the right way is, you have all been told now. Do that, and we'll get you home again safe and sound."

It sounded good. He wondered whether he believed himself or not.

He sent out the pickets at low sun and they confirmed his expectations: the two patrols, one from Little Sante Fe and the other from Coldwater Grove, had already passed each other and were on their way home; the garrison at Aubry had only the twenty-one men in it and Colonel Pike, who was not likely to pursue them but, rather, to wait for reinforcements, and the prairies to the west were absolutely clear.

And so they came swarming up out of the marshlands of the High Blues, the first hundred in U.S. uniforms, up through the thinning woods and out onto the plains of Kansas behind the farm woodlot owned by old man Adams, who was rumoured to be deaf. Quantrill sent Cole Younger, dressed as a Yankee colonel, to the farmhouse to tell Adams and his family that they weren't to be frightened because they were only a Union patrol out on manoeuvres.

It was his first mistake.

Once Younger was gone, old man Adams saddled a horse and rode to Aubry, where he found Colonel Pike seated at a small desk smelling of rum. He told the colonel he had counted eight hundred of them, and even though some of them wore blue uniforms, they were all border ruffians, and they had come winging up out of that swamp like a swarm of skeeters looking for blood. "It's Quantrill!" he screamed. "I tell you it's Quantrill! The man that come to my house was that Buddy Younger!" The colonel might have been a little tight, but he knew when a man was sufficiently worked up to tell the truth and sent a messenger up to General Ewing at The Landing with the news. Then he wrote a note to the two patrol commanders at Little Sante Fe and Coldwater Grove saying Quantrill had just breached the border with eight hundred men and there was no way he was going out looking for him with fifteen.

It was five hours before the men from Little Sante Fe and Coldwater Grove converged on Aubry, five and a half before they were on the trail, a man with a lamp lighting the way. By the time Pike reached Paola, it was midnight and he knew Quantrill had probably already got to wherever he wanted to go.

176

NINETEEN

After the raid Quantrill had Will Toothman, bound and gagged, brought to him in the bushes of the Marais des Cygnes River. He dismissed the men and removed Toothman's gag, stared at him until the boy dropped his eyes.

"All right, Toothman," he growled, "start at the beginning and go until I tell you to stop!"

The sweat ran from his forehead. "Give me a drink first," said Toothman.

"Tell me the goddamn story!"

The man's mouth was full of phlegm but he talked through it, and as he spoke, Quantrill's face recorded the terrible truth. "Me and Skaggs," he began, slow, the words barely audible, "we saw you standin' on your horse and we looked at each other and when you was done the two of us went down to the water and Skaggs, he says. 'There ain't goin' to be anyone around to see what a fella does and live to tell about it.' Me, I says, 'You heard Charley, you heard what he said.' But I knew it, it wasn't goin' to be no different than usual, soon's I got there, same's before, I'd follow him 'round like always. 'I'm goin' to get me a woman,' says Skaggs. 'That's why I come.' Me, I says, 'You ain't s'pose to touch any women.' 'Who's goin' to see you do it!' says Skaggs. 'I already got a big one jest thinkin' on it,' an I could see myself he had this big bulge in his pants. Well, I made up my mind, soon's I got to Lawrence, I'd stay clear of him. I was with

177

Todd, I knew Todd was watchin' everybody.

"All the way to Lawrence I stayed shy of Lark Skaggs but ever'time he saw me, why he'd point at his crotch and laugh and laugh, and so by the time we got to the top of the hill and I looked down on Yankeetown I knew I was hooked."

"You sonofabitch!" snapped Quantrill and slapped him with the back of the hand so hard that Toothman fell to the ground.

Lawrence lay across the high grassy prospect above the river, asleep. A ravine began in the south and coursed due north through the town to the tannery perched above the river. The town site looked to have been laid out to a mathematical formula and made to point its axis along the lines of true north. The streets ran perpendicular to each other, and each residential block was subdivided into twenty-four lots, each block with an alleyway bisecting the rear quarters of the houses that squared away with their equal number on the other side of the street. The town appeared to derive nothing from the natural terrain but preferred to impose its order everywhere. It was ten by twelve blocks long and twelve blocks wide, with a large open park, square, in the lower half of the village. Streets running north and south were named after states of the Union that had abolished slavery, streets east and west after such abolitionists as John Quincy and John Hancock. The settlement sat on a height first admired by General John C. Fremont for its geographical outlook, but later settlers seemed to prefer the site for its political prospects.

The wide gravel streets of the town were cordons of white houses representative of the plain New England style, wood, with a discreet amount of gingerbread and bright colour, protected each by a white picket fence and flower garden. A number of fine wood and brick commercial structures lifted their crowns above the residential areas and brought a touch of class to an otherwise dull place, not the least of which was the Eldridge Hotel, a four-storey brick building which lately had come to serve as command headquarters for such men as Senator Jim Lane and Charles Jennison, among others, and as a conference

178

place for visiting government men. The hotel stared across Winthrop Street at the courthouse and looked down upon the Journal House and the Willis Brothers' Stable, and, especially, further along, the City Hotel, which it had supplanted as the settlement's leading hostelry. It turned its back too on the Johnson House, now strictly a boarding house for Union officers and visiting military personnel. It seemed to have nothing to do with the churches along Vermont Street, the Presbyterian Assembly Hall, the Second Baptist Temple, and the Black Baptist Tabernacle.

The rich and powerful had built across the bridges, to the west, where the land began to lift toward the grassy bluffs of Mt. Oread, which really was no mountain at all, but rather a high hill. It seemed as if some people were determined to find a place where they could look down on others, and this was the perfect place for it. A long yellow cornfield spanned the western edge of the village on down to the river, and beyond the field, the grass became bush and bush tree, which grew in increasing numbers toward the west.

It was a little after six when they came.

They fell upon the town, rolling out to the east across the grassland, swinging in a wide arc and like a tornado with deadly accuracy.

"When we rode into town," said Toothman, bleeding from the mouth, "I was right behind Skaggs, reachin' out for the tail of his horse, my heart beatin' like it would break wide open. I was goddamn scared!"

The first ones to awaken at the campground must have sat up when they heard the thunder, they must have looked up at the sky to track the eye of the storm, but as is often the case in Kansas, the storm struck them first. It was a whirl of flaring eyes and nostrils, ringing hooves, explosions of Colt revolvers. There were no Yankee survivors at the white campground, but when Cole Younger's men reached the Blacks, they had many of them vanished into the woods at the top of the ravine. They left them

179

and joined Quantrill's men and Holt's recruits as they poured down Massachusetts Street toward the hotel, and the two companies swung out, half to the top of the street and half around behind the hotel. Bill Gregg brought his men around Kentucky Street and along the picket fence at the rear of the hotel, dismounted and covered all the rear exits. Jarrette's men had already climbed to the flat roof of the Willis Stable, Dick Burns' people stood in the windows of the courthouse, and Colonel Holt came in through the churchyard, while Jimmy Little and Ol Shepherd slipped into the Journal House and climbed to the roof, slinging themselves flat and pointing their guns at the Eldridge.

Not five minutes had elapsed since they rode into town and suddenly it was silent. A light wind played in the streets, lifting small whirlwinds of dust.

Quantrill rode alone into the street in front of the hotel, exposing himself to any gunfire. He dismounted and, quickly, from several doorways, came Cole Younger, James Younger, Frank and Jesse James, Bill Gregg and George Todd, building a circle around him.

Silence.

Then they heard a window being heaved open. Quantrill knew it was a window in one of the conference rooms. A man's white shirt dangled from a broomstick, and a high voice was heard.

"Who are you?!"

The men stared at each other as if in the crush of events they had forgot and needed to be reminded.

"Quantrill!" screamed George Todd.

"And what is your intent?"

"Send us Jim Lane!"

"We are not armed . . . but we won't come out unless you promise to treat us as prisoners of war!"

"Send out Jim Lane and you go free!"

It was silent for a while.

"Lane is not here!"

"Jennison then!"

"Jennison is not here!"

180

"Who in hell *is* there?"

"Captain Banks! I'm the provost!"

"Well, Banks, you come on out here with your hands on top of your head and make sure everybody else in there comes along with you unless you want to be roasted alive!"

"Either that," shouted Frank James, "or stay inside and you can be a hero!"

At last they came out. There were forty of them. They had been to a late night meeting of the railroad committee, but the subject had not been iron horses. It was Quantrill and rumours of Quantrill. They had read a letter from General Ewing stating that there was no substance to the rumours, and so far as Quantrill was concerned, it would be folly for his men to test the border patrol, which day and night was committed to keeping the bushwhackers at home.

The captives were lined up in the street and marched to the garden behind the City Hotel. It was a large garden with stone walls and an iron gate, and there were apple trees in it with hard small apples that made the best pies in Kansas. Quantrill watched them being led off, turned to Cole Younger and said, "Well, Buddy, this is no time for speeches. There's work to be done!" Cole Younger waved to a couple of men who ran into the hotel lobby and began to break open all the oil lamps. Quantrill stepped up onto the edge of the walk and looked out over his assembled troops.

"Burn!" he shouted. "Secure that armory! Capture Jim Lane! Cut the cable to the ferry! Away! Away!" He took off his Kossuth and waved it over his head, laughing madly. He felt good. It was his turn. He walked out into the street, turned and saw the first flames in the hotel lobby.

Jimmy Little had found just what he was looking for in the Willis Brothers' Stable. He hitched up a team and brought it to Quantrill. It was a newly-built buckboard, with red wheels, gilded with gold, and it had a leather seat with a fancy long black-and-white whip.

"It ain't as good as Jarrette's chariot," he laughed, "but it'll do you!"

181

He got into it and rode down the street.

"Soon's we see you whip off that hat of your'n, we got onto our horses and fell in behind Todd," said Will Toothman, having been joined on the ground by the man who had beaten him (who now stared into his face as if being told a nursery rhyme which had dragons in it). "Only thing is, we kinda hung back, waitin' for a chance, seein' what the other fella was goin' to do, almost like we was darin' each other to do it, waitin' to see the other fella do it and then say it was his fault, if he hadn't led you to it, you wouldn't've done it.

"Well, we was ridin' hell-bent-for-leather out toward the river when all to once I see ol' Lark cuttin' across this field toward an ol' broken down mill. 'You sonofabitch!' I yelled after him. 'I ain't goin' with you!' Well, I went across the field, kinda slow, waitin' to see if maybe he wasn't jest takin' a piss or somethin', comin' back soon's he was done or somethin'. But there he was, wavin' at me. 'I ain't comin'!' I says, and I went over to him and he says, 'Someone run inside as we was comin' along the street.' I see his nose all blown-up, like a bloodhound that had seen a coon. He had his gun out and he was goin' inside. 'If they catch you,' I says, 'you're in big trouble. You know what Charley says.' He tells me to shut up and goes over to the door, sniffin' the air like a goddamn coonhound, as I said. 'Listen!' he says.

"Me, I listened for a long time, I didn't hear nothin'.

"'I tell you somebody's runnin' in there, tryin' to hide on us.' He had this crazy ziggyzaggy look on his face and then I see him put a hand over his crotch. 'Just as we come round that corner,' he says, 'I saw 'em goin' in here.' He cocked an ear. 'Listen.' he says. Me, all I can hear is guns goin' off all over town. I can see our boys runnin' everywhere, and then I see you comin' along in this fancy wagon, and I says, 'Hey, Lark, here comes Charley!' and he grabs me and pulls me into the mill and we wait until you're gone, and Skaggs, he says. 'They're in here somewheres.'

"I says, 'How many?' He says, 'Two'. I say, 'You sure

about that?'

"Ol' Skaggs, he looks at me, his lips festerin' away, he says, 'A man and a woman.' And he says it again, 'A woman,' like that, all slobbery. I set there smellin' that mill, that wet dry dusty grain smell, you know, cool musty dark.

"'There must be a million places to hide in here,' I says, 'you'll never find them'.

"And Skaggs says, 'Me, I can smell a woman's crotch two miles off with the wind in the wrong direction. Why, right now I can tell exactly where that bitch is, so stick close to me and keep quiet!' All those long belts hanging there, the birds up in the lofts singin' away, the stillness, I can still hear that stillness." Will Toothman wiped away the blood and cranked an eye up into the blue sky. "And then," he said, "somewhere below us, we hear it at the same time, pebbles . . . little pebbles fallin' into the water like somebody kicked them there."

The house knelt behind two dead cottonwoods, set in that direction to catch the morning light, and the yard was swept clean. Red and blue bottles hung in the branches, like chimes, reflecting the light, and along the edge of the walk, a few spindly flowers had survived the oppressive heat.

Mrs. Lane stood in the doorway.

Quantrill parked his buggy and walked into the yard, paused with one foot on the stoop and lifted his hat. "Captain Quantrill, m'am," he said, smiling. "I came to have a word with the General Senator Lane."

"I have already told your ruffians he is not home to visitors."

"I'm not a visitor, m'am."

"He's not home."

"Where is he?"

"Leavenworth."

"We know better, m'am!"

"You know nothin' but lies, Quantrill."

"We got ways of knowing. We know, for instance, he was at the railroad meeting last night and afterwards he came to this very house."

"He's smarter than you. He knew he was being watched and so he went to Leavenworth in the middle of the night without telling anyone."

"Step aside."

She put her arms out and touched the doorframe.

"Where is he, Mrs. Lane?" he said, pulling out his revolver. He knew he was beginning to look a little foolish. "I know he's home because I can smell him."

"If you force your way into this house, I shall notify the proper authorities."

"We *are* the proper authorities!" he said, pushing her to one side and walking into the hallway. Jimmy Little followed him into the house, but stood at the door waiting for trouble. Quantrill walked through the rooms, pulling out drawers, opening closets, and, at last, entered Jim Lane's bedroom which had been used by two people the preceding night. Lane's clothing hung in the closet and there was the appearance of haste about the room: a coin here, a dropped shirt there. One window, which dropped to the back porch, was standing open. He came back down the stairs and went up to Mrs. Lane. "There's only one way to find out where he's hiding, m'am," he said. "Only the one way."

"Yes," she said. "When you're wrong, you make them pay for it, don't you?" Her composure was beginning to break, her voice to crack. "I should have listened to my husband in the first place. We should all have listened to him!"

"It's too late, m'am."

He walked out into the yard. "Dick!" he shouted across the street. "I found your piano. It's right there in the parlour like you said. McCorkle's silver is in the dining room. It's a real museum, boys! But the lady says General Lane is not here, so you better get in here and clean this place out before we burn him out!"

"What about my piano?"

"Leave it for now, Dick. You never played it in the first place."

184

He walked out through the yard and sat in his buggy, and she came along behind him and stood at the fence.

"You tell your husband next time you see him, m'am," he said, "it would've been more honourable for him to stay home to protect you."

"It isn't fair!" she sobbed. "Maybe he deserves it but I don't. Look at my house . . . I worked my whole life for it."

"Nothing is fair, m'am. Not even having to work all your life for a miserable roof over your head."

He sat in the buggy watching her house, and she stood with her back to it watching him. The men had it surrounded in anticipation of Lane's eventual cries of surrender but none came. It was a dry house, even drier after a hot summer, and its rooms were brittle and dense, close with old furniture and inflammable objects. The windows exploded and the town was full of its conflagration. He wanted to tell her he didn't know whether he hated her or not, whether he felt good about what he was doing, whether even at the beginning, on that late spring day when Lane brought all his new men over for a cup of tea, when he watched her hovering above him, whether he hated her or felt good about being in her house. Perhaps it was because of the distance that separated them, she and all the other women of Lawrence, the untouchables, exempt from the blowing sands and parched creekbottoms, moving unseen behind Boston glass and New Haven shutters, perched atop stools before spinets in high lace gowns from New York. But then he had not come back for her, he had come to put the question to the Senator, the General, the Redleg leader Jim Lane, who now most likely hid somewhere out in the cornfields.

This would have to be his consolation, this burning and looting. Maybe that was all he needed, maybe he should be content with that. He climbed into his buckboard and rode off down the street, immune, turning but once to see Mrs. Lane walking toward the house as if she intended to cast herself among the flames.

"It was all dark shafts and broken stairs and empty bins,

ladders, all leadin' down toward the water wheel,'' said Will Toothman, leaning closer now to his listener, who sat with his head bowed, as if hearing a confession. ''Down there where wood met water, don't you see? There where the wheel turned in the creek and the loose gravel stones lay around the wheelroom where somebody clingin' to that wheel might just happen to kick a stone or two into the water.

'''Down there!' whispered Skaggs.

'''Let's go back and do what Charley told us to do,' I says. 'How do you know, maybe there's somebody down there with a gun?'

'''Two kids', he says, 'and one of 'em's a girl!'' So Lark, he creeps around like a toad, wall to wall, gettin' closer and closer, and, me, I'm right behind him because now I'm feelin' a kinda excitement too about all this, you see. I got two heads now, one of 'em in my pants, jest like Lark, and two heads is dangerous when it comes to women. Anyways, I see Skaggs kneelin' just where that long belt run down into the hole, and then he took to the steps like a man who seen an open bank vault and me right behind him, and when we come to this railing above the hole, we seen 'em.

''Two of 'em, a boy and a girl, the boy maybe ten twelve, somethin' like that, and the girl, older, maybe fifteen, the pair of them crouchin' there lookin' up at us, cornered just where that wheel turned, above the creek, sluicin' down over the broken wall, and Skaggs, he says, 'That your brother with you?' But she don't say nothin', she's plumb scared, I'll tell you, well wouldn't you be, lookin' up into two Colt pistols? Oh, she was a real beauty, I'll admit. Long blond hair . . . good tits on her, I—''

''What did that goddamn Skaggs do!'' said Quantrill, angered again.

''Well, he . . . spoke to the little boy, he says, 'Is that your big sister?' But he, the little fella, he was just sittin' there, holding' onto her, scared, he didn't say nothin' at all. Me, I says, 'Let's go back.'''

Will Toothman stopped, held his head, his eyes searching the ground as if he had dropped something at his feet.

186

"What happened next?"

"Well, I . . . Lark Skaggs shot him. He took aim at the boy and shot him. The boy just flipped up in the air and fell into the shaft and you could see him being spun out through the water into the creek, and all the girl could do was stand there and scream her fool head off!"

There wasn't much shooting in the streets. He rode slowly along like a tourist, watching men pull people out of houses and tie them to trees or fences, children winding in and out of their parents' feet, whining, hysterical. Jimmy Little rode up to him, tied his horse to the buckboard and climbed in beside him.

"I went to the Griswold's like we said," he groaned, wiping the soot from his face. Little was sweating, his face red, eyes distended, his speech was slurred. "Only they saw us comin' and came out into the yard with guns. We had to shoot to defend ourself, Charley, me and Ol' Shepherd, Jess' and Frank, so we shot them. There was Griswold and Trask, that newspaper man . . . and Harlow Baker the Redleg."

"What about Senator Thorpe?"

"Dead."

"Goddamn it, Jimmy! I wanted hostages! What are we goin' to offer them for those women in The Landing, a wagonload of famous corpses?"

"Jess' says they had guns, I saw the guns!"

"Christ! Can't none of your boys shoot to wound no more? What's goin' on? We wanted those hostages!"

They went to watch the Republican Building burn. It cut off the sun and plunged Lawrence into a dark red cloud. George Todd came running to them, saying the place was full of loot brought to Lawrence from Blue Springs. "Too much of it to take back," he said.

"No hostages, no loot," said Quantrill, watching one of his men (he didn't recognize him) driving along ahead of him a couple dozen people with their hands in the air. "Well, maybe with the mayor of the town, ol' Collamore, that should be worth a dozen women."

187

"I stood there and watched him climb down the steps and into the hole where the girl was. Her back was to the wall, she had no place to run. He took her by the hair and dragged her up the steps and struck her across the face. That stopped her from screamin'. Kinda woke her up a little. Me, I couldn't do anything, I couldn't come closer, I couldn't run, I was rooted to the floor. I wanted to see what she looked like without clothes on, but that was all. Jest curiosity, you know, but I didn't want to...you know."

"What did he do next, Toothman?"

"He told her to take her clothes off. But she jest stood there. It was real quiet, cool, in there, jest the pair of them standin' there like they was havin' a friendly conversation, like they jest met."

"What did he do, goddamn it!"

"Well, she didn't want to take off her clothes, naturally. So he says, 'Grab her arms!' to me. I can't move. 'Grab her arms!' he says again. 'No,' I says, 'I ain't goin' to have nothin' to do with it!' And so ol' Skaggs, he pulls out his gun and points it at me, he says, 'Get ahold of this lady's arms, Jackass!' and so I took hold of her arms and he ripped that dress right off her."

When they climbed down from the buggy, an old woman came up to them, her dress torn, mumbling, clawing at them, pointed to the back of the house. Andy McGuire was walking out of the house carrying a sewing machine. "My ol' lady always said she wanted a sewing machine," he said. "This one'll do."

"What's she saying?" said Quantrill.

"Ol' lady Collamore?" said Andy, as if noticing her for the first time. "The mayor's out there in the well. I figured it was a good place for him. He won't go too far that way."

"He's in the water!" they heard her say. "Come quick, he's drowning!"

They ran out to the well.

He peered deep into the rocky hole. It was dark at the bottom. "Mayor Collamore!" he shouted. There was no answer. He looked at Jimmy Little and the moaning woman. "Step back, let in the light." He peered down into the sheeny halflight and saw, back and shoulders, silent, headless, the shape of a man.

"Damn!" he said. "There goes my last hostage!"

Joel Crabtree and Bill Hulse ran across a yard toward a house and flattened themselves against the wall. They broke the windows with their boots and fired idly into the rooms, and, as they rushed in through the front door, a man bolted from the back one, only to encounter Andy Blunt's men, who waited in the alleyway and, as soon as they saw him, killed him in the garden.

Twenty or so young boys stood at one corner with their hands on top of their heads as Bud Spence played with his revolver in front of them. One of the boys had filled his pants and was sobbing.

"Now you know," he said, "how we feel over there in Blue Springs, boys."

John Noland and Jimmy Reed walked down the boards in front of the shops along Massachusetts Street emptying their revolvers into the spaces between the planks. He could see from his buggy where those who had fled the fireworks to hide under the walkways had met their fate.

Harry Trow and Foss Key were in the doorway of a flaming house trying to wrestle a frantic woman away from a man lodged in the half-opened door. The children stood in the yard screaming at her to escape from the flames. Trunks had been set about the yard, and a man was breaking them open with an axe, throwing the clothing and books onto the grass and pocketing the jewelry. The flames belched from the windows. Foss Key at last had her in his arms, pushing her down the steps and out into her waiting children's arms. When he got back, Harry Trow had both the boots off and was about to run with them.

"Please!" shouted the woman. "Carry my husband out of the fire before you go!"

"Why?" said Harry Trow. "He's already dead, ain't he?"

They raced off, one boot apiece, and she was left to contemplate her husband wedged into the doorway while the flames came after him. At last she turned away, drawing her children close, looking for refuge in other fires.

All Massachusetts was on fire. The Eldridge Hotel was engulfed and tottered inward; the Republican Building, the stables, stores, sheds, all burned. In front of the courthouse, Frank James stood tolling the bell, his brother Jesse laughing at him like a country boy getting his first taste of the city.

He rode through the bloodshed realizing suddenly he had made a mistake. It was not going to be easy prying Yankees out of houses and shooting them in the street because they all had wives and children, ten or twelve apiece. It was hard for men of conscience, as were the boys from Blue Springs, to shoot a man in front of his screaming wife and bawling babies. He had made it even harder for them by telling them they couldn't touch women and children. It was the women who were shooting at his men as they rode through the streets.

Either that, or they acted like men at a church outing. He saw three men carrying trunks out into the yard of one house, driven by an angry woman who seemed more interested in her furnishings than in her husband, who lay bleeding in the yard. He saw four men sitting around a porch holding soup bowls out to an old lady who lectured them for their inconsiderate manners. He saw five men bringing rolled-up carpets and laying them neatly in the yard, while another stood waiting with the torch. When his men's backs were turned, he saw a man crawl out of one of the rugs and hightail it for the ravine.

It would have been better to drive the men out into the cornfield and into the ravine, where they could pit themselves against other men. This was a different kind of war he had invented for himself, and he was going to have to learn from now on how to shoot women and children.

He looked up into the black tunnels and considered shooting women and children.

His carriage struck something and woke him: he turned and saw the dead man in the street, in a long green nightshirt, holding something in his hand. He went back to him and kneeled before him.

190

"You run me over you sonofabitch!" said the man, but it was plain to see he would die anyway. He lifted the man's hand and saw the watch. "What time is it?" said the man.

"Seven o'clock," said Quantrill.

TWENTY

In the dining room of the City Hotel you could scarcely hear the noise in the streets, and the smoke in the room might have come from the fireplaces. Quantrill had never been admitted into this room when he worked in the kitchen for Mr. Stone, but he had peeked into it when the worthies dined, and vowed that one day he would eat there. It was still a pleasant room, though shabbier than he had remembered it to be. The wallpaper had been designed in Paris and manufactured in Brooklyn, the cut-glass chandelier was from Boston, silverware and china from Sheffield, linens from Dublin. The intricate lace curtains caught and sustained the daylight and made it seem somehow old. Before the men the table was laden with eggs and ham, fresh corn, a chicken, white beans in a sauce, hot rolls and an urn of coffee — and in the centre of it all a large green bottle of French wine.

"They never let me in here," said Quantrill, turning to look at Nathan Stone and his wife, against the kitchen door, like captives. "Ol' Nathan told me you shouldn't see the help. Ain't that right, Nathan?"

"Ordinarily," said Bill Gregg, with his bib tied around his neck, "I don't drink wine for breakfast."

"This ain't breakfast," said George Todd, filling all the glasses, tilting above the table unsteadily, smoke-filled eyes. "This here's a celebration!"

"I propose a toast!" said Jimmy Little, standing, "You sit,

192

Charley," he added, watching the others rise. Colonel Holt was on his feet, Frank James, Jesse James, Cole Younger and George Todd, all standing around looking over at him, waiting to see who'd laugh first.

"Here's to Charley Quantrill," said Jimmy Little. "He brought us here, now he can get us home without losin' our heads!"

"Hear! Hear!" said the others, drinking and then once more falling to their plates.

"Way I hear it," said Todd, "Senator Lane wanted everybody to have a gun under his pillow but the mayor, old Collamore, he said he wouldn't be mayor to an armed camp, but he went so far as to let everybody put his name on a gun which was stored down in the armory."

They roared with laughter.

"I saw a couple of your boys, Colonel Holt, goin' along the boardwalk just shooting through the cracks," said Quantrill.

"You should've been there," said Jesse James, "when we cleaned out the Johnson House. They said they didn't have nothin' against people over in Missouri, they went over there and burned 'em all out 'cause they was under military orders!" Quantrill glared at him: he should have insisted that Frank tell his brother no children should be seen at the table. "So we lined 'em all up against the wall and told 'em we had nothin' against 'em either, we was only followin' orders."

"Shut up, Jesse!" said his brother.

"We cut the cable to the ferry," said Colonel Holt, ignoring Quantrill's pointed remark, "and we heard 'em coming down to the water, the whole United States Army in Lawrence. There wasn't more than a couple dozen of them, and all they could do is try to lob a little lead into town."

Quantrill had not yet picked up his knife and fork. "Last time I looked at our list, I counted fifty names on it, that and about ten hostages."

"It's damn lucky for the Yankees," said Bill Gregg, starting in on seconds, "there ain't no wind today. Why if it was windy, one little match would've burned the whole damn place down."

"You ain't eatin', Charley," said George Todd, his mouth stuffed. "Mr. Stone," pointing with his knife at the man leaning against the wall, "he ain't goin' to say nothin' to you now. You're his employer, ain't you? Ain't this what you wanted? A little revenge on these sonsabitches?"

"Charley ain't hungry," said Jimmy Little, "because he's got somethin' on his mind." They all stopped and looked at him. "What's on your mind, Charley?"

"I don't know who they are," he said, seriously, "but they're our men. I thought I'd met them all, but I sure as hell don't recognize them now. What in hell is goin' on around here anyways!" he said, breathlessly. "We lost all our hostages. I see dead men in the streets that don't appear nowhere on our lists!"

"You can't write a war down on a little piece of paper and expect to follow it," said Frank James, smiling. "It's hot out there in those streets."

"When I was riding along," said Quantrill, quietly, "I see this guy runnin' a knife in and out of a man like he had somethin' against him!"

"You got to watch these sonsabitches, Charley," said George Todd. "People with names on little pieces of paper get up and walk around, and when your back is turned, they try to shoot you."

"The man I seen doin' it was Arch Clements!"

Even Todd stopped chewing.

"Now you boys are supposed to be runnin' this show the way I told you to do it and I want to know why Clements is down here in the streets when he's supposed to be up on Mt. Oread with Bill Anderson on lookout." They appeared to have nothing to say, and Quantrill turned to look at Frank James. "Now, you're supposed to be in charge of Anderson and his little band of cut-throats, Frank. Where is he, where's Anderson?"

"Well," he began, paused as if uncertain whether to say anything. "He come to me, you see. I told him 'No, you go back up there like you're supposed to.'

"Then he come to me," said Todd, "and I tried to talk to him, told him to get to hell out of my territory."

194

"Him and Clements was hookin' up some horses to wagons when I saw him," said Cole Younger, "and so I says, 'What are you doin' here?' and he says, 'Ain't this that place owned by John Dean, Charley is always talkin' about? Well, I'm puttin' together the wagon train so's we can take all the loot back to Blue Springs like Charley says.' I told him to get back up on Oread but he wouldn't go."

"So you just left him. You wouldn't come to me and tell me about it, would you?" Cole looked down at his plate as if suddenly he wasn't hungry anymore. Quantrill peered above the heads of his men at the Stones, who stood watching him. "Get to hell out of here, Nathan!" he shouted, and when neither of them moved, he pulled out his revolver and aimed it at them. It was embarrassing, the men looked at each other. When they were alone, Quantrill looked around the table. "We had this all worked out so it was neat and clean," he said, recovering from his anger. "We wanted somethin' to take home again and feel good about afterwards."

"It ain't neat and it ain't clean," said Jesse James, smirking, "but it sure as hell is fun!"

"I want you boys to eat up and leave me alone in here. Frank, I want you to bring in Anderson even if you have to bring him in by your gun."

"I'll jest tell him you want him for a scalpin' detail," said Frank James. "That way you couldn't keep him away."

"I held her while Skaggs went and got some old gunny sacks and threw them down onto the floor," said Will Toothman. "I tried to whisper into her ear jest to relax, you know, try to think of somethin' else and it would all soon be over and she could go home again and nobody would know, but she kept on bawlin' like that, and Skaggs, he says, 'Lay her out on these things, Will', and this little girl, she jest kinda melted, sorta went all soft, and I laid her down on them gunny sacks. She was all white, you know, but she had real nice breasts, little pink nipples, and I was gettin' all hexed up myself then, watchin' her. She didn't try to run off or nothin', she jest lay there, sobbin'.

195

"Skaggs sat on the floor, listenin' to the gunfire, smilin' over at me. He pulled off his boots and set them next to each other, and then he stood up and dropped his trousers and I could see he had a real big one on him, just slobberin' away, was ol' Skaggs, talkin' to himself, talkin' to me, talkin' to the girl but not makin' no sense to any of us I could see. 'Takin' this thing in my hand,' he's sayin', 'runnin' through the trees, you can see him swingin' there, that juice jest comin' in and out', sprayin' it ever'where . . . and then I run him through with the knife two three times and that juice jest sprayin' ever'where and I took that knife in my hand 'n I jest slitch-slatch! and the damn thing come right off in my hands an' it was still hard as a nun's tit . . . an' then I stick it 'twixt my legs and gawdamighty! I jest couldn't hardly stand it, it was the strangest feelin' . . .'

"And then he unbuttons his shirt and falls onto his knees in front of her, all drawn up now, pushin' back into me, but Skaggs, he pries her legs apart, she says, 'No! No! No!' but that only makes him feel good, and he pulls her out flat and says, 'Hang onto her, Will, hang on!' and me, I'm holdin' onto her hands, she's flat on her back, and from that angle, all of a sudden, I see this little girl looks just like my sister, and I start to get a funny feelin', I'm sick, I want to throw up...and ol'Skaggs, me holdin' her arms, watchin', Skaggs thrusts himself onto her and I can see him diggin' to get inside her when . . . I jest couldn't he'p myself, I jest vomited all over the pair of them!"

Anderson came into the room by himself. He was in no hurry until he saw the food on the table, whereupon he tossed his hat to the floor and fell into a chair, reaching for the tureen. Quantrill stood, suddenly, reached across the table and pushed him backward, so that, unexpectedly, the chair tipped and Anderson went sprawling onto the floor.

"Sit down in that chair and listen to me, Anderson!" he barked. He walked over to him, set the chair upright, and steered Anderson into it. The young man wore the remnants of a Yankee uniform but had draped himself in gold jewellry and rings. "You're supposed to be up on Oread, now why ain't you?"

"Nothin' to do up there.'

"I seen Arch Clements running a man through with a knife."

"These are big boys, Charley," said Anderson, his sneer returning. "You gotta be mean with 'em."

"I heard Clell Miller strung up a couple of men on Massachusetts."

"Clell? We strung up lots of 'em. I don't remember the ones on Massachusetts."

Anderson looked around the room. "Nice place you got here," he said, rising, putting his hat back on his head. "I'm sorry I can't stay but I got work to do."

"Sit down, Anderson."

"Naw," he said, in jest, "I can't really accept your invit—"

Quantrill drew his gun and pulled back the hammer. "Sit down, like I said."

Anderson considered the odds. He knew it was not wise to push Charley Quantrill too far: he was too fast, too deadly, and especially when, as now, his eyes had come straight out of their well, looking twice the size of any man's eyes. He pushed his hat back and fell into the chair, and Quantrill laid the pistol down on the table in front of him.

"Don't make me go for it, Anderson," he said, matter-of-factly, "because you wouldn't have a chance right now." He fixed his eyes on the man in the chair. "I want an explanation and it better be a good one."

Anderson avoided the eyes, turned to look into the window. It was getting dark, the streets were full of smoke, the light in the room oppressive, heavy, as if the sky was bringing a tornado toward Lawrence, yet of course the storm was already there, already obliterating it.

"All right," he said, redirecting his eyes across the table at his inquisitor. "I'll tell you everything, I'll confess to everything. We're in this thing with you, my boys and me. We like the work, we like the money. We come to join up with you that time because we figured you was better at it than anybody else. But you got a funny way of doin' things, Charley. We can't figure

197

you out. You don't allow people to do what they got to do. It ain't a Sunday School outing, you know. It's a war!''

''There's only one way to go about this war and that's *my* way!''

''Every man in this outfit is good as you. That's why nobody can't beat us no how. Why if these boys ever let you down, you're done . . . washed up.''

''There's been a lot of extra shooting, Anderson,'' said Quantrill, darker. ''A lot of burning, some we planned and some we didn't.''

'You mean to tell me—''

''I mean to tell you I want this thing done right and I don't want a bunch of crazy men runnin' around killin' just because it's fun!''

Anderson sniggered. ''I must not be hearin' too good today,'' he said. ''You're openin' your mouth but nothin' seems to be comin' out of it.'' It had come down to a mere trade of insult. ''This ain't quite like you, Charley. This is too big, ain't it? You're happy with small potatoes.''

Quantrill gazed at his loaded revolver and suddenly realized how helpless he was.

''Go get your boys,'' he said, level. ''I want you to bring them to the hotel. I'll send someone else up on Oread before it's too late.''

Anderson rose, pulled his hat forward; it was as if he had read Quantrill's thoughts about the loaded revolver. ''I didn't hear that, Charley,'' he said with an assurance Quantrill had not heard in him before. ''I never heard you say that.''

''You're under arrest, Anderson.''

''You goin' to arrest me?''

Quantrill felt the tremor run through him, reached for his gun.

''So,'' said Anderson, smiling, ''you're goin' to shoot it out with me, is that it? You want me to draw on you, is that it? So's you can cut me down? Ain't that goin' to sound sweet out there in the streets? Charley Quantrill shot down one of his own men in a saloon shootout while the rest of his men was goin' about the

198

serious business of war!''

His hand was on the gun when Jimmy Little burst into the room. Little drew up, eyed the pair of them, guessed the nature of their quarrel, and proceeded with the news. ''Charley,'' he said, ''you got to come, Harry Trow just told me about ol'Lark Skaggs.'' The two men looked at him. ''Him and Toothman, they had gone missin' and Trow went lookin' for them and found their horses tied up outside an old abandoned mill and he went inside and found the pair of them astride some little girl!''

Quantrill looked at Anderson. He had the look of a man who had just been shot.

''Go, Charley,'' smiled Anderson. ''Go fight your war and I'll go fight mine!''

''That didn't stop him,'' said Toothman, ''he jest went on humpin' away, guzzlin' her face, chewin' away at her ear, and the poor little girl breathing deep, like she was just comin' up from under water, her eyes all glazed over, face all red from his heavy beard scrubbin' away at her . . . and then, all of a sudden, he started to growl like a dog, snarl, and I could see his humpin' gettin' faster and faster and then he looked up at me like he'd seen a ghost and shuddered and snarled and took to her face again and I could see him eatin' her ear. Why, there was blood all over her face, him nibblin' away like a dog, I tell you!

''Then he stops, he groans and lifts himself up and I can see she's all covered with him and all, and her face is quiet, calm, and I can see she's plumb fainted away, and so I let go her hands. My stomach's all torn up, I can't see straight anymore and all I can think is I want to kill that sonofabitch . . . but I can't, I'm jest sick, that's all, you know. He puts his pants on and gets into his boots and he says, 'It's your turn, Will' and I says, 'Let's go' and he says, 'Goddamn it, it's your turn'. I can see he's serious, dead serious. 'I wanna see you two do it,' he says. I look down on that little girl, her head to one side, blood comin' out of her ear and out of her crotch and I'm thinkin', I'm goin' to kill this sonofabitch if it's the last thing I do. And he says, 'Get those trousers off, Will,' and I says, 'No.' And ol' Skaggs, he come at

me and pulled down the suspenders and dropped my trousers
down to my heels, pushes aside my shirt and of course and he can
see there ain't nothin' there but a danglin' man, a little danglin'
man, you know. I can't get myself up, and you know what that
sonofabitch did? he got right down there in front of me and
started pullin' on me! He says, 'You two goin' to do it and that's
all there is to it! Goddamnit, get hard!'

"Me, I can't get hard, I can't even look at myself. I'm
lookin' at his face and realizin' I been a goddamn fool all my life
followin' this man around, like I was his shadow. Oh, he come
apart, Lark Skaggs! He come right apart, watchin' me standin'
there, a man with a piece of loose flesh hangin' to me. He jumped
back and swore at me again and commenced to pound me with
his fists. 'When I tell you to do somethin', you do it!' he says.
'Even if you can't do it, you do it!' And he pushes me over to the
girl, leans me over her and says, 'Do it! Do it!' screamin' away at
me like a wild man.

"And so I look down at this little girl there on the floor, her
eyes dartin' back and forth, she knows what's on my face, like
she can read my mind, and, seein' me there, beginnin' to cry like
a silly boy . . . why, she reached up for me and touched my hand
and started to pull me down to her, her face all puffy and red, her
eyes all bloodshot, ear bleedin' away, she just sees I'm in trouble,
and she pulls me down onto her, like. 'Now do it!' he says, comin' around, fallin' on his knees so he can watch me do it . . . and
where I touch her, I just turn red, it hurts me . . .

"And then I knew I couldn't do it, not even if she wanted
me to do it. I had somethin' else to do and I knew I had to do it. I
calculated how to do it, how to get off'n her and past him, so's he
couldn't stop me, stand in my way. I pretend for a minute,
waitin' my time, watchin' the little girl . . . and then, when it
come to the moment when I knew what I had to to . . . why I done
it.

"It's the only thing I done in my whole life I'm proud of
doin'."

It was like that time when he was a boy. He slipped into the

200

dank mill, hearing the deep vowel somewhere in the pit, a kind of moan. He crept along a wall, staying low, his eyes searching the semi-darkness, smelled the sourness, and he came to a staircase, slid down, his gun in front of him, out across the floor to the railing, hearing the moan. He peered over the edge of the floor and saw a man on his belly, in a pool of blood, Toothman or Skaggs, and a woman on her back, naked, staring up at him, moaning that deep dark pain.

Somewhere in the mill one of them still held a gun.

That would be a fitting conclusion: to be shot down by one of his own men.

"I don't know where you are, you sonofabitch!" he shouted, "but when I find you, I'll have your cock and balls out on the road! You haven't got a chance!"

Toothman jumped out from behind a wall. "Don't shoot!" he cried. "I never touched her! He did! Skaggs! And I shot him dead for it!"

Little came up behind him and went to the girl. She was alive, but that was the bad part. Something had gone from her and it had nothing to do with having been raped by a madman. The world had cracked, there would be no tomorrows in it, it would be only a noise in the night, a terrible light in the mirror. Quantrill knelt beside her and touched her on the shoulder.

Her screams brought others to the mill.

He wondered whether he shouldn't kill Toothman and then go climb into his buckboard and head out for California or Canada or wherever it is they go when they have to go on living when they should be dead.

Randy Venable came and told him about the Yankees.

"How many Yankees?"

"Couple hundred."

"You think they know the way we're headed?"

"Hard to say."

"George," he said, and Todd rose to him, "pass the word, the Yankees are coming and we assemble in the park for our ride home." He climbed down from the buckboard and went to

201

Nathan Stone, who watched from the doorway of the City Hotel. "You got the only hotel left in town, Nathan," he said. "I hope this time you won't let Colonel Eldridge get his saddle onto the horse before you do. His hotel is gone. It's a real chance to make a name for yourself."

"Don't you worry about my name," said Nathan, spitting out his words. "From this day on your name will disappear from the English language. A man'll be thrown in the hoosegow if he even says it out loud."

Once they reached the ridge above town, he paused at the summit and turned to survey his work. He seemed transfixed, his eyes orbed and clear as glass, saying nothing, and when he forced himself to turn, the last man out of Lawrence, he was surprised to find that the picture was so deeply scored in his mind that it appeared to him to be nothing more than a portrait of burning towns ahead of him.

TWENTY-ONE

He had brought 453 to Lawrence and now had only 452 to see safely home. The one remaining, Lark Skaggs, he carried on his back like a dead albatross. He sat in the shade with Will Toothman, while the rest of them stood around in the sun, tired, touchy, bleeding; they looked like men who had drunk too much, slept but not rested. It was 103° in the shade in the bushy retreat of the Upper Marais des Cygnes River. Jack Jarrette stood in front of Chief Bighand and his band to make sure that, for every fresh mount the men received, they gave the Chief a Kentucky steed. It was only a matter of shifting saddles and they would be off again. The scouts took the best of them and set off for Paola, and George Todd and his men took the next batch and returned to Brooklyn to face the flagging fortunes of Major Pres Plumb, who had had to leave half his fighting force in the brush oak cover at Cole Creek suffering from sunstroke. Quantrill sat alongside Will Toothman, the pair of them watching Bill Gregg's men making the trade, and then there was only the pair of them left.

"I figured I'd just shoot you, you sonofabitch!" said Quantrill, but all the heat had gone out of his voice. Only the hard eyes remained, fixed on him. "You heard my orders, why didn't you follow them? Christ!" He stared at a dead snake Todd had shot when they arrived at the river. "I haven't got a goddamn thing to show for it. Nothing. Just this girl laying in the mill screaming her fool head off when I lifted her head and tried to . . ." But he couldn't remember what he wanted to do. "I don't know what got into you. What in hell did you go to Lawrence for anyways?"

Toothman looked at the riders mounting. He suddenly felt very sorry for the man at his side, but he didn't know how to tell him that. "I had it in me to do it," he offered, softly, "I wanted to do jest what I was s'posed to do but . . . well, I don't think I can jest blame ol' Skaggs, I must've had it in me. Hell," he said, turning, fixing his eyes on him, "I'm jest flesh and blood like the next fella. There's nothin' special about me. Maybe you expected too much out of fellas like me."

Quantrill examined him. "Where you from, Toothman. You haven't got a Missouri accent."

"Kentucky."

"What are you doin' out here?"

"Lookin' for. . .somethin'."

"What?"

"Hell if I know."

It was clear sailing all the way back to the border. After a couple of stands at the Fort Scott Road and at Ottawa Creek, George Todd's men at last broke up Major Plumb's force and rode to rejoin the main troop. A couple dozen Yankees rode into Bull Creek, where they had found a place to rest, but Todd took his men and went after them. The scouts returned saying the border was dead ahead and clean as a whistle.

Under a moonswept sky, they crossed the last high ground and vanished among the cottonwoods along Big Blue.

Major Plumb found enough men to ride across the border the next morning but the trail they followed came suddenly to an end, and it looked as if at that point, Quantrill had gone straight up into the air.

TWENTY-TWO

She sat on a kitchen chair in the centre of a bright braided rug. She wore a white satin gown, generous with lace, low in front, and her hair had been piled high on her head and run through with a peacock feather. A scarlet cummerbund was laced about her narrow waist, a bouquet of wildflowers planted on her knees and held together by two gloved hands. The room had been decorated with boughs of pine and cedar, and a scent of French perfume reached him as he contemplated her from the doorway.

"I'm going to forget what I said," she smiled. "It ain't as if I've been sitting around getting dressed for the occasion." She extended the flowers to him. "I been up to Independence today."

Quantrill accepted the flowers and took off his hat. "I couldn't come right away," he said. "I had things to do." He was low, but he tried to cheer himself up by kissing her on the cheek. "It was a good thing you weren't there."

"They said you killed two hundred people," she said. "The town is in ashes. A banker told me he heard the damage done would come to over one million dollars. It's in all the papers from Maine to Texas." Her eyes were a little glassy as she continued. "It come as a surprise, a complete surprise. They said they had had warnings before and nothing happened. Nobody saw you coming or knew where you come from or how you got home again without losing anybody." The tears began to run down her cheeks. "There's a special meeting in the White House and Abraham Lincoln is going to make a speech about Lawrence. Why, one man even told me this would turn the whole war around in favour of the South."

She held out her hand and he went and kneeled before her, pressed his head to her lap and felt her hand running through his hair.

"You've done it," she announced. "You've accomplished what you set out to do, you've taken the war to your enemy."

He lifted his head and stared at her.

"Kate," he said, clenching his teeth, "it was a disaster."

"Yes,' she said, resting one hand on his shoulder, the tears falling onto her dress.

"A lot of innocent people died," he said, his eyes unfocused, "a lot of houses burned, mistakes." The smile faded from Kate's face. "I knew I had made a mistake, but it was too late. Not that, Kate, not in going. I had to go. It was an evil city, there were evil men living in it, it was a city of loot, warehouses, barns, houses stocked with the planters' goods, pianos, beds, tables, silverware. They had it coming to them."

Kate leaned forward, dropped the flowers and held his face up to hers.

"What happened, Charley?'

"I don't know, Kate. Something went. I didn't know these people, none of them. I was a cashier, that's all. The rest of them seemed bent on each other's destruction. It was hard to tell my own men from the Redlegs. I had . . . no control over them, they did what they wanted, that's all. It had nothing to do with me. And then . . . I heard about Will Toothman and Lark Skaggs." He told her the story, in detail, and when he was finished, he went into the bedroom and stared at the wall.

She came into the room and pressed herself up against him, threading her arms through his and holding her hands over his belly. "It was Anderson, wasn't it? You should have left him here."

"Anderson? He was all right. It was the Lark Skaggs that ruined me."

206

She dropped her hands and began unbuttoning his pants. "What you need," she said, "is a good night's sleep." The pants fell to the floor, and she began on his shirt. He turned to face her. "There's always tomorrow, Charley," she smiled. "Time for you to rest."

"It isn't rest, Kate. I need you."

Jimmy Little had come with him bringing two more men, and, together with Kate's watchman, it made four, and they took turns during the night, sleeping out the warm night in sleeping bags alongside the creek. They stayed out of sight for two days, and on the third, Jimmy came down out of the trees and showed them the notice he had pulled off a tree on the Blue Springs road. "Ninth of September," he said at the door. "Everybody out of the county, no excuses this time. If they find you out on the road day or night whoever you are, they shoot and ask no questions." Kate and Quantrill read the notice. "Come down from Ewing, but some says it come out from Lincoln."

"Total war," said Quantrill, looking up. "Jimmy, what does it mean?"

"Total war, like you say. There's three thousand men up at Independence and The Landing, and like in one long line of men, they start south on the Ninth of September, two weeks. People got two weeks to get out of the country. It'll become a no-man's-land. Then, when they got the top of the Divides empty, they can spread out and come down into the creeks."

"If we stay?"

"Stranded," said Jimmy, grimly, "like an old boat."

"If we go?"

"Where? We ain't got nowhere to go. We're already there, Charley! Our backs up against the wall."

"Leave us for a while," said Quantrill, folding the notice. "Tell Gregg and Todd I want to think for a while. Keep the men low, Jimmy. Don't risk nothing until I come back, and keep an eye on that rat Anderson."

"Once I nailed myself up in my room." They walked, as

207

usual, along the creek; she held to him as if, should she let go, she would sink up to her neck in sand. "My mother used to force me to go to the choir practices," he said. "She sat alone out there in the dark watching us practise, waiting until I made a mistake, and, on our way home, she would pull me along like a bad dog at the end of a collar and talk about the sour notes. She sat at the piano, it didn't matter how late, and she would play the song and make me sing it over and over until I got it straight, and my daddy, he'd come out of the bedroom and say, 'What time is it?' and 'My God, Caroline, can't you shut that boy up?' The next Sunday, he came to our church and stood up in the middle of the choir hymn and shouted out loud. 'That boy in the third row is out of tune!' he said. I was so embarrassed I ran from the church and hid in the weeds along the creek. I couldn't go home, I couldn't go back to the church. I stayed there all night. In the morning, I went home and my mother said, 'You bad boy! you're in the Devil's hands now!' and I went to my room and took out a can of nails and started to nail myself into my room."

He went to see Andrew Walker.

The roads were busy with wagons and farm animals plodding along toward the deep South, and Quantrill's men lay in the trees watching the exodus, observing the well-drilled phalanx of Union horsemen as they moved across the tablelands and searched for Quantrill's men. Quantrill himself was alone, coming up from behind Andrew's barn, leaving Charley in a small opening in the woods and continuing on foot through the high grasses until he reached the back door of Andrew's house.

"Andrew!" he shouted in a whisper, once inside the door. The room was empty. The walls were devoid of the pictures, cabinets of food, only a small mouse watching. He walked through the house. Overhead, something creaked. He looked about, considering a trap. He pulled out his revolver and went to the steps. Slipping up the stairs, he lifted the latch and watched it swing on its hinges. "Who's there!" he said. He fired once. "Come on out!"

He heard movement behind the wall, braced himself.

"We're coming out."

Familiar voice. It was George Todd, smiling sheepishly as he came into the room, and behind him, like a slave, Nancy Slaughter. He knew at a glance that the pair of them had been living in the house for some time, for the room had the look of comfortable habitation.

"Don't start lecturin' me, Teach!" said Todd, gruffly. "People livin' in sin, all that crap! I got as much right to a woman as you have. Well, ain't I?"

"Andrew has gone south," said Nancy Slaughter. "He gave me his house. I'm a . . . Yankee, didn't you know? I signed all the papers. It's mine now, the place. Andrew could've stayed, but his mommy and daddy, you know, his wife, Christ! He did what they wanted him to do. They went to Texas, I think!" She came to Todd, snuggled close to him and ran her hands over him in a familiar way. "My husband went with them, the coward. He beat me, you know. He was a mean man!"

"I guess I'll know where to find you if I want you," said Quantrill, pocketing his gun and turning.

"I don't need you!" shouted Todd, his words slurred in his anger. Quantrill turned to look up at him. Todd thought twice before he said it. "Gregg knows where I am, you know where I am, I know where I am. Is there enough darkness in that, Charley? After the war, after it's all over, why don't you come up to the Red River Valley and look me up, Charley. We'll talk about darkness."

He laughed outrageously.

Quantrill came to the meeting late.

Todd was already holding forth, sitting on a log, putting final touches to a doll, talking to them in an off-hand manner, hoping they wouldn't see through it to the real meat of his idea. "There don't seem to be any real good reason to take it back," he said, breaking his sentences as he concentrated on his work. "All they would do with it now is have to load it on a wagon and drag it all the way to Texas." He waited for signs of disagreement and proceeded to make his point. "I say we split it up between us, what do you boys say?'' He looked over at Cole Younger, the James Brothers, Jimmy Little, Bill Gregg. ''No point in cutting in Anderson. He'll want more than his share.''

''No way,'' said Jimmy Little.''Anderson'll make trouble 'less he's cut into it. By the way, George, where in Hell is it? I thought it was s'posed to be down at Luther Mason's.''

''Luther Mason? He got burned out,'' said Todd, working close around the nose and eyes of the doll. ''I didn't give it to no Luther Mason.''

''Goddamn it!'' barked Jesse James. ''Where is it then?''

''Don't get sassy, boy!'' said Todd, carving. 'There ain't nothin' to it but a lot of fine clothes and jewelry, old clocks, things like that. What you goin' to do with it, Jess? Ride around in a woman's dress with pearls around your neck?''

Frank drew his brother back. ''Let's talk about the money. Where's the money?''

''Baltimore Thomas put it into the bank vault up at Sibley. He knows the banker. All he wants is a cut.''

''Now let's not go up to Sibley,'' said Jimmy Little, ''and rob a bank and find out it's our money.''

''How much money is there?''

''Frank,'' said Todd, ''let me ask you a question. What would you do with the money if you had it?''

''I'd put it in a bank in Sibley, insure it, and *then* go and hold up the bank.''

Quantrill stood to one side like an actor waiting for his cue. ''You got all the answers, ain't you, Frank?''

''I got a few,'' said long-jaw Frank James, tilting a little to watch Todd cut out the eyes of a doll. ''You got that thing wired together right? A fella like you is likely to put their ass where their brains should be.''

Todd paused, heaved a deep sigh and stared at the floor, trying to curb his anger.

Jesse leaned close to his brother and said, ''Don't rile the artist, brother, he might get things right once.''

Todd's jaw tightened. He heaved the doll at Jesse but it missed him, flying straight into Quantrill's face.

"Sorry," said George Todd, collecting himself.

"I say we strike while the iron's hot!" said Bill Gregg, who saw it his duty to inject a serious note into the meeting. "I come down here with Jimmy tonight, we rode together, and we agreed, the only ones we can't beat are us!"

"I say we hit The Landing!" said Jesse James. "Find those bastards who killed the women and put them to the torch!"

"It's closer than Lawrence," said Cole Younger.

"All it needs is a little organization," said Bill Gregg. "I know the Big Blue like it was the main artery from my heart to my trigger finger."

Todd, recovered, jumped into the middle of it. "We got a hundred men . . . we could do it. Listen, this time, we don't just go in, see? and pick out names on a list, we go in there shootin', it don't matter. Those bastards are building a fortress and it ain't made out of masonry, it's iron and blood, Yankee blood. Go right in, I say, and cut the bastards throats, kill everything we see!"

"Count me out," said Quantrill. He said it when he saw an opening, imparted a certain tone of resignation to it. "I don't see it. I don't think we can do it."

"What did he say?" said George Todd, snapping his fingers at Frank James. "Did you hear what Charley said? He said we could count him out. The man who has the goddamn world by the balls says count me out." He climbed to his feet and walked to Quantrill, looked down at the doll, picked it up, dusted it off, rearranged it and held it out in front of him. "Listen, Charley," he said, in a mock ceremonious voice, "This here little marionette is my final masterpiece. It's as far as I can go. I can't get no closer to meat and potatoes than this, and so I'm goin' to give it to you after all." But Quantrill merely looked at him, his arms at his sides. "It's a token of everything you ever done for us, don't you see?" His hard thin lips cracked a little, and he drizzled a small laugh. "See, all you got to do is lift up her little dress," he said, with one hand lifting the skirt of the mannikin, his eyes fixed on Quantrill's eyes, "and you can see what she's got there underneath it all." He laughed out loud. "See?" Todd had put his knife to all the incidentals in the doll's anatomy, and his knowledge of the parts was faithfully revealed.

Quantrill took the doll in one hand, and, without releasing his eyes from Todd's face, heaved the doll high into the air. His revolver was out before anyone saw it, and three shots reverberated across the campfire clearing.

Two shots had missed the cartwheeling doll, but the third had made splinters out of it.

He returned his revolver to his belt. "I don't think I'm ready for any speeches from you just yet, George." He looked around at the others. "It's time to lay low. You know it, I know it. It don't pay to go on any of these suicide raids George Todd wants. Buddy," he said, looking at them one at a time, "and Frank, Jimmy, Jack, Bill Gregg...you boys know what I mean. They got us sealed off for now. They've got two thousand men between us and Independence and The Landing. We're scattered, we ain't all in one place. I tell you it isn't right. You listen to me and you'll make it down to Texas this winter, where we can plan our next move. You listen to Todd and Anderson..." but he paused, looking around the fire. "Where in hell is Anderson?"

They laughed.

"Anderson," said Jimmy Little, "is runnin' around the county lookin' for women."

"How many did he take with him?"

"A couple dozen."

Quantrill dropped his head, cleared his throat. "I'm goin' to be over at Dillingham's with Kate," he said, in a low voice, "and if you need me you know how to reach me. I need a picket or two to keep an eye on me. Other than that . . . "

It was quiet for a while. Quantrill looked over at George Todd, who had seen the death of his marionette and had not fully recovered from it.

"George," he said, trying to smile. "I appreciate that girl, and you're right, meat and potatoes. You I hold responsible to keep the boys out of sight. If anything goes wrong, I'll know who to blame. Bill, you know the rules. Jimmy, Jack . . . we only got another month, then we head south. Don't try nothin' too risky.

You understand?"

On his way to his horse he saw Will Toothman, who stepped out from behind a tree. "Charley," he said. "I'm still here. Anderson come for me but I told him I wasn't goin'." Quantrill smiled at him. "I thought maybe you'd like to know."

"You should've gone, Will," he said. "There'll be women . . . and song . . . and lots to drink. What would old Lark say if he knew you passed that kind of excitement up?"

Toothman watched him ride out of camp. "I told Anderson I wasn't goin'," he said to himself, "I said, it wasn't right then and it ain't right now."

TWENTY-THREE

The first of October they set out for Texas in a cold blue rain. Small parties riding close followed the intricate leafstrewn paths to the creek bottoms, clearing the scouts who reported their safe passage by birdcall deep in the bush to others along the line of march. They rode dressed as Yankees, their heads low. Jimmy Little brought up the rear and made sure no evidence of their movement was left behind. The second morning they gathered in a clearing south of Carthage, cold and sleepless, and formed squads of fifty as they rode the Neosho Road toward Fort Scott. The sun came out, and they followed the dusty roads for three days, Davey Pool running the front scouts, George Todd the rear. Kate rode alongside Quantrill in the centre squad, outfitted in a Yankee officer's uniform, her hair trimmed like the rest of them, her hat low over her eyes.

Davey Pool came back to Quantrill one morning and reported his men had stumbled upon a Yankee foraging party, who informed him they were stationed at Baxter Springs, which was undergoing reconstruction. Quantrill seized the opportunity at once and led an attack on the fort, found a wagon train containing the headquarters company of General James Blunt scurrying for the fort. He overran the train *and* the fort, for good measure, and by four in the afternoon, they were all stretched out in the shade enjoying Yankee food.

About a hundred miles south of the Canadian River, Davey

Pool's scouts met the advance party of the Confederate States Army, who informed Pool that they had come to lead him safely behind the lines. It was another day's ride to the waterhole, where General Douglas Cooper sat among his officers, high in the saddle, surveying them as they rode in among the trees.

He sent for Quantrill, whom he addressed from the saddle. "Captain Quantrill," he said in a slow liquid voice. "I send you hearty greetings from General Henry McCullough, commanding officer, who advises you and your men while in this District to observe and obey all military regulations." An officer rode forward and handed him a small book containing said regulations. "You shall be quartered at Mineral Springs, where your fellow Missourians have built a shelter. You should understand you will have to build your own enclosures. In due course you and your men will receive instructions as to your military duties."

He spurred his horse, turned with his staff officers, and rode away without waiting for a response.

"He didn't even say thanks," whispered Jimmy Little, his eye on Cooper's scouts. "The goddamn fool didn't even say thanks."

Mineral Springs was far enough from McCullough that he didn't have to look at them, close enough to keep an eye on. A few rough hovels had been put up under the trees along the creek, but most of the refugees from Missouri still lived in their covered wagons. It was a desolate place, barren, flat, dusty. People from Fire Prairie, Missouri, had tried to farm the sandy gopher-stricken ground, but without success. Most of them survived on jackrabbits and handouts.

One morning Quantrill arose to find fifty men had slipped away in the night, among whom were Bill Anderson and Arch Clements, the others those who had clung to Anderson ever since the ride to Lawrence.

"Good riddance," said Will Toothman.

"Not good," said Quantrill.

It took two weeks to construct the camp — two log bunkhouses and two loghouses, one for Quantrill and Kate, one for company meetings. Todd did the stonework, and Bill Gregg saw to the construction of the bunkhouses. Kate stayed out of the way at a loghouse some distance away until her own was finished. In Bonham, sitting in front of General McCullough's desk, Quantrill had one riot act after another read to him. "I understand some of your men have deserted you," he said. "I also hear they have taken up their natural trade as bootleggers and common thieves. That must stop!"

A letter came to Mineral Springs one morning early in November. It was from General Sterling Price, who said he was attempting to convince the Confederate High Command that Quantrill's men were loyal soldiers and worthy of respect and official status while in Texas. Some of the brass, he said, still considered Quantrill a murderer and brigand, especially now that he had sacked Lawrence. Quantrill knew he had to show the letter to his men to prove the point he had made to them about McCullough's intransigence. Kate prepared a meal for the officers, who came and stood out in front of the loghouse. Quantrill went out to them and read Price's letter.

"We don't owe him nothin'!" said George Todd, as they walked in and sat before a table steaming with yams, hominy grits, soup and sidepork. "This is our own goddamn war, we do what we want to do when we want to do it!"

Cole Younger could not contain himself: he heaped his plate high with the food. "It's like we done somethin' wrong," he said. "We ain't done nothin' wrong."

"What was wrong," growled Todd, "was winnin'!"

"It ain't like Price to write a letter like that," said Frank James, calmly. "I can't figure him out."

"He's stood with us right from the start," said Jimmy Little, who sat beside Quantrill.

At least he ain't against us like everybody else."

"Buddy's right. The way he sees it, if he can get Charley to tell him why Lane done what he done, maybe then he can tell Jeff Davis why we done what we done."

"Frank used to stand up in the schoolroom and talk like that, and all the rest of us would laugh," said Jesse James. He had not been invited, but he came anyway. He and his brother

216

Frank were inseparable, and, although they often fought, no man could come between them. Frank James always figured if they invited him, they invited Jesse too. "He never could get all his words in the right order. Me, I saw we won Lawrence fair and square. We never done anything because Jim Lane made us do it. We done it because we had to do it."

"Things went bad in Lawrence," said Quantrill.

"Now don't go gettin' preachy on us," said Todd, talking louder than usual. "We been all through this before. Things ain't quite so neat just 'cause you like it that way. Maybe up in heaven where it's all clouds . . . but down here in hell, all you got is a gun and you got to use it."

"Charley's right," said Jimmy Little, trying to sound neutral. "If General Price is goin' to get us a fair shake." he said, "he's got to have our word we was doin' what we had to do. It's that, pure and simple. I don't know what we're gettin' so wrought up about."

They ate quietly for some time. Cole Younger was relieved of the necessity to use his mouth for words, and bore his way through two helpings; Jack Jarrette, the neat one, spent his time cleaning off his plate with three slices of Kate's bread; and Bill Gregg sat quietly and respectfully.

"I sure had fun at Lawrence anyway," said Jesse, wandering into the silence like a boy poking a live rattler with a stick. "What's wrong with havin' a little fun now and then?" Little Jesse had an innocent face, and he knew how to use innocence like a gun. "But we ain't havin' fun no more," he said, turning to his brother. "Frank, I ain't havin' no more fun. I want to go home. Let's go home—"

"You are out of order, boy!" barked George Todd. "You ain't even speakin' to the question."

"What was the question?" said Younger, having finished his second helping and looking for another.

"Nobody asked a question, far as I could see," said Jimmy Little, watching Quantrill. "Listen to what Charley has to say 'stead of actin' like a squad of Prooshians!"

"Charley asked us what we was goin' to do about Price's

217

letter," said Todd, injured by Little's sudden sincerity. "He told Charley to make a formal report not on what we done but what they done to make us do what we done. It's like a trial, see, Price is our lawyer, and he wants to know what he can say to the judge so we won't get the noose."

"What we got to confess?" said Jack Jarrette, stirred into anger. "Eye for an eye, tit for tit!" he said, too late to take it back. He smiled at Kate, who stood at the door, apologized by making a funny expression on his face. "I say write the letter. Who started this scalpin' business anyhow? We found Abe Hallar out at Texas Prairie without a scalp. You remember? That was a long time before Anderson went around cuttin' off ears at Council Grove. And it was Gentleman Jim Lane who started the practice of stringin' people up to apple trees. Just put it down that way, Charley, let the chips fall." He sat back, laughed, picked at his teeth. "The only thing everybody's mad at is we're a hell of a lot better at all this than they are."

Laughter relieved the burden of George Todd's anger.

"We used to be good at it," said Jesse James, still teasing George Todd.

"Jesse!" Cole Younger belched. "You're such a saddlesore. Why don't somebody take that boy out to the kitchen and give him some dishes to wash?"

"We used to be good at everythin'," said Jesse, undisturbed. "But now, well, I just happen to know it's all over. We're finished. There ain't no Quantrill Company no more. Some of us is even goin' our own ways now."

"What are you talkin' about, Jess?" said his brother.

"Anderson's one."

"He never was part of this outfit anyways!"

"Well, what about Ike Flannery and Nat Kerr, they went along with him?"

"Good riddance, I say," laughed Cole Younger.

"Well, then . . . what about Bill Gregg?"

They knew they had not heard from Gregg for some time, and, turning to look, saw him with a spoon halfway to his mouth, looking trapped.

"What about Bill Gregg?"

"I was over at Bonham last week," said Jesse, spitting out his words, "and I was in the general store when I see him comin' out of the post and he had some papers in his hand. He didn't see me but I seen him and I went in and asked them and they said they had just signed up Bill Gregg, was I int'rested too?"

"Is this true, Bill?" said Quantrill.

Gregg looked around the table once, twice, resigned by heaving a sigh and dropping his fork to his plate. "Little Jesse," he said, bracing himself forward on his elbows, "has got to be taken out and given a good woodsheddin'."

"Answer the question!" shot Quantrill.

"Look," said Gregg, giving reasons instead of submitting to the grilling, "I jest took the next step, that's all. Charley, you keep wonderin' where the next step is goin' to take us. Well, I jest took it, that's what I done." Quantrill merely stared at him and said nothing. "You heard McCullough; he said, 'Why don't you boys join up and help us win this war?' Why, you even said it yourself, you said, we can't go 'round pickin' off patrols and robbin' banks and holdin' up coaches. Look, that war up there on the Kansas prairie, that ain't the real war. That's out East, in Virginia and Tennessee and along the Mississippi." The other men were embarrassed and stared at their empty plates. "Why, Charley, you even said to me the other day when we was all alone, you said we are losin' this war and it's all because of Lawrence."

"I said nothing of the kind!" said Quantrill, his eyes blazing.

"You said we was done even before we got home again. Look how you hung your head up there along the river, you and that Will Toothman. Christ! I had to come and get you or you'd never come home again!"

"Toothman was tellin' me about that sonofabitch Lark Skaggs!" said Quantrill, rising angrily and upsetting his water glass.

The two men stared across the table at each other.

"You come out of the bushes, Charley," said Gregg, honing

his words like a lawyer, "and took us boys of the Divide, farm boys, boys with a grudge, our folks losing their farms. We don't know what to do, and then you come along. You showed us what we could do. You took us as far as we can go, Charley." He darkened his words. "We got to the point where we came apart, over there at Lawrence, like you said. You can do what you want to do if there's just a few of you, but when you get all these new people comin' in, people like Anderson and Clements and Lark Skaggs, these people don't have your high ideals. You got to sit on them and you can't . . . you can't and I can't," he said, turning to face George Todd. "Todd thinks he can," he said, his voice betraying his cynicism. "Todd, he has your wizardry, Charley. He can see farther than the rest of us, he can shoot, ride . . . but he's different too. He don't understand what this is all about." He turned to appeal again to Quantrill. "That little poem you got, Charley, about the Devil and how we ought to rip out our gizzards if we violate the rules, all that, they laugh about it behind your back. George Todd laughs at it."

"I do not!" snarled George Todd, rising.

"You don't know these men any more, Charley. You can't just glad-hand them and then read a poem to them, give 'em water and cornpone and make them sit in the creeks until you ride them up into an army of well-trained Yankees holding those new Henrys in front of them. No, you can't do that anymore. The only way you can go on is go over and join up with Anderson . . . either that, or turn it all over to George Todd." Gregg turned to look at Todd again. "Todd ain't got so many rules and regulations to hold him back. It don't mean a thing to ride straight into the Henrys and automatic Colts, Charley. What's a few dead men anyways?"

"You sonofabitch!" said Todd. He threw his drink into Gregg's face. "Take that back."

"I don't take none of it back," said Gregg, walking out from the table, pushing his chair back into place. "I don't have to take any of it back. I don't belong here no more. It was time I was gettin' over to Bonham anyways. I . . . ride out tomorrow for Alabama . . . I . . ."

220

Bill Gregg looked once at Quantrill as if he wanted to say something, but changed his mind and strode straight out the door.

Todd jumped from the table, rushed out into the yard and climbed onto Gregg's back, and the two of them fell against each other heavily. The men came out of the bunkhouses to watch, and the officers, one by one, walked out of Quantrill's little house and lined up along the front of it. Charley sat alone at the table, watched by Kate from the doorway of the kitchen. Suddenly, he leaped to his feet and threw himself through the door, knocking down Jimmy Little as he flew straight into the wheeling bodies of the combatants.

First Gregg hit him, took away his timing, hurt him, and as he turned to face them again, Todd brought his right knee up into his groin and dropped him face down into the sand.

Later, when it was dark, he looked up and saw Kate's face hovering above him. Behind her, like a distant star, Will Toothman stood, his hat in his hand.

Quantrill wrote the letter himself.

There is only one way, he said, to defeat the enemy and that is to engage him on fields where he has the disadvantage and by means he considers undignified. Those in power are there because they have mastered the conventions, and those who will remove them from power must engage in unconventional war. If the Confederate States were to adopt this as a military rule, then the South would endure, but if it fights the Yankees on the battlefield, it will lose the war.

He sent the letter and waited for Price's answer. By mid-December he had waited long enough: he saddled Charley and rode into Bonham. The man behind the desk told him that the General was not available, that he was at a meeting and could not be disturbed. Quantrill twirled his hat in his hand for a moment, heard the voices in the General's office, and contemplated his next move. "I'll wait," he said. His name was written into a book and he was advised to come back another day.

"Thank you," he said, walking toward the General's door.

"Not that one!" barked the aide.

But it was too late.

He threw the door open and looked in upon five men seated around a table and passing papers back and forth. They were surprised to find him there, and the General rose slowly and began to fume.

"I'm sorry, sir!" said the aide, trying to push Quantrill out of the way. "He took the wrong door!"

"No," said Quantrill, wheeling the man away from him, "this is where I wanted to go."

"But we're having a meeting!" said one of the men at the table.

"May I see you a moment, General?"

"Well?" said McCullough, "you see what is going on here. Do you want to interrupt?"

"Yes."

"Well, then!" said the General, recovered. "What is on your mind? Out with it!"

"I . . ."

"Gentlemen," he said, "this is him. This is the man I was telling you about." They watched him as the General spoke. "The very man I was telling you about." He paused and looked at Quantrill. "Come, Captain, you wanted to see me."

"Yessir," said Quantrill, uncomfortably, "I hadn't got an answer back from General Price and I—"

"Ah," laughed McCullough, "but you see *we*," and he indicated the men at the table, "we have, you see." The General looked at them. "You will recall that little . . . item we discussed," and at Quantrill again, "I have received instructions from headquarters to employ you and your men as I would any others," and smiling, "so you see, your letter to Mr. Price was successful."

"Employ?"

"Yes, employ. You know I think you and your men are a bunch of cut-throat bastards that ought to be cleaned out, but that . . . apparently, is not what headquarters thinks. Your men shall be advised that if they wish, they may go into regular service, and if they refuse, if they wish to remain under your command, then they may do that too. So you see, everyone should be happy."

"We have agreed that you shall serve on patrol duty," said one of the officers at the table, a small man with sharp eyes. Like the others, he was dressed in an immaculate uniform. "You shall serve under General McCullough, who is responsible for your conduct."

"What General Smith means," growled McCullough, "is I tell you what to do and you do it or I can jail you for insubordination!" He enjoyed his little joke with the others. "Now, Captain Quantrill, if you play your cards right, you see, by March, you'll be free to return to Missouri with your men, but if you displease me, if you fail to carry out my commands. . . ." He had a knack for the theatrical and wheeled away into another subject. "Since you seem bent on disturbing us, perhaps I should now inform you of the duties I expect you to carry out."

"Yessir," said Quantrill, his jaw set.

"Some of your boys, I am told, are in the moonshine business." He stood for a moment to let the words sink. "The stills are up along the river. Now, I'm not going to deny that, as commanding officer, I don't barter with them. I do. I am trying to regulate the sale and trade of moonshine, don't you see? That's my way. I serve justly and with honour. I make sure my Indians don't get lyewater when they want moonshine."

Quantrill said nothing.

"Yes, it's coming from your own boys, Captain. I don't know who they are, but presumably you do. Now, I want you to bring in the guilty party, do you understand? I want you to bring him down here and arrest him." His eyes narrowed. "And if you don't, if you find this an onerous task, if for some reason that causes you troubles, why then, I shall have no alternative than to come out there and clean the whole pack of you out of there."

"Yessir,"

"I'll give you one week to bring in the guilty parties, and if you fail, why I'll come out there and clean you all out!"

"Seven Indians died of it," said a man at the table.

"One week!"

223

TWENTY-FOUR

You smelled them even if you couldn't see them from the road. They were down along the river, invisible from the bluff, hidden in trees. Quantrill led the way down the hill, slipping from tree to tree, watching the men come down behind him, until he reached the bushes just above the shed. There he sat on his haunches and prepared the dynamite fuses as George Todd and Jimmy Little settled alongside him, watching the others thin out along the hill.

"You're sure Anderson's not in there?"

Todd leaned close and whispered, "We don't know who in hell is in there, Charley. We followed a man on horseback this mornin', but none of us knew him. He was all bundled up. Davey Pool tipped us off about him because he knew he was the man who buys the stuff from whoever it is inside that still."

"Anderson's boys."

"You don't know it's Anderson," said Jimmy Little. "We been watchin' Anderson. We know he ain't in there, that's for sure."

"Too bad."

"Maybe if we wait a couple days."

"We don't have time."

Todd sat down and fixed his eys on the wall of men stationed along the hill. "Christ, Charley," he said, "why don't we just bust right in there and kill everybody? We got the men for it."

"Because," said Quantrill, busy with the fuses, "we don't

224

know who is in there. Isn't that what you said?"

It was a tumbled-down unpainted shed perched disconsolately out over the edge of the rock on one leg and belching white smoke. He slipped down the last remaining steps and fastened the powder to the leg of the shed and unravelled the wires back up to his plunger.

"Fine," he said. "Signal to Buddy, tell him I'm ready to go."

"I like workin' for the law," said Jimmy Little. "It's nice to know you're doin' something *right* for a change."

"I can't see no difference," said Todd, signalling with his arm.

"Pipe down!" said Quantrill, blowing his hands and crouching. "I want to hear this thing when it goes off."

It was a disappointing explosion.

But the leg broke away, the building lost its balance and fell to its knees, something burst on the inside, boiling water leaked out around the foundation and hissed when it struck the cool water, and then there was a series of explosions, fire and smoke everywhere.

Only two men escaped from the fire.

One of them was Andrew Walker.

Kate went for the doctor while Quantrill and Jack Jarrette cleaned Walker and applied salves to the wounds. Their patient was delirious at times and called for 'Lizzie', with whom he engaged in a couple of long and intimate conversations. The doctor ordered them out of the room and went to work, returning to the outer room by late afternoon.

"He'll live," said the doctor, "but he's badly burned and frightened. He should be better by the morning, but I can tell you more the next time I see him."

During the long hours that night Andrew held several incoherent conversations with Lizzie, words of which consisted mainly of blurred vowels surrounding islands of words such as 'Bonham' and 'business' and 'money'. Just before dawn Quantrill dozed off, his head against the pillow in his chair, and when he woke again and looked at the bed, he found Andrew Walker staring at him.

"Where's Tuck?" he said, distinctly.

Quantrill rose and went to his bedside. "Tuck who?"

Andrew Walker stared at him blankly. "Tuck," he said again.

"It's me," said Quantrill, leaning on one knee so that his face was even with Walker's. "Quantrill. Charley Quantrill."

"Hello, Charley." It was a different voice, one closer to the one Quantrill knew, and a slight smile slipped into the wooden white face. "Charley, what are you doing here?"

He told the man in the bed the whole story, and when he was finished, the sun was high in the windows and the light warm and comforting across Quantrill's shoulders. Kate came into the room and brought the two of them breakfast.

"Stay, Kate," said Quantrill, as she was about to leave. "I want you to hear Andrew's story. You . . . won't be in the way." She smiled and settled beside him on the floor.

"I won't start at the beginning," said Andrew, slowly, as if inventing each word he spoke. "We had to come in one wagon," and he closed his eyes to see it all clearly, "because they came and took us and put us into a wagon out on the road. There were a dozen other people there already, the Jessups and Jake Lambert . . . others, I forget now . . . and we joined a long line of wagons at Lone Jack, people with their belongings tied to horses, and the Bluebellies came through and broke everything and threw all the food onto the road and beat everyone. They said they were looking for Quantrill's men. I found my folks halfway to the Indian Territory, in another wagon way in the back . . . there must've been three hundred wagons on the road, and the Yankees rode alongside on horses and shot whoever they wanted to . . . especially those who wouldn't give them apples and bread. Clara Nestor. They shot her because . . . she kept falling off the wagon all the time. They got tired of propping her up, tying her to the tailgate. One time when she fell off, tied up, they just rode over her. They didn't bother to shoot her, they just rode across her body. She was . . . eighty-one, or so I heard.

226

"She was crazy at the end. Her kinfolks would turn their backs to her and she'd go and roll off the end of the wagon right in front of the horses of the next wagon, you know."

He lapsed momentarily into a daze. His eyes were open, his face drawn, lips quivering, remembering. "We got to Texas and found a refugee settlement . . . just a circle of wagons. People living out of wagons, killing rattlers and boiling them, sickness and starvation . . . the children walked around with cups in their hands looking ninety years old, all skin and bone, you could see their skeleton underneath." Quantrill thought of George Todd's art and realized the sonofabitch knew what he was doing with a knife and a block of wood. "And then my mother took sick and the Army came and took her away. When I last saw my father . . . he merely sat and stared at the fire. He wouldn't even talk to you."

"Poor man."

"He's finished, Charley," said Andrew, stronger now. "His way of life, his way of thinking, the way he farms, it's all gone. It'll never come back again. He grew up in Virginia and Kentucky, he worked on the plantations, he knew cotton and he knew niggers. He never hurt a nigger, Charley. He loved his niggers. He set up a school for the children, he hired a white teacher, and he made them go to church, and if anyone ever touched one of his niggers, my father would kill him. It was like one of the family." Quantrill enjoyed hearing Andrew talk because it made sense out of everything he was doing. "But that's all gone now. The plantation. . . is in ruins, the niggers gone, who knows, up to Canada with all the rest of them. It's all over, Charley," he said, tears beginning in the bearings of his eyes. "It don't matter whether the North or the South wins this war. My father is a man who has lost everything, even his memory. He can't remember a thing. He doesn't even know me when I go to visit him."

They waited, Kate whispering in his ear, "Give him a little time." After a while, he smiled at them and put out one hand, which Quantrill took into his own.

"I can't wait to get home," he said.

"Where do you live?"

227

"Blue Springs, Missouri." He laughed then, tilted over and laughed. "Yes, soon's this is over, I'm goin' home again." He looked at them. "My sister Nancy has bought us all from the bank. She left her husband, took all his money up to Independence and told them she wanted to register, and then she told them she wouldn't help the bushwhackers if they would give her my father's plantation back again. Did you see her when you were there, Charley?"

Quantrill waited a while. "Yes, I did, Andrew."

"Where?"

He hesitated. "In your house."

Andrew looked puzzled.

"What was she doing there?"

Quantrill smiled at him. "Andrew," he said, "what were you doing in that still?"

"Still?" barked Andrew, hauled quickly back into the pain and discomfort he felt. "What still? Was that a still?"

"Come on, Andrew!" said Quantrill. "I know all about the still. It would help me out if you would tell us who is running that still. Are you running it?"

Andrew's face went through a number of changes in colour, he sighed and confessed. "No," he said. "I'm just a middleman, Charley. I . . . I buy moonshine for General McCullough." He tried to still the pain. "I'm in business for him. Provisioner, you know. I buy and sell mash liquour for the soldiers."

"And Indians."

"Maybe."

Quantrill leaned close to him. "How sick are you, Andrew?"

"Sick? Who's sick? I'm telling you the truth. I'm square with you, Charley."

"Then I want to ask you a question, and I'll need an honest answer."

"It will have to be an honest question then."

"Do you sell moonshine to the Indians?"

"Yes," he said, unflinching.

"Then you know about the lyewater."

228

"Yes." He was biting his lip, his eyes narrowed. "I know about the lyewater."

"Did you sell lyewater to the Indians?"

"I didn't know it was lyewater."

Kate said, "Who knew it was lyewater, other than the Indians who died of it?"

"The man who owns the still."

"Who's that?"

"Wild Bill Anderson owns it."

The following day they took Andrew Walker home to Lizzie. It was out behind Jim Crow Chile's roadhouse among a half-dozen shacks built out of old wagon beds and stuffed with straw and wild grass, hers the one down beside the creek all by itself, surrounded by yew trees that trailed their long arms down over the top of it in sad wreaths. She was in the doorway, and as Quantrill neared her, he could smell the mash on her. She was wearing men's boots under a long green dress that she used at night when she sat at the tables.

"Hello, Lizzie," Andrew said, smiling guiltily.

"What in hell happened to you?"

"It's a long story. Lizzie, I want you to meet two friends of mine, Charley Quantrill and Kate—"

Lizzie turned, disinterested, and went back into the shack.

"You don't give a damn about me, do you!" he suddenly shouted, trying to find her shape amidst the darkness of the shack. "You don't give a damn I was damn near killed yesterday!"

"No, I don't!" she said.

Andrew stared up at Quantrill. "Charley," he said, "leave me alone. Just . . . go away. Leave me here. I'll talk to her. She's just . . . scared, you know. See, I didn't come home last night and all."

"All right, Andrew," he said, trying to smile.

"Now, I want you to listen to me, Charley," he said, placing a hand on Quantrill's arm. "You let me handle Anderson, you hear?"

"No," he said. "I got my orders, Andrew. I got to take him in."

"Let me talk to him."

"What? And tip him off?"

"Charley," said Andrew, "Anderson's a dangerous man. He's watchin' you and your men all the time. He's got gunmen around who shoot to kill. You won't get within a mile of him, not even if you took all your men with you. He'll run. He's clever." He laughed. "You know, he reminds me a lot of you when you first started . . . a small bunch of hardheads, hellbent boys, livin' out in the woods, got a real live picket. You know you can't beat that."

"Andrew," he said at last, "if you go anywhere near him, if he gets any idea what I'm going to do to him, I'll be dead. Now, here's your chance to return the favour I did for you and your father. Go into that house and stay there until I tell you to come out again."

Andrew smiled and nodded.

Kate and Quantrill rode out onto the road. He took one final look at Andrew Walker, moored in the yew trees with a woman standing in the doorway shouting obscenities, burnt and painridden as a result of his own business practices. "Poor Andrew," he said, and he meant it.

"Don't worry about him." said Kate, her eyes fixed on the horizon. "He'll survive. You'll be working for him one of these days."

"Never."

He went straight to the bunkhouse.

George Todd sat in front of the men dangling two marionettes and making them dance. The men laughed when Todd spoke out of one side of his mouth and then the other. It was all about a man who went into a tavern and saw another man he didn't like, pulled out his gun and killed him. The men thought it all very humourous and applauded roundly when both wooden dolls lay at George Todd's feet.

"I have it straight from Andrew Walker," Quantrill said.

230

"The man behind the still was Bill Anderson and his boys." He looked out over the two hundred faces, side-lit from the windows. A jug circulated among them, and several were smoking, so that the air in the bunkhouse was close and rancid. "Walker is only the man who runs the mash, it's Anderson's business, he's the one who sold that lyewater, and he knew it was lyewater."

They merely observed him quietly. He got the feeling they considered him part of the afternoon's entertainment.

"Todd," he said, walking over to the men seated on the crate, "I want you to prepare the men for an attack on Anderson's camp. Jimmy," he said, looking around, "you and Frank, Jesse, you come along with George, and we'll work out the details." He got up slowly, looked them over. "I don't like it any more than the rest of you. I know you got family over there at Anderson's fire. But . . . there's nothing we can do about it. If we don't go over and take Anderson into McCullough, McCullough'll be out here for you and me this week, and I for one don't aim to spend my days rotting inside a Confederate jailhouse."

He turned and left without saying another word.

"I didn't dare stay," he said, laying his hat on the table, her fierce eyes on him. "If they turn me down, Kate," he said, facing her, "I'll have to go away. You and I . . . we'll have to leave. I'll just have to wait now and see what they want to do."

"You mean," she said, "you'll have to wait now and see what Todd tells them to do."

He thought of striking her in the face.

All that stopped him was the face itself. Kate looked at him with such an unflinching expression that it scared him. Yes, she was right, it was the case, it was all up to George Todd.

"That's what I mean," he said, at last.

She came to him and held him to her for a long time, until, suddenly, there was a knocking at the door. Kate looked into his eyes as if to recharge him, gave him a slight shove backward. Then, turning, he coughed and straightened himself.

It was George Todd, who stood, feet apart, his hat in his

hand, his jaw set, unsmilingly. "The men," he said, "have decided it ain't right to go in there firin' away at kinfolk." Quantrill looked across Todd's shoulders and glimpsed them in the shrubbery around the bunkhouses, watching the two men in the doorway. "They want you to know they ain't afraid of Anderson nohow. And they ain't afraid of McCullough either."

"Who are they afraid of then?" said Quantrill.

Todd's jaw slackened. "It just ain't good to go around shootin' one's kinfolks. John Edmunson's over there, Josh's brother . . . Hiram George, Jimmy's brother . . . Sid Creek, Oliver Bunch, Ike Flannery . . . Ike's cousins are with us, you know that."

"What are they afraid of?"

"Look, Charley," said Todd, a harder edge to his words, "if sellin' a little lyewater to Indians is what we got to pay to stick together down here until we can go back to the Divides, the boys are willin' to pay it. And if McCullough comes lookin' for us, why we'll just pull up stakes and head out now for a place where we can be appreciated. The men are bored anyway. We don't like it down here in Texas."

"They're afraid of you, George," he said.

"What I mean to say," Todd said, snarling, leaning so close that Quantrill could smell the mash, "if you got a grudge against Anderson, well you'll have to go over there and settle it by yourself. We ain't goin' along."

Todd took a more provocative stance.

Quantrill could see them in the trees watching and he remembered the little show they had seen coming out of Todd's hands. He shook his shoulders as if he wanted to make sure there were no strings attached to them. Todd stood waiting for Quantrill to close the door and go back inside, because he knew that was all he had left to do. Without his men, Quantrill was just another man, and, with Quantrill's men, Todd realized that he could do anything he wanted to do.

"George," he said loud enough that the men in the yardhouses could hear him, "I need you now more than ever." He knew what he was about to say would turn the balance one way or the other. "I been working on what we're goin' to do when we go back to the Divides next spring. We got to be smarter this time than ever before, and you know I never let you down. I never lost a fight to Independence, and if I'm going to do that again, I'll need you more than ever. I need men with brains to steer me through it."

Todd tried to sound like a public man. "Charley, the men have decided what they are goin' to do. You go and follow your own goddamn rainbows and leave us alone. We got our own fights, we don't need none of McCullough's, 'specially when it means fightin' kinfolk! As long as you can 'preciate that, why then you'll find the boys behind you all the way, but me and the boys," he said, turning slightly, "Buddy Younger, Jimmy Little, Frank James, Jack Jarrette . . . boys you know and trust, we want you to know we ain't being disrespectful, we just ain't goin' on this one. Look, we went anywhere you told us to go, we always done it; why the boys woulda rid off the end of the world with you if you'd told them to do it. But this time," he said, his eyes burning bright, "this time we're stayin' home."

Quantrill stared at him for a moment and walked around him and headed for the men in the trees. They watched him come, saw him stop when he came to Jimmy Little.

"Charley," said Jimmy, after a moment's silence, "I hate Anderson harder than you. It ain't right for him to sell lyewater to Indians. Even me, I can see it ain't right." Quantrill's eyes tore Little's composure apart, and the man turned away from him. "I ain't got anything more to say. It ain't right, I know it ain't right."

"Why ain't you ridin' with me, Jimmy?"

"I ain't shootin' Joe Crabtree. Joe, he saved my life up at Kemper Stage. If it weren't for him, I wouldn't be here today."

Quantrill stood, waiting for him to turn.

He went to Jack Jarrette, who leaned down from a branch like a monkey.

"If you can give me one reason why I ought to ride with you this time, I'll go, Charley," he said. "Why, I'd ride clear to the State of Maine if you give me a good reason to do it."

233

"McCullough's orders," he said, quietly.

Jarrette leaned through the tree and spat his words. "Well," he said, "you tell McCullough he can shove them orders up his ass, I ain't goin'!"

Frank James said, "You stopped givin' reasons lately. Ever since Bill Gregg walked out on you, you run out of reasons. A fellow's got to know where he's ridin' and why he's doin' what he's doin'. Now that don't seem to be too hard, does it?"

"There's one thing worse than school," said Jesse James, from the top of the tree, "and that's vacation. There just ain't nothin' at all to do summers 'ceptin' work, and I hate work more'n I do sentence writing."

Cole Younger flashed his golden tooth. "We never lost," he said, "but we never won nothin' either. I can't wait for this god-damn war to get over with so's we can get down to some serious work, like robbin' banks and stuff like that."

Quantrill smiled at him.

"Where we goin', Charley? We take in Anderson, and then who's next? You? Me? Once McCullough gets started, he won't be happy 'til he's got ever' one of us in the hoosegow." Cole Younger came and stood in front of him, looking for words. "Where we goin'? What are we goin' to do when we get there? The boys and me, we want to know."

"Buddy," he said, turning so that the others could hear him, "there's no stopping Yankees up there on the Divides. There's no stopping them anywhere, so far as I can see. We figured Lawrence would do it for us, but look, it only made them hopping mad. Lincoln got mad, everybody got mad. We took up the wrong side in this war, boys. We lost out there. I don't mean the Yankees are right, you know that. But no matter, we were on the losing side." He turned away from Cole Younger and went back to Jimmy Little. "After the war they'll hunt us down and kill us like we was jackrabbits. Everywhere we go, we'll be the badmen. You go straight, they'll keep an eye on you. You bend over, they'll get you in the back. It's only a matter of time. Somewhere, sometime, they'll come lookin' for you. You take to hidin' out in the woods, and they'll come after you. You buy a farm and lead a good life, they'll come lookin' for you.''

"You paint a gloomy picture," said Jimmy Little.

"Something's happenin' in this country," he said, going to Harry Trow, "I can feel it under my feet. It's like the ground is shakin', like it's an earthquake everywhere, and it's all comin' from somewheres out East . . . it's hard to say where exactly, but I'd sure like to find out." He went to Frank James. "I know how to move, Frank, and I know how to stay alive while I'm movin'. This is more than you boys can do on your own. You stay with me and I'll get you there and back again, just like at Lawrence."

"We got to know where we're goin'."

"You won't know, Frank, until you get there."

"You ain't preachin' to the Mormons, Charley. Just a bunch of farm boys from Missouri. We don't aim on ridin' nowhere, 'lest it's down to The House of a Thousand Delights!'' The men laughed at that. "We're homeboys, Charley. We ain't goin' out onto the roads lookin' for some place to land."

He walked among them for a while until he came to George Todd, in front of whom he stood and looked up at the sun. "There's two ways to go," he said. "East and West . . . me, I aim to go East. There's gold that way," he said, pointing out over the bunkhouses, "and there's money that way," he said, thumbing back toward his little loghouse, in which Kate Quantrill stood, watching him from the door. "I don't have nothin' definite worked out in my own mind yet . . . I won't know what it is until I get there."

"I don't know nobody out East," said Frank James. "I don't make it a habit to go around shootin' people I don't know."

"Who said anything about shooting?"

"What else is there?"

"I aim to find out."

"It don't make no sense no matter how you slice it!" barked George Todd, taking ahold of Quantrill's shoulder and spinning him around to face him. "We got a war to fight up at the Divides and that's where I'm headin'," he said, walking out toward the men. "That's the way we're all headed." He walked back toward

235

the bunkhouses, his legs churning up the dust. The men watched him move and began to fall in behind him.

"Jimmy!" he said, following Todd. "Tell George what I told you about Washington and Philadelphia and places like that!" Jimmy dropped his eyes, turning, following Todd, saying, "Stay away from Bill Anderson, Charley!"

"Jack," he said, appealing to the man that fell out of the tree in front of him. "Tell George about the future, tell him about all the wars in the streets."

Jarrette smiled at him but followed Jimmy Little toward the bunkhouses.

He was alone in the yard at last, hearing the doors of the bunkhouses slam shut one by one.

TWENTY-FIVE

She stood in the window watching him walk slowly back to the house. He walked like a man who'd forgotten how to use his legs, pausing at the door, his back to his men. Will Toothman had followed him all the way to the door. "You've lost all of them," he said. "They belong to Todd now. I belong to Todd, I don't belong to you." Quantrill did not turn, stood merely with his hands up against the door as if maybe he thought he could push it off its hinges. Will Toothman turned and went back to the bunkhouse but found all the doors secured against him. After a while he wandered out to the corral and took up a conversation with a mare.

It rained all day. Quantrill sat in a straight-back chair in the middle of the room, his eyes fixed on the window, waiting to see who would be the first man to break loose from Todd's jail. He put his money on Jimmy Little . . . maybe, Jack Jarrette then. Jack, he figured, had more brains, he could see farther than the others — they had had long talks about the future, what it would be like, what kind of people would be walking the earth, how they would live and love and kill...or Frank James. Frank never liked George Todd, distrusted him, called him 'that goddamned Metis'. Kate tried to talk to him, but he ignored her, refused to move, as if his skeleton had rusted closed on him and he couldn't move. He stared at the bunkhouses, or was it something beyond the bunkhouses which only he could see?

237

She left him and went for a walk in the rain. The faces in the windows of the bunkhouses looked like jars, but the eyes moved as she turned toward the corral. She saw Will Toothman sitting in a hollow tree talking to himself, and called Charley to her, fed and curried him, threw a saddle onto his back and rode him out across the prairie. He was in good shape, his legs strong, his chest powerful. She could feel him moving beneath her, lay back and gave him his head, flew. It was darkening when she returned and unharnessed him. Toothman was still there jabbering, and the faces in the windows had eyes that swept along with her.

"They're crazy too," she said, looking down at Quantrill. "All of you are crazy."

It wasn't until she had drawn the shades and lit the lamp that he dropped his gaze. He slumped, then, as if he had at last surrendered to his worst thoughts. She brought him a cup of coffee, gave him a knowing smile. He moved, looked at her, then took the cup and drank from it.

"Kate," he cried, "that isn't the problem. I know they're crazy. I've known it all along. They haven't got a mind of their own. They just do what you tell them to do. I've always known that. I tell them what to do when I can get away with it, and if I can't, then George Todd does . . . and if he can't, there's always Anderson. That's not my problem."

She handed him a bowl of oxtail soup. He stared at it for a long time as if he didn't know what it was.

"Eat it, it's soup," she said.

He finished it off in no time. He looked the better for it, but it didn't help his disposition. "You know, I keep thinking about Andrew Walker," he said, hollowly. "He said his life is over, all he ever believed in, that the war was lost. I rode with Andrew because for the first time in my life I knew somebody who cared about me, him and his father. I didn't give a damn about their Causes, just as I didn't give a damn about Jim Lane's Causes . . . and now, to see him at the end of the road . . . in an old shack with a tart . . . no further to go." But he never finished; he looked confused for a while, but then reached for her hand. "Maybe it's time for you and I to ride out of here together. We could go

238

wherever we wanted. California, Oregon Territories, Canada.
Why couldn't we go to another country and start all over again?
They wouldn't know us in Canada. You know," he said, smiling
with a ghostly look on his face, "I heard the niggers talking on
their way down to Texas that time Mark Gill sold them to a
fellow down there . . . they said, somewheres out west, beyond
the rocky shore, way out in the mists of the sea there's a ring of
islands somewhere . . . where it's always green and cool, it never
snows and the nights are always cool and dark . . . no sand-
storms, no rattlers, no wars. Just wood and water. Salmon so
thick in the river why you can just walk across it on their
backs."

"I was wondering what you were looking at all day," she
said, kneeling beside him, resting her head on his lap. "You were
looking for some place to run away to."

"I'm twenty-six years old, Kate. In another twenty-six years
I'll be an old man. That's something to think about."

She raised her head and contemplated his face. "God,
Charley!" she smiled, "it sounds too good to be true . . . living
somewhere up in those woods with you." Suddenly, the smile
evaporated, she stood up on her knees and gripped his arms.
"But I've got to give you up . . . now." It was difficult to hold
her tears back. "You talked about the ground moving under
your feet and you said you knew something was afoot in this land
and if you knew what it was you would take them straight into
it."

"Words," he said, half smiling. "I always talk when I can't
think of anything to say. The more I talk the less I have to say."
His face took on a long sad slant. "Ever since I was a little boy,
I've been told to go stand somewhere and wait, and every time,
I'm just standing there, and I hear something moving
somewheres and I have to go have a look at it. I had a dream
once, I'll never forget it. The ground shook and broke up and
everybody ran away from the hole in the ground, but me, I ran
the other way, threw myself onto my stomach and peered down
into the fire . . . and suddenly my head fell off!"

"Charley, you've got to stop dreaming."

239

"That's what I do instead of sleeping. I never sleep. I'm either awake or I'm dreaming."

"Sometimes," she said, her voice hardening, "you're wide awake and still dreaming. Like right now." The room had got cold, lighted only by the one lamp that cast an eerie light up against the rough wall. Kate had tried to make the little loghouse liveable by hanging bright Indian prints on the walls, but in the half-light, they had assumed a sinister aspect. "You think somewhere out on that perfect emerald island in the Pacific you're going to find peace. It won't happen, Charley, and you know it. You said it yourself, everywhere you look you see Lawrence. You can't run away from Lawrence when it's everywhere you run to!" She climbed between his knees and stared at his face. "You know you've got to go over there and arrest Anderson on your own because if you don't . . . it's all over, the men belong to George Todd. You know that, don't you!" His eyes were deep in his head now but they were fixed upon her. "And you know if you ride into Anderson's camp all by yourself, you'll never be able to arrest him because his men won't let you. They won't shoot you, no, they'll let Anderson do that, and nobody would know or care. They'd take you out onto the prairie and leave you for the rattlers. No, even if you drew on Anderson and killed him, there's always Arch Clements in the shadows and he'd kill you . . . or what about his crazy brother Hank or Ed Hink, they're all crazy."

"They say it rains all summer up there on those islands," he mooned. "And it's just green as the world used to be when it was new."

"The only way you can get away with it," she said, undeterred, "is to leave out of here in such a way that the men in the bunkhouses know you intend to go do it. That's all they ever believed about you, that when you made up your mind to do something, you did it. I know them, Charley, I know they won't be able to stay behind. Even Todd, if he sees the others go, he'll go too. You'll be able to arrest Anderson if they want you to. If they want to stop you, they'll stop you one way or another before you get there."

240

He laughed at last. "Kate," he said, leaning forward and placing a hand on top of her head, "your mother was right. She said, 'Go not with a wrathful man lest you learn his ways and tangle in his snare.'"

She touched his face softly. "You're not a wrathful man," she said, "you're a killer."

He took her into the bedroom and closed the door.

TWENTY-SIX

Kate was wrong. He was more than halfway to Anderson's camp and the plains were as empty behind him as they were in front. Somewhere at that moment one of Anderson's men would be watching and passing the word along that he was coming, coming alone. Always alone, with the men, even with Kate. Perhaps then most so because she brought out the loneliness, and made him look at it. He had said nothing to her when he left. The sun sat on the hips of the eastern hills and poured its yellow influence into the valley. His boots reverberated in the hollow air. Will Toothman was asleep in the tree and snoring loudly. The whistle that summoned Charley did not wake him, nor the sounds of saddling the horse that Kate had somehow cleaned and groomed for his last ride. This was the way it ended: straight into the jaws because there was nowhere else to go. No Canal Dover, no Lawrence, no Blue Springs, no Bonham, no Mineral Creek. Only a bootlegger's shack and, that too, a fraud, delivering death rather than illusions. Better to keep riding west, keep on moving, to those green islands, the boat that would take you out into the Pacific, see where that leads to. Full circle back to Canal Dover, Lawrence.

Still a road around Anderson, a road that would take him west?

Suddenly he saw the sharp light. It came from a rise to his left. It would be a gun barrel or a mirror, perhaps an eye-glass. A

242

signal.

No, there was no road around Anderson. The only road was the one he was on. He turned to look back along the trail and saw that it was still empty. He had the sun in their eyes, that was one thing . . . but he lacked the second element of his wizardry, surprise. He knew Anderson had already been told he was going to have a single visitor.

"Go, boy!" he said, suddenly, kicking Charley into motion. He gave him his head, leaned with him and felt the wind clear his head, make his blood flow faster, give him the edge he needed, rolling now, in around the riverbank and up along the draw toward the rise above Anderson's camp.

He rode into a mean collection of tents and scrapheaps, trash scattered alongside the creek, campfires, and in the centre of it all, a large tent he recognized as his own, Anderson having stolen it from him the day he ran away. It was a blue Yankee tent, tall enough to stand in, with a breezeway from pole to pole. He saw them coming out of their tents, rising from their bedrolls, sleepy-eyed, perhaps groggy from mash, and, as he raced across the campground, a small weasel of a man came out of the blue tent and stood in front of it with his hands on his hips.

He was unarmed.

The two men who had been up on the rise came running down into the campsite and rushed alongside Anderson and pointed their carbines at Quantrill as he reined in. His cloud of dust sailed off to the north.

"Good mornin', Edmunson," he said to one of the gunners, and turned to the other. "Huffacker. Nice to see you two boys again." They said nothing, an eye closed, sighting at him, waiting for the word. God! he was a fool! There was no way to turn now. "Good mornin', Bill! Hope you're enjoin' my tent." Anderson did not look frightened. Curious perhaps, as if he expected to be falling for a bad joke but wanted to see what it was. Quantrill tried smiling to hide his confusion, his sudden cold fear. "I always had bad dreams in that tent. What about you?"

"Just git!" snarled Anderson.

243

It seemed hard for him to say as much. The eyes were mere slits of light, and when he opened the mouth, you could see him flick his tongue like a snake.

"Now," said Quantrill, riding to within a few feet of Anderson, "is that any way to greet an old friend?"

"You git!"

Like a banshee, Arch Clements charged out of nowhere, a riflebutt jammed into his shoulder, his face red and splotchy. "Shoot the goddamn fool!" he screamed as he came. "Don't take no chances! Kill him!"

"Don't you even want to know why I came?" said Quantrill, watching the beast close on him.

"I don't give a goddamn why you come!" snarled Clements, peering down the sight. "You come to git killed!"

The sun was in Clements' eyes, and he was momentarily blinded by it.

"Then I s'pose I have to tell you myself. Why I came, that is," he said, trying to remain clearheaded. Charley rolled under him, danced, feeling the danger. Quantrill looked around the campfire and found the men standing in front of the tents, and, off to the left, he saw the pickets riding in from the flats like buzzards with an eye for the pickings. "Why, I came over to arrest you, Anderson," he said. "I came to take you in."

Anderson cocked an ear at him. "You what?"

"I came to arrest you for selling lyewater to the Indians. I got a warrant for your arrest right here in my pocket," patting his pocket and smiling. "It's signed by General McCullough. You know him, don't you?"

"No."

"He's the man you're working for."

"I ain't sellin' no lyewater to no Indians. Where'd you hear somethin' like that?"

"Andrew Walker told me."

"Andrew Walker!"

"He says he's working for the General too."

"I'll tell you one thing," said Anderson, his teeth flashing in the morning light, "I ain't workin' for you, Quantrill. Even if I

244

was sellin' lyewater to Indians, it ain't got nothin' to do with you. I don't work for you no more. My men don't work for you no more. Nobody works for you no more. I hear George Todd don't work for you no more and I hear even Jimmy Little, he don't work for you. I don't guess nobody works for you no more."

Quantrill laughed (or tried to sound like he was laughing) and said, "I haven't got that in writing and as far as that goes, you," and he turned to look at the men before their hovels, "you and your boys, all of you are still part of the Quantrill Company."

"Quantrill Company!" laughed Anderson, and Clements started to laugh, and then Huffacker and Edmunson, and soon they were all laughing. "You boys ain't ridin' nowheres I can see. Besides, if you want to know who's sellin' lyewater, you go talk to George Todd and Jimmy Little and they'll tell you who's sellin' lyewater to Indians."

Quantrill looked down at Edmunson and Huffacker. "Now, John and Mose," he said, his voice beginning to crack, "you boys put up those widow makers, I'm goin' to take Anderson with me. He broke the law. You and me, we broke the law too, but we never got caught at it like Bill Anderson. If you boys want to go back to Blue Springs and fight in that war next spring, you better not stand in the way, because if I don't take him in, then McCullough will bring in his troops and take you boys in."

"Get out of here!" screamed Arch Clements.

"Arch," said Quantrill, "you're going to have to find somebody else to shadow from now on. Tell you what, you can shadow me if—"

"You goddamnsonofabitch!" he screamed, dropped to one knee, aimed the gun at Quantrill's head and pulled back the hammer.

Only confusion registered in Clements' face when he heard the explosion that wasn't from his gun, when he tried to pull the trigger but found a hole in his shoulder where the strength and will should have been, when, instead of looking at the man on the horse, he was staring at the ground. Nothing at all registered on Anderson's face as he turned to look up the hill and saw the men up there. Fast as a rattler, he made for the cover of his tent. John Edmunson wheeled in midair and fell to the ground and Huffacker scrambled out of sight. Quantrill rammed his heels into Charley and spun him out through the trees and into the prairie to where his men circled the way he had taught them to do, pumping the campfire full of lead shot.

Well, goddamn that woman.

P3